Pm

PURSER

Purser, Ann
Weeping on Wednesday

33090006533774   **LOSA**

WEEPING ON WEDNESDAY

The Lois Meade mysteries by Ann Purser from Severn House

MURDER ON MONDAY
TERROR ON TUESDAY
WEEPING ON WEDNESDAY

WEEPING ON WEDNESDAY

Ann Purser

This first world edition published in Great Britain 2003 by
SEVERN HOUSE PUBLISHERS LTD of
9–15 High Street, Sutton, Surrey SM1 1DF.
This first world edition published in the USA 2004 by
SEVERN HOUSE PUBLISHERS INC of
595 Madison Avenue, New York, N.Y. 10022.

British Library Cataloguing in Publication Data

Purser, Ann, 1933-
    Weeping on Wednesday. - (The Lois Meade mysteries)
    1.   Meade, Lois (Fictitious character)ʾ - Fiction
    2.   Cleaning personnel - England - Fiction
    3.   Country life - England - Fiction
    4.   Detective and mystery stories
    I.   Title
    823.9'14 [F]

ISBN 0-7278-6027-5

Typeset by Palimpsest Book Production Ltd.,
Polmont, Stirlingshire, Scotland.
Printed and bound in Great Britain by
MPG Books Ltd., Bodmin, Cornwall.

One

'Hello? Is that Mrs Meade? Mrs Lois Meade?' The voice was hesitant, quiet.

'Yes, this is *New Brooms*. *"We sweep cleaner!"* Can I help you?' Lois was sitting in her office, feet up on her desk, reading the classified section of the *Tresham Advertiser*. She was looking for new staff, and had an advertisement in today's issue. Her question was met with silence. She tried again.

'Hello, Mrs; er? . . . Are you there?'

A throat was cleared, and then the quiet voice said, 'Um, yes. I saw your advertisement, and thought I might suit. I . . . er . . . haven't done anything like this before . . .' The voice trailed off again.

'Well, d'you want to give me some details about yourself? Or I could call in and see you?'

The answer was quick this time. 'Oh, no, that won't be necessary. I'll put something down on paper today and get it in the post, and then I could come and see you, if you think I might be suitable.'

Lois frowned. She liked to interview prospective cleaners in their own homes. It was always more revealing than pages of autobiography. She remembered only too well a previous applicant, smart on the streets but a slut at home. Fortunately Lois had not employed her, and just as well. That one had turned out to be enemy number one, and was now safely behind bars.

'Give me your name and address,' she said now, 'and your phone number, and after I've read your details I'll get in touch.' Probably no good anyway, she decided, putting down the phone. She read what she had written on her notepad: *Miss*

1

Enid Abraham, Cathanger Mill, near Waltonby, and then a
telephone number. Lois shook her head. Sounded more like a
below-stairs housemaid than one of the New Brooms team.

Lois had been a cleaner herself. That was when they lived
in a small house on an estate in Tresham, the local big town,
and she'd chosen to take jobs in villages around. Every day
a different house, a different family, and all intertwined in
village affairs. She'd had a unique position, being at times a
not unwilling eavesdropper, and often received confidences
from wives or husbands who swore her to undying secrecy.

After a scandal which rocked the village, the doctor
she'd worked for in Long Farnden had moved away, and
the Meades bought his house cheaply. It had had murderous
associations, and nobody wanted it. But Lois knew every inch
of the house, and had been fond of the doctor and his wife.
She had no qualms about making an offer, and now she and
her family spread themselves in the unaccustomed space.

Lois Meade, the listening ear and receiver of secrets, had
not passed unnoticed by Detective Inspector Hunter Cowgill,
and he had enlisted her help on a couple of occasions. Both
times had involved murder, and endangered both Lois and
her family, her husband and three children. For this reason
she had more or less, but not quite, promised her husband
Derek not to succumb ever again to the wiles of Hunter
Cowgill, and since the last murder case had been wound up,
she'd heard nothing more from him. Until yesterday.

Now she forgot about the strange woman on the phone, and
thought again about Cowgill's call. She'd put him off with an
ambiguous answer, but she knew he'd be back. Never give up,
that was Cowgill's motto. And he knew that she'd be tempted,
that she was fascinated by the jigsaw business of detection,
and the dark world of crime and punishment. She'd been on
the fringes of it herself during a mildly misspent youth. Once
she'd ended up in a police cell, and had been really frightened.
Persistent truancy from school had led to her being taken in
and given a real bollocking by the police. They'd asked for her
parents' name, and she'd given another girl's details. She'd
always hated that prissy cow, and the bust-up that followed
had been worth it!

Lois laughed aloud, and her mother, coming in with a mug of coffee, looked at her in surprise. 'Share the joke?' she said.

'Nothin' really, Mum,' she said. 'Just remembering what an 'orrible daughter I must've been.'

'Yes, you were,' agreed Gran equably. 'Still, you got better as you got older. How're you doing? Was that a possible on the phone?'

Lois shook her head. 'Doubt it,' she said. 'Strange woman. Didn't say much and sounded sort of scared, as if she'd had to pluck up courage to ring. Not the sort we want in New Brooms.'

The telephone rang again, and Gran turned to leave the room. 'Better luck with this one,' she said.

'New Brooms,' said Lois into the receiver. 'You read the advertisement? Good, yes, give me some details and we'll take it from there.'

She picked up a pen, and began to write.

Two

'Looks like more hopeful cleaners,' said Derek. He had brought a handful of post in from the hall of the solid red-brick house where he and Lois lived with their three children: Josie, a typical fifteen-year-old with the useful stubborn feistiness of her mother; Douglas, a cool rising-fourteen; and Jamie, nearly twelve, and special to his mother and his gran, who also lived with them. And then there was Melvyn the cat, named after an unsuitable boyfriend who'd nearly spirited Josie away from them for ever.

Lois slit open one of the envelopes and pulled out a sheet of plain white paper, covered with neat handwriting in black ink. None of your computer-literate students here! 'Ah,' she said, looking at the address, 'it's the one I told you about. Miss Abraham, from Cathanger Mill . . .'

'Blimey, Mum,' said Josie, 'sounds like something out of a horror movie . . .'

'Yeah, *The Creature from Cathanger Mill*!' Douglas stood up from the breakfast table. 'School bus'll be here in a minute . . . You lot'd better be ready.' He sloped off out of the kitchen and Lois heard him climbing the stairs at a languid two at a time.

Jamie shoved his chair back with a rasp and followed his brother, and Lois noted his attempt at the sloping gait. Her baby . . .

She smiled, and Derek said, 'What's funny? You said she sounded deadly . . . a real no-no?'

'Haven't read it yet,' she said, returning to the letter. It was very well written, with no mistakes in grammar or spelling as far as Lois could see, though she was the first to admit that she was none too clever herself in that department.

'Well?' said Derek. He knew Lois well enough to know that her interest was caught by something in the letter. 'Don't keep us in suspense . . . what does she say?'

Gran turned from the cooker with a frying pan full of sizzling bacon and added, 'And for goodness sake sit down and have something to eat, Lois. You're not going out on an empty stomach again, I hope!'

Lois sat down, spreading the letter out in front of her. '"Dear Mrs Meade",' she began, '"Further to our telephone conversation, I am writing to give you some particulars of myself and my past experience".'

'Very good,' said Josie, nodding wisely. 'She's been taught how to write a letter, that's for sure. Go on, Mum.'

'Get yourself off upstairs!' said Derek. 'If you miss that bus, I'm not taking you to Tresham in the van again. Go and get yourself together, gel, or else . . .' His stern words could not hide his fondness for his first-born. The boys frequently accused him of favouritism, just because Josie was a girl, and though he denied it hotly, both he and Lois knew it was true.

'"I am forty years old, unmarried, and came to Cathanger when I was nineteen. Before that, we lived in Edinburgh, where my father was caretaker in a school. Mother originally came from this area, and wanted to move back".'

'Wonder what her mother's maiden name was?' said Gran. She'd lived around Tresham all her life, and claimed she knew everybody worth knowing.

'Doesn't say,' said Lois. 'Anyway, it's not important for New Brooms . . .'

She read on to herself, until Gran said, 'For goodness sake read it aloud – sounded interesting, like the beginning of a story.'

'"I worked in a chemist in Edinburgh",' Lois continued, '"and was promoted, though I was very young. It was in the old town, and had been established a long time ago. I loved the work, and was sorry when we had to leave. Since living in Cathanger, my mother did not thrive as we had hoped, and I have been unable to take a job. But I have run the

5

house, cooking and cleaning, and so feel I could be of use to you. Circumstances have changed lately, and I have some free time, so could fit in with your requirements to some extent".'

'What circumstances?' said Derek suspiciously.

'Doesn't say,' said Lois. She frowned. 'Bit odd, isn't it,' she added, and continued to read. '"I would be happy to come for interview, if you felt able to give me a try. Yours very truly, Enid Abraham (Miss)".'

Gran began to collect the breakfast dishes and take them to the sink. 'That's what I call a proper letter,' she said approvingly. 'I hope at least you'll talk to her?'

Oh yes, thought Lois, I'll talk to her. And although she was fairly sure Miss Abraham would not do, there was something about the letter, the neat handwriting, the black ink, and the polite formality of it all, that whetted her appetite to know more.

'OK, Mum,' she said, 'I'll give her a ring now, if that'll make you happy. I bet she's a pillar of the Women's Institute. Probably does the flowers in church, an' all that. Be a nice new friend for you?'

As usual, she had hit the bullseye, and Gran laughed. 'And what's wrong with that?' she said. She added that if Lois would just finish her breakfast and get out of her way, she'd be able to get the mid-morning bus into Tresham to do a bit of shopping.

Detective Inspector Hunter Cowgill sat in his car, parked inconspicuously among others in the village hall car park. It was Long Farnden playgroup morning, and there were four or five other cars around him. He had just received a call from the local constable, Keith Simpson, who said something funny had been going on in the adjoining playing field. 'Funny? Be a bit more specific, man!' he'd answered, and Simpson had told him that somebody had been digging with a spade down at the bottom of the field. Very strange-looking holes in the ground. The spade was still there. He'd be investigating, of course, but if Inspector Cowgill was in the area, he'd like him to take a look. He

6

hadn't liked to disturb the earthworks, he'd said, and the smile in his voice had irritated Cowgill, whose wife had been particularly sharp this morning. Sharper than usual. He sighed and got out of his car, pulled on wellington boots to deal with the November mud, and set off for the bottom of the field.

Squelching through puddles still lying on the surface after recent heavy rain, he came upon the 'earthworks'. The spade was still there, an old one with a wobbly handle. There were hollows in the ground, and hillocks where someone had piled up the earth. Cowgill sighed. He had no idea what had been going on, and really did not care. Simpson should have sorted it out himself, without bothering the chief. He took out his handkerchief, snowy white and perfectly ironed as always, and blew his nose violently.

'My God, what a trumpet!'

Cowgill spun round, and saw Lois Meade. Her old coat and bobble hat failed to conceal her undoubted charms, and she struggled to control a large dog pulling at the lead in her hand.

'Lois!' Cowgill recovered his equilibrium and put away the handkerchief quickly. 'What on earth are you doing here?'

'What I always do every morning,' she said, smiling. 'Taking old Polly's dog for a walk. She's nearly eighty-five – Polly, not the dog – and can't give it enough exercise. Get's me out for a walk, so it's a good thing for both of us. How about you?' she added, knowing his well-honed ability to avoid answering questions.

'Investigating a major crime, of course,' said Cowgill dryly. 'It's these hollows and hillocks. Constable Simpson thought they looked suspicious, especially as he failed to catch the hardened criminal who was digging here. And here is the murder weapon,' he added, lifting up one of the spades.

Lois peered at it. 'Looks like Derek's!' she said. 'Just wait 'til I get hold of Douglas . . .'

'So have you any valuable clues for me?' Cowgill felt his spirits rising. Lois always had this effect on him.

'Oh yes,' said Lois blandly. 'It's a bike run . . . the kids do all kinds of acrobatics on them. But it'd be no good at this time of the year. Much too muddy. Still, if you want to arrest the villain now, I can give you particulars . . . and his criminal record . . .'

'All right, all right,' said Cowgill. 'But I'm glad I've met you. I want to have a talk about something serious . . .'

'Not now, chum,' said Lois, setting off with the straining dog. She shouted over her shoulder, 'The less I'm seen talking to you the better. See you!' she added cheerfully, and was halfway up the field before Cowgill had collected his thoughts.

Three

M onday, and, as usual, a team meeting in Lois's office at midday. She'd had half a dozen replies to the advertisement, and wanted to sound out the others to see if they knew any of the names. This was partly a genuine wish to tap their local knowledge, but also, as she'd said to them at the outset, her policy was to make them all feel part of decisions taken as a team. They came to realize that this was rubbish, and that Lois never took any advice from anyone, but mostly they went along with the fiction happily enough.

One of their number had vanished into the hands of the law – though remembered with some affection – and Lois now had only three cleaners: Bridie, her daughter Hazel, and Sheila Stratford, plus herself, and Josie in school holidays. She was looking for another two. There was enough work coming in now, and she wanted another male cleaner. Some jobs were better handled by a man. Still, she had to listen to the views of the others.

'Could be he or she,' she said to the assembled team. 'We want the best person for the job, don't we?'

Hazel Reading sniffed. 'It was good having a man about. Women bicker, when there's only them.'

Lois raised her eyebrows, but said nothing. Bridie Reading had been Lois's best friend since schooldays, and she and her daughter Hazel both worked for New Brooms. Hazel, sharp and suspicious, was now approaching twenty. She had, for a while, been involved in drugs and knew the score. She'd kicked the whole thing herself, but still knew a great deal about the scene, and kept Hunter Cowgill informed on the young and corrupt who got up to no good in Tresham and around. It had been coincidental that both Lois and Hazel had this other, undercover work in common, and it gave them a special relationship – sometimes close and mutually protective, and at other times edgy and suspicious. Still, they rubbed along, as Lois intended they should.

The third member of the team, Sheila Stratford, was solidly rooted in rural life, and was not without strong opinions when challenged. She was married to a farm worker, had a daughter and grandchildren living close by, and came from generations of Stratfords now lying peacefully in Waltonby graveyard. When her husband said he thought she had enough to do at home without going out skivvying, she had tried to explain that working for New Brooms was different. It was a business, she'd said, almost like having a career. He'd laughed at that, but raised no further objections.

Now Lois met Hazel's challenge and said, 'Haven't noticed any bickering in New Brooms. But I see what you mean. Right, shall we get on now? We'll start with our usual schedules, and then have a look at the new applicants. I'd appreciate your help on those.'

When they came to Enid Abraham, she read the letter out and looked round enquiringly. Hazel and Bridie shook their heads.

'The name rings a bell,' said Bridie, 'but you don't see anybody about down there, except an old man out in the yard sometimes. Keep themselves to themselves, folk say.'

'Spooky place,' said Hazel. 'I've been by there at night, and there's never any lights. This Miss Abraham sounds all right, though . . . bit old-fashioned . . .'

'Do you know them, Sheila?' said Lois, and wondered why she looked uncomfortable. Sheila had lived in Waltonby, the nearest village to Cathanger, all her life and was the most likely to be forthcoming.

'Yeah, I know them.' Sheila stopped and bit her lip.

'Well?' said Lois, frowning.

'There's four of 'em,' Sheila said hesitantly.

'Three, don't you mean?' said Lois.

'No, four, the old man and his wife, the daughter, Enid, and a son.'

'A son?' said Lois. 'She doesn't mention having a brother. Are you sure?'

'Sure as eggs is eggs,' said Sheila firmly. 'He worked with Sam on the farm for a bit. Didn't last, though. Funny bloke. Something happened, and he left. Haven't seen him since. Edward, his name was, and wouldn't answer to Ted. Sam said he thought himself too good for the job. They didn't get on . . .'

'Mm, well, I'll have a word with her,' said Lois. 'Worth a word, do you reckon?' She looked at Bridie and Hazel, and they nodded. They weren't really bothered one way or the other. It was the bloke on the list that interested Hazel, and Bridie's thoughts were on her next job, her favourite, cleaning at the vicarage for Reverend Rogers.

Three other women were dismissed as not flexible enough, or without a car, and one had no telephone. 'Why do they apply?' said Hazel.

'Some don't read the ad properly,' said Lois, picking up the last applicant's details. 'Now, this one is twenty-two, working at present as a nursing auxiliary and likes the idea of going out and about round the countryside.'

'Where does she live?' said Sheila.

'*He*,' said Lois, with a dramatic flourish that made Hazel laugh, 'lives over in Fletcham and shares a cottage with his partner. Comes from up north, and is number four in a family of seven. Not a bad letter – here, Sheila, pass it round.'

Fletcham was a village of about the same size as Long Farnden and Waltonby, with which it formed an irregular triangle. The villages had been known for some years as the lucky three, since none of them had lost valuable young men in either of the two Great Wars. Lois had had one or two enquiries for help lately from Fletcham, and was keen to sound out the lad.

'What's his name?' said Hazel.

Lois knew that if there was any dirt sticking to this one, Hazel would know of it, and answered in some trepidation. She liked the sound of him, and didn't want to be put off. 'William Stockbridge,' she said firmly. 'Likes to be called Bill, thank goodness.' Sheila Stratford nodded approvingly.

11

She had always said that Edward Abraham was no good – anybody who'd rather be Edward than Ted was a stuck-up twerp, in her opinion.

To Lois's relief, Hazel shrugged. 'Don't know him,' she said. 'Never come across him – does he say what his partner's name is?'

Lois shook her head. 'Read the letter, Hazel. I think you'll agree he's worth a try.'

So it was settled, and after the others had gone, Lois sat in her office with a plate of Gran's sandwiches in front of her, and made the necessary telephone calls. Enid Abraham had answered herself, and insisted she came to see Lois in Long Farnden. She would explain, she said, why that would be more convenient.

A pleasant girl's voice answered Bill Stockbridge's number, and made the necessary arrangements. Tomorrow at ten thirty would be fine. Bill would be off duty then, and would look forward to seeing Lois. And, by the way, her name was Rebecca.

'How'd it go, gel?' Derek sat in front of the television, watching the local news.

'How did what go?' said Lois.

'Your meeting – the list of possibles, all that,' he said, his eyes still fixed firmly on the screen.

'OK,' said Lois. 'What's that you're watching?'

'The news – some bloke's disappeared. Seems he owed a lot of money around here, and he's done a runner or something. They had his sister on a couple of minutes ago, and she looked frightened to death. Dodgy story, if you ask me.'

'What was the name?' asked Lois idly. Her mind was still on the interviews she had set up for tomorrow.

'Can't remember,' said Derek. 'They come from over Waltonby way . . . Cathanger . . . you know that rundown old mill house? It's outside the village, in the middle of nowhere.'

'*Cathanger*, did you say?' said Lois, concentrating now. 'Was the name Abraham, by any chance?'

12

'That was it,' said Derek, and then the penny dropped. 'Oh my God,' he said, 'that's the woman you got a letter from, isn't it? Must've been her on the telly.'

He got up and turned to Lois. 'Now listen to me, young woman,' he said, and put both hands on her shoulders. 'You can forget all about Miss Enid Abraham. Before we know it, we'll be right in the middle of another bloody mystery, and Sherlock Cowgill will be round here pumpin' your brains and makin' use of us all. So no, no way, Lois, and that's an order! I don't want you havin' nothing more to do with that slimy cop. If he gets in touch, tell him a definite no!'

This was a long speech for Derek, and Lois hadn't the heart to tell him that the last call she had received in her office had been from Detective Inspector Cowgill, and it had been about the Abrahams.

Four

B ill Stockbridge was first on Lois's list, and she felt confident and cheerful as she knocked at the cottage door. The garden, she noticed, was neat and tidy, and the windows were clean. As the door opened, a pleasant smell of washing powder greeted her. This was important. Lois had formed many an accurate judgement of clients from the smell of their houses. The vicarage at Waltonby, for example, had wafted old cabbage and damp all over her when she first called on the Reverend Rogers. Now that Bridie had taken over, lavender wax polish and freshly made coffee cheered up the elderly cleric twice a week.

'Hello! Come in, please.' The door opened wide, and a stocky young man stood grinning at her. Sandy-haired, with a dense crop of freckles over his nose, Bill Stockbridge looked fit and strong, as if he'd been out for a run over the moors before breakfast. His light blue eyes smiled too. Yep, this was more like it.

'It's not a usual job for a lad,' said Lois, thinking she might as well get this one out of the way at once. 'I have had a male cleaner before, but it didn't work out in the end. Why do you want to do it?'

Bill Stockbridge laughed heartily. 'Rebecca says she knows what my dad will say,' he said. 'He's a farmer in Yorkshire. Tough as they come. Could turn his hand to anything. That's why I fancy this job. On the farm we did everything and anything. Mum pitched in all year round, and if she got sick, we did her jobs around the house too. Scrubbing and polishing is nowt new to me!'

This piece of information was certainly new to Lois. All the farmers she knew – and Sheila Stratford had told hair-raising

14

tales – were of the 'Y'don't keep a dog to bark yerself' variety, and wouldn't dream of boiling an egg for themselves, let alone get busy with a duster.

'What does Rebecca do?' she asked. Was this one of those role reversal partnerships?

'Teacher,' said Bill. 'Takes the infants' class in Waltonby village school. Loves it, luckily. She's always lived round here. That's why I followed her south; we met at a party, and I could tell I'd have to get in there fast to stand a chance. She's very pretty,' he added, with a proud smile.

'What's her surname?' said Lois. It wasn't really relevant, but you never knew when such things would come in useful.

'Rogers,' said Bill. 'Her uncle's the vicar.'

Of course. The vicar was chairman of the school governors, and would have put in a good word for her. They'd got a new headmistress now, since old Betts had gone, and according to Sheila Stratford, it was much improved. So, a farmer's son with a bit of imagination, and a vicar's niece. It all seemed very respectable and suitable for New Brooms.

'Right,' said Lois. 'I'll let you know in a day or two. But I will just say this. My team of girls is a good one. They work well together, and I'd expect you to do the same. Everything open and fully discussed at our meetings, and if there's trouble with any of the clients, I expect to be told straight away. And no gossip, not with clients, nor anywhere else. *I* need to know everything that goes on, but nobody else does. All right?'

Bill nodded. He'd not been expecting anyone like Lois. An efficient woman, yes, but Mrs Meade was different. And quite fanciable, too. But he knew without being told that chatting up Lois would be out of the question. Well, it all seemed very promising, and he whistled happily to himself as he shut the door behind her.

Heavy black clouds had drifted over the earlier clear sky, and Lois wished the car heater worked. Ah well, as soon as she had enough in the bank, she planned to invest in a shiny white van with *New Brooms – We Sweep Cleaner* emblazoned on the side. Now she pulled her coat collar up, and wondered if it was going to snow. As she approached Cathanger Mill the road narrowed, and trees hung over it, making a natural tunnel. In summer this patch was truly beautiful, with dappled sunlight coming through the leaves, and a small bridge over the mill stream. Lois's boys biked from Long Farnden and joined others hanging over the water and dipping for minnows. Well, Douglas was too cool for that now, she smiled to herself. But Jamie and his friends would be back for perhaps another summer. Now, with no leaves on the trees and the bare branches interlaced over the road like arthritic old fingers, it was a dark place, full of shadows, and Lois shivered. Perhaps it wasn't such a good idea to have a quick look round Cathanger before meeting Enid Abraham.

She almost missed the turn to the mill, and had to reverse back into a field opening a few yards beyond. It was not that the road was unfamiliar. She had been this way more times than she could remember, but had never had reason to give the mill more than a glance. In fact, as she'd said to Derek not so long ago, she always accelerated along this stretch, especially in winter. It was a silly fancy, he'd said. Everybody locally said it was one of the prettiest places for a picnic by the stream. So Lois kept her feelings to herself, but now she remembered, and felt reluctant to get out of the car. Still, she'd better get on with it. Her appointment back at home with Enid Abraham didn't give her much time, and it would look strange if any of the Abrahams caught her snooping around the mill now.

She closed the car door quietly, and sauntered back up the road, trying to look as if out on a casual stroll. An icy wind whipped her scarf back from her throat, and she tied it more tightly. The mill house stood back from the road, and was approached by about two hundred yards of narrow, twisting track. Grass grew down the centre, and ruts and potholes abounded. Not exactly a warm welcome, thought Lois, as she walked on past. She glanced back at the house through a hole in the overgrown hedge. It was so dark now that even though it was the middle of the day, a passing farm vehicle had its lights on. But there were no lights coming from the house, and she could see nobody about. A dog barked suddenly. It was a frantic, hysterical bark, and then Lois heard a gruff shout: 'Shut up! Down!'

That's quite enough of that, Lois told herself, and walked quickly back to her car. She drove off with as much speed as the twisting lane would allow, and was glad when she came to the Long Farnden sign. She cruised along the High Street at an obedient thirty miles an hour to her own gate, and drove in with a feeling of relief. Why relief? She could not have said. All farmers shouted at their dogs. Enid and her mother could have been out shopping. And the brother wouldn't be there. He'd done a runner, hadn't he?

'You were a long time,' said Gran, as Lois walked in. 'Any good? Bill Whatsisname?'

'Stockbridge,' replied Lois, sniffing the clean warmth of the kitchen, and bubbling beef stew on the Rayburn. 'Yep, he was really nice. Farmer's son from Yorkshire. Girlfriend teaches in Waltonby village school. Cottage clean and tidy, and no problems that I could see.'

'Why does he want to be a cleaner?' said Gran, going for the jugular. Lois shrugged. 'Maybe he's heard New Brooms is the place to be? No, but seriously, I think he may not last long. He's been working at the hospital for a while, since he came down to be with his Rebecca. Now he says the idea of going round the villages, being on the move, appeals to him. He didn't really say, but I bet it's not that easy to get farm work these days. All done by computers.'

Gran laughed. 'Don't you mean robots?' she said. 'Anyway, I know what you mean. Bloody great machines in the lanes and whizzing over the fields. Men not needed, not like they were in the old days.'

Lois could see a rambling tale about picnics in the harvest fields coming up, and so excused herself, saying Miss Abraham would be here in half an hour, and she just needed to organize one or two things. Gran muttered on about another missed meal, but Lois said she was looking forward to beef stew for tea, and meanwhile she'd have a cup of coffee.

'Coffee!' humphed Gran. 'That'll do you no good . . .'

But Lois was already in her office, checking phone messages, and preparing to receive Enid Abraham, spinster of the parish of Waltonby, writer of good letters, and probably totally unsuitable for the work Lois was offering.

Five

Gran went to open the door. She loved to do this. What some would call nosy, Gran regarded as healthy curiosity.

'Good morning!' she said brightly, looking approvingly at the neat figure in front of her. Well-cut grey coat, sober scarf.

Miss Enid Abraham, clutching a well-worn black handbag in both hands, said nervously, 'Is this right for Mrs Meade? I have an appointment . . .' Her voice trailed off apprehensively.

Lois came out of her office and took over. This maid-of-all-work act of her mother's irritated her, and she knew exactly why she did it. She liked to be kept informed, did Gran, and it never occurred to Lois that she herself might just be a chip off the old block.

'Come in, Miss Abraham, please,' she said, leading the way into her office. 'D'you want to take your coat off? It's quite warm in here, and you'll not feel the benefit when you go out again.'

Enid Abraham's face broke suddenly into a broad smile, miraculously transforming her colourless features. 'Oh, goodness,' she said, 'I've not heard anyone say that since my grandmother died! Oh yes, thank you, I'll just put them on the chair.' She slipped quickly out of her coat, and folded her scarf. 'It is really cold now, isn't it,' she said, turning back to Lois and sitting down in the chair by Lois's desk.

Lois nodded and smiled. Perhaps it was going to be easier than she had expected. She felt slightly uncomfortable, like some upper-class dame who'd inserted an ad for a mother's help in *The Lady*. Well, she wasn't, and the sooner they got things on to the proper footing the better.

'Now, Miss Abraham,' she said firmly. 'I'm looking for a cleaner. Someone who's not afraid of hard work. We don't gossip, and the girls are used to taking orders. We operate as a team, and you'd have to be happy to be out in all weathers and all times of day. You do drive, don't you?'

None of this had wiped the smile off Enid Abraham's face, and she replied mildly, 'I drove here, Mrs Meade.'

'In your letter,' continued Lois, still in the stern, no-nonsense voice, 'you said you could fit in "to some extent". What did you mean exactly?'

Enid Abraham shifted in her chair. 'I'd prefer not to be out after tea . . . that is, supper . . . as Mother is a bit nervous about . . . well, if it could be any time before fiveish . . .'

'How about early in the morning?' said Lois. Some of her clients liked their homes or premises to be sparkling before the working day started.

'Oh, yes . . . that would be fine. Father is always up early . . . we have a few beasts in the barn. They're in for the winter. Summer, of course, they're in the field . . . Anyway,' she added swiftly, 'I could certainly be available as early as you like.'

'Beasts?' said Lois incredulously, remembering *The Creature from Cathanger Mill*.

'Oh, that's just the old country word for cattle,' said Enid Abraham. 'Mother and Father were both country people. Father's family had land in Norfolk, but he wanted to do something different. Neither were Scottish, of course, but he'd seen an advertisement for a business for sale in Edinburgh, and they went up there soon after they were married.

She was silent for a moment, and Lois said, 'So what happened?'

'Well, the first business failed . . . and the next. He lost heart then, and ended up a school caretaker. He was happier when we moved down here, back to farming in a small way. Until, of course, Mother . . .' All at once the smile was gone. Her mouth shut tight, and she looked down at her hands.

'Why didn't you want me to come to the mill?' said Lois. She had forgotten this, in the unexpected pleasantness of talking to Miss Abraham. Now she waited. It was quite a wait, and Lois could hear Gran clattering about in the kitchen, offended that she'd been sent packing to the nether regions of the house.

Finally Enid Abraham looked up. 'It's Mother,' she said. 'She's a bit nervous about people coming to the house. Nothing serious, but we humour her if we can, you know. We're a bit isolated at the mill, anyway, so it doesn't make much difference to us.'

'Who is us?' said Lois. She had to ask. 'We saw you on the telly . . . about your brother. You didn't mention a brother in your letter.' She hesitated, seeing all traces of colour drain away from Enid Abraham's face. 'It's no business of mine, of course,' Lois added quickly. 'But it must be common knowledge now, after the news, an' that . . .'

'Yes,' said Enid Abraham quietly. 'I didn't want them there. The television people came down to the mill, and I talked to them so they would go away quickly. Mother, you know . . .'

'And your brother? Are you worried about him?' This was chancing her arm, Lois knew, but then the private lives of her cleaners were her concern. She had learned that the hard way.

'I'd rather not talk about him, if you don't mind, Mrs Meade,' was the reply. 'He has always been difficult . . . though when we were children . . . Anyway,' she added quickly, 'between you and me, Mrs Meade, it would be such a relief to me if he could make a life somewhere else.' Then she sat upright and the shutters came down, and she was the neat, remote, single woman of unblemished character once more.

There was a lot more to say about Edward Abraham, as Lois was to find out, but for the moment the subject was closed.

'What a nice woman,' said Gran, when the visitor had gone. 'Did you take her on?' Enid Abraham had smiled wistfully as Lois said she would let her know.

21

'Not without thinking about it,' said Lois abstractedly. It was going to be difficult, this one. She felt, like her mother, that Miss Abraham was a nice, gentle and clearly well-educated woman. She seemed completely without side, and her neat, clean appearance boded well for the job. There was no reason, on the face of it, why she shouldn't hire her. But then, what about the brother, and the mother, and the gruff father, and the dark and dismal mill house . . .?

When Derek came in for his tea, she had made a decision, and was not at all sure whether Derek would agree with it. Not that it mattered, she told herself defensively, but another point of view was always useful.

'You must be mad,' he said. 'I thought I told you—'

'I know you did,' said Lois. 'But she turned out to be a very good sort of woman, just right for us.'

'Huh!' said Derek. 'Well, nothin' I say'll make any difference. I'm used to that. So it's your affair, me duck. Don't blame me if it goes wrong. And the minute that Cowgill puts in an appearance, she gets the chop. Agreed?'

'Right,' she said. She always agreed when Derek got masterful. He seldom held it against her when she did the opposite. 'I've got no worries about Bill Stockbridge,' she continued, 'except whether he'll stick at it.'

'He'd be better sticking to farming,' said Derek, reaching for the teapot.

'Here!' said Gran. 'Give me that! We don't want ginger twins, do we?' She chuckled and poured him another cup. 'Well,' she continued, 'I didn't get a chance to talk to Miss Abraham' – this with a meaningful look at Lois – 'but she looked just the ticket to me. She'd get on with the others all right, too, if she's used to handling a difficult family. I might be able to help her out,' she added briskly.

'No, Mum, you keep out of it!' said Lois firmly.

'So that's all the thanks I get,' Gran said huffily, 'for working my elbows to the bone—'

'For God's sake!' said Derek. 'Can't a man get a bit o' peace in his own house? Women!'

*　　*　　*

22

It was about an hour later that Derek picked up the paper, leafing idly through the property pages while Gran listened to *The Archers*, her favourite radio soap. Everything stopped for *The Archers*. Lois said Gran learned more about the country from *The Archers* than she did from living in the middle of it. Derek said that he was buggered if anybody could learn anything about the country from *The Archers*! Just like all the other soaps, he reckoned, with a few mouldy sheep baaing in the background.

'Hey,' he said now, 'look at this.'

'Sshh!' said Gran.

Lois leaned over Derek's shoulder and peered at the paper. It was a house-for-sale advertisement, with a small, smudgy picture. 'That's that farmhouse just up the road from Cathanger Mill,' he said. Her hair tickled his face, and in spite of himself he turned and kissed her cool cheek. 'Bin empty for years,' he said, as she kissed him back. 'Old Joe Bell used to live there, and let it go after his wife died. Mind you, it's one of them old stone farmhouses that are solid as a rock. Wouldn't take much to get it up to scratch. Still, look what they want for it!'

'Blimey!' said Lois, relieved that he'd cheered up. 'Not worth five hundred the way it is now. Still, it's got a few acres. Some townie with kids and a pony will buy it, you bet. Restore it to something it's never bin, and move in with the four-by-four and a mother's help. Beats me why they have kids, that sort, if they can't even be bothered to look after them!'

'Well, we'll see if anybody's fool enough to buy it at that price,' said Derek.

Tumpty, tumpty, tumpty, tum, went *The Archers'* tune, and Gran turned off the radio. 'That Brian Aldridge,' she said. 'A leopard never changes its spots. If I had my way, I'd put him up against a wall and shoot him.'

Six

In a newish estate of executive dwellings in a well-heeled suburb of Birmingham, Rosie Charrington sat at an elegant little writing table she had bought for a song at a car boot sale. She turned over a pile of newspapers, each time going straight to the property pages. Rosie and husband Sebastian, a local vet dealing mostly with dogs, cats and hamsters, had decided it was time to move out to the *real* country. It would be good for the children, Maria and Felix, to get some fresh air into their lungs. It would be a whole new social life for Rosie and Sebastian, and if they chose wisely Rosie could still be within reach of motorways that would take her swiftly back to civilization when required. And if Sebastian could get that job with a veterinary practice advertised in the area they had chosen, he could get back to the large and, to Rosie, fearsome farm animals he loved best.

Her moving finger stopped on a smudgy photograph. She peered more closely. 'Bell's Farm,' she read, 'situated in one of the county's most desirable areas, close to the M40 and M1, and maintaining its rural charm. Four acres of pasture, with delightful stream. Barns and stabling, many original features. In need of some restoration.'

Excitement rose. This was it, Rosie felt it in her bones. Sebastian had said the best thing was to get a property where they could rebuild and restore to get it exactly how they wanted it. She looked at the price. More or less within their limits, and Sebastian was good at bargaining. 'Bell's Farm,' she said aloud. It had a good, plain ring to it. They'd need to change her car, of course. Sebastian had a company Ford, but she'd need one of those off-road jobs. Pile in all the children, and Anna, and they'd have to get a dog . . . or two . . .

24

'Mrs Charrington?' It was Anna, a Polish girl who looked after the children and had failed to master much of the English language in six months' stay. 'I go for the children?' she said, looking up at the old shelf clock.

'No, no,' said Rosie. 'It's your free time. I'll get them, and then nip into the supermarket for some food for tonight. I've got something exciting to show you later on,' she added, and never thought to wonder if Anna would like living in the country, where there would be no other Polish au pairs to befriend, and where there was only one bus per week to get her into town.

Not many miles away, in the reception class of Waltonby village school, Rebecca Rogers was tidying up her classroom after her pupils had gone home. She'd been out in the freezing playground, making herself available for any worried mum whose child had not yet settled down, though it was two months since the start of the new school year. Most of her little ones soon accustomed themselves to the new, strange routines, especially those who had been to playschool already. There was really only one, whose parents were older than average and had clung overprotectively to this little girl, keeping her a precious baby until the law said she had to go and join the cruel outside world of Waltonby village school.

'Miss Rogers?

Rebecca blinked. 'Sorry, Mrs Stratford,' she said. 'I was miles away. Can I help?'

Sheila Stratford, one of New Brooms' cleaners and Waltonby grandmother, stood smiling at her. 'I just wondered if you were carrying on with the milk bottle tops collection, like last year? My granddaughter's just gone up a class, and I've got a bagful here. But I can take them away if you're not . . .'

'Oh yes, of course! Here, I'll put them in the cupboard. They're getting scarce now, with everyone into cartons. These look nice and clean too – not like some.'

'Ah well,' pounced Sheila, spotting an opportunity to raise the subject she'd hoped would come up, 'I've been well-trained. Working for Lois Meade, y'know. "We sweep cleaner" and all that. Her standards are very high.'

Light dawned, and Rebecca smiled. 'Ah, you mean the cleaning business my Bill has signed up with? Yes, he's really looking forward to it. Mind you,' she added, perching on the edge of her table, 'I was surprised. Thought he'd want to do farm work, like he always has. If I'd been asked – which I wasn't! –' she looked confidingly at the motherly figure in front of her – '*if* I'd been asked, I'd have said he'd be better handling bullocks than dusters, though he takes his turn around the cottage. I have to give him that.'

'Well,' said Sheila, 'if it don't work out, my Sam might be able to find him some work. Still,' she said, with a guilty look, 'I probably shouldn't say that, Lois havin' decided, an' that. Anyway, I mustn't stand here gossiping! That's one of Lois's rules . . .'

Rebecca reckoned that Sheila Stratford rated gossip as one of the necessities of life, and before she could escape, said quickly, 'This Mrs Meade – is she nice? Bill didn't seem too sure. Not what he expected, he said.'

'Nice?' Sheila hesitated. 'Well, not like your uncle, Rev Rogers, is nice and kind . . . not soft in any way, y'know. But you could trust her with your life. An' she's loyal to her cleaners . . . providing they're loyal to her. She's a good mother, too, in her way. And her husband, Derek,' Sheila added, brightening up, 'he's really nice. Lovely bloke. Puts up with quite a lot, one way and another . . .' Then she put her hand up to her mouth in a mock stifling gesture. 'There I go again!' she said. 'I must be off, before you get everybody's life history at New Brooms!'

'Cheerio, Mrs Stratford,' said Rebecca, 'I expect we'll meet again.'

'Bound to,' said Sheila, and made for the door. Then she turned back. 'Oh, by the way, did you see our Waltonby's in the news? Cathanger Mill? That Abraham chap, seems he done a runner. Your Bill'd be interested, seein' as Miss Abraham has applied for a cleanin' job with Lois. I know one thing,' she added, in a final exit line, 'I wouldn't have nothing to do with that Abraham lot, not for all the tea in China!'

Later that evening, when Bill returned from the hospital, Rebecca mentioned the Abrahams. Neither she nor Bill had seen the news item, and had never heard of the Abraham family. 'But I've driven past it,' said Rebecca, putting another log on the fire. 'Spooky-looking place. Bloomin' great dog came out barking its head off, and chased the car all the way up to the empty farmhouse.'

'That farmhouse is on the market,' said Bill, not much interested in spooks. 'D'you fancy going for it? We could do the renovations ourselves.'

But Rebecca shook her head. That would be a commitment she was not ready for. This warm little cottage, rented from the church, suited her fine. There were too many uncertainties ahead to think of putting down roots with Bill just yet.

Seven

E nid Abraham drove her small, grey car slowly up the track to Cathanger Mill. It was growing dark, and the weak lights showed up the potholes and ruts. She could not use the headlights for fear of alarming Mother. Not that it mattered. She could have found her way through this obstacle course with her eyes shut.

In the summer, Enid would walk about the mill garden and field at dusk, often staying out until all the light had gone, but in winter the evenings were long and dreary. Mother would sit in one room with the door firmly shut, and Father and Edward stayed silently in the kitchen, the day's newspaper shared between them, seldom exchanging a word. She was ignored by all of them. Novels saved her life. She went regularly to the library in Tresham, as she had today, taking out four new novels a week, and these she would read quietly in a chair by the kitchen range. Halfway through the evening, she would make a cup of tea for all of them, receiving no thanks from Mother, and a curt nod from Father and Edward.

Once or twice, she had suggested joining the WI in Waltonby, but this had been dismissed as unthinkable. Edward had been particularly sarcastic. 'My God, Enid!' he'd sneered. 'I never thought you'd come to that! Jam and Jerusalem? You'd be better employed straightening out our accounts . . . take a book-keeping course or something.'

But when she'd found an accounting course run by the WEA in Long Farnden village hall, Edward, the turncoat, had said it was ridiculous to be out in the car in the evenings when all she needed was to know how to add and subtract, and surely she could manage that with her past experience in the chemist's?

So, she had acquiesced, as usual. Then one day recently, searching through a drawer in Mother's room while she was asleep in the chair, she found an old bag full of lace-making things, and remembered how long ago in Edinburgh she had been to classes and learned the old skills. They'd praised her aptitude, and she'd made lovely lace and sewn it on to fine cotton handkerchiefs as gifts for the girls at work. After they'd moved, and everything changed, she'd forgotten about lace-making.

Now, fetching the bag, she began to sort the bobbins and cottons. The low wattage light in the kitchen was not good, but she moved her chair nearer to where Father sat reading, and as her fingers moved swiftly, sorting out the muddle, she began to hum softly. Perhaps it had been the reminder of happier days that encouraged her to apply for the job.

'What're you making that noise for?' said Father, without looking up.

'Because I'm happy,' said Enid.

Now he looked up, frowning at her. 'What've you got to be happy about?' he grunted.

'I'm happy because I've got a job, a cleaning job,' said Enid.

'A job? Did you say a cleaning job?' Walter was incredulous, and Enid had a moment's pang of remorse at adding yet another worry to his burden.

'I'm wasting my life here,' she said quickly, 'and this is a chance to do something. Not very challenging, I agree, but it's a start.'

He stared at her, and knew from the set of her mouth that she would not be dissuaded. 'You fixed it, then?' he said sadly.

She nodded. 'I start on Monday,' she said.

The Abrahams had no television, and Mother had forbidden them to have the radio. She said there was never anything but trouble, trouble, trouble. News of the outside world came in the pages of the *Tresham Chronicle*, which Father picked up from Long Farnden village shop every morning when he went in for his cigarettes. His one self-indulgence, he said, puffing through sixty a day and discarding packets all around the house and yard. Enid hated the smell of cigarette smoke. Father had never smoked until they came to Cathanger. Now his shoulders were bowed, and his cough kept her awake at nights.

She began to straighten the bobbins. It might be all right, she told herself optimistically. Things could improve, if only Edward would settle things and make a life for himself, preferably somewhere else.

Eight

'Why couldn't you just hire a couple of nice ordinary women, with ordinary kids and no trouble?' Derek, in an exasperated mood, sat in front of the dying fire opposite an unrepentant Lois. It was late, and the central heating had gone off half an hour ago. Lois moved her chair nearer to the fire and said, 'I don't know what you mean, Derek,' though she did know, perfectly well.

'Nothing difficult there,' said Derek. He thought how young she looked, hugging herself in the growing chill. You'd never think she was a mother of three, ran her own business and was about as bloody-minded as it was possible to get. Oh yes, and an amateur sleuth into the bargain. He resisted the temptation to grab hold of her and rush upstairs to have wonderful, energetic sex, which she was also good at.

'Just think, Lois,' he continued. 'You've taken on a young bloke who's worked briefly as a hospital auxilliary, but mainly on a moorland farm, used to being out of doors, roughing it in all weathers, one of the lads, and a useful scrum half. And you're goin' to set him on cleaning people's poncey houses!' Lois nodded and smiled irritatingly.

'And then,' he carried on, trying hard not to notice how long and lovely Lois's legs still were. Right up to her arse, his dad had said when he first took her home on approval. 'Then,' he said, 'there's Miss Abraham. Anybody else would see that she won't be any good. Too old, too posh, and from a place straight out of a Hammer Horror! Cathanger! Blimey, that's enough for a start!'

Lois laughed now, her best open, straightforward laugh, and Derek gave in to temptation. 'Oh, all right,' he said. 'Have it your own way. You always do, anyway. Come on, gel,' he added, reaching out and pulling her to her feet. 'Time for bed, an' that,' he said.

'Specially that,' Lois replied, putting her arms round his neck and nuzzling his ear until he picked her up bodily and carried her to the foot of the stairs. 'Put me down,' she whispered, 'else you'll be runnin' out of steam.'

Derek, already regretting his chivalric impulse, put her down with relief.

Next morning, Lois sat in her office, idly looking out of the window. She was waiting for a ring-back call to a new client, the estate agent's small branch office in Fletcham. If she got this job, she planned to send Bill Stockbridge along. It would be a good start for him, she'd thought. Better than him having to get used to some woman who might follow him about to check he was dusting the tops of the picture frames.

She knew Derek was right. But right from the launch of New Brooms her cleaners had been more to her than just machines who had to function efficiently in the workplace. Bridie had been her childhood friend, and she remembered the day Hazel wriggled herself efficiently into the world, one of those babies who seem to know the score from the start. They were close to her already, before starting to work for her. Then there had been Gary, a misguided charmer, for whom Lois still had a sneaking fondness, though he'd left under a cloud. And dear old Sheila Stratford, who chose to work outside her own village, treating the job with New Brooms as if it were a fast track career with limitless prospects.

No, nice ordinary women were not for Lois. It was more interesting her way.

A car pulled up on the opposite side of the road, and Lois snapped to attention. Cowgill, seated behind the wheel and looking straight ahead, took out his mobile and dialled. Damn! Lois picked up her phone and said, 'Something wrong with your feet? I thought policemen were supposed to plod round their beat, inspiring confidence in the local community and all that rubbish.'

'Morning, Lois,' said Hunter Cowgill. 'You can't have forgotten you've forbidden me to be seen with you? No alternative but to—'

'But to sit outside my house with absolutely no reason for being there,' interrupted Lois. 'Anyway, what do you want?'

'To talk to you,' said Cowgill briskly. 'More an exchange of information, really. About the Abrahams. You know a bit about Enid now, I'm sure, and I can fill you in with some more about the family. There's a problem there, as you've probably heard. I need your help, Lois. Two thirty, Alibone Woods? It's not going to rain . . .'

'I suppose I can be there,' said Lois reluctantly.

'Good.' Cowgill was in authoritative mode now. 'And in my own defence,' he added, 'I've just been to your village shop. They've had a break-in. So I have every reason to be in Long Farnden. Bye, Lois. See you later.'

She watched him, and he did not once glance towards her window. The car slid off down the High Street, and as far as she could tell, no one noticed. Of course, she could not see that a small grey car had been parked outside the shop, and that Miss Enid Abraham had been bent over the biscuit selection whilst Inspector Cowgill had discussed the break-in with the shopkeeper behind the counter.

The ring-back call came in, and Lois forgot about Cowgill for the moment. The estate agent's office was small, three rooms in all, with a sub-manager and girl clerk working there five days a week. They needed to keep it tidy and clean, said the girl, because they had so little space. 'And you won't catch me going round on hands and knees!' she said brightly. 'Can you help us? Perhaps you can give us a special rate, as there's really not much to do.'

'No, no special rates,' said Lois flatly, thinking that estate agents deserved their evil reputation. 'I think you'll find we give good value for money. Our team is the best, and you won't have any reason to complain. Would it be all right if I call in this afternoon to discuss it?'

'Oh, right,' said the girl in a more subdued voice. 'Yes, that will be fine. See you later then, Mrs Meade.'

33

The morning went quickly, with Lois attending to paper-work and working out the schedules for next week. Bill would start at the estate agent's, with luck, and Enid Abraham would be going with Bridie to the vicarage to work alongside her and get used to the routines. Lois had decided this was the best way to train new staff. Gran had said surely there wasn't much to learn; it was a poor sort of woman who couldn't clean a house decently! But there was quite a lot more to it. Lois had done the job herself. Professional cleaners invaded a client's private space. It was very important that they did it with tact and efficiency, leaving homes as they found them, but with a cheerful shine. The client must wave them goodbye with a pleasant feeling of well-being that had not been there before.

'Are you out this afternoon?' Gran said at lunchtime. She had made a mushroom omelette, and frowned as she watched Lois clearing her plate in minutes. 'Have you any idea what you're eating?' she said.

'You sound like somebody's mother,' Lois answered. 'But thanks, Mum,' she added quickly. 'That was great. Got to be going now, and I may not be back in time for the kids getting home. Will you be here?'

'Of course,' said Gran, smiling happily. 'Aren't I always?'

The woods were dark, although it was only halfway through the day. A thick mist hung over meadows that bordered the wood, and Lois regretted agreeing so readily to meet Cowgill. She'd have to think of a better place than this, if their arrangement was to continue.

'Thanks for coming.' He stood by their chosen tree trunk, tall and unsmiling, immaculately turned out as always. Must have a very dutiful wifie, thought Lois, noticing the snowy-white handkerchief showing from his breast pocket.

'Tell me about the Abrahams, then,' she said. 'I haven't got much time. Thingy's in Fletcham want a cleaner, and I'm going there after here.'

'Useful for your new chap – Stockbridge, is it?'

'Is there anything you don't know?' said Lois. 'Anyway, get on with it. I suppose it's about that brother. Enid's brother?'

Cowgill nodded. Edward Abraham had been on the fringe of certain dodgy deals in the area for some years, he said. Nothing criminal. He was too clever for that. But he was a nasty piece of work, and nobody liked him. His father was, in Cowgill's opinion, frightened of him, completely under his thumb, although Edward had sponged off his parents on and off all his life. 'To tell the truth, Lois,' Cowgill said, 'I don't know how they live. The old boy's got a pension, I suppose, and dabbles about in his smallholding with a few bullocks. But that wouldn't keep the three of them in socks.'

'Four of them,' said Lois. 'There's the mother as well.'

'Mother?' said Cowgill. 'Since when?'

'Since always.' Lois shrugged. 'She's some kind of a recluse, according to Enid. Gradually losing her marbles, from the sound of it. Rules them all from a shuttered room where only Enid is allowed. She clammed up on the subject after a bit, and anyway, it's not really my business. I liked the woman – Enid, that is – and reckon she'll do a good job.'

Her voice had a defensive edge and Cowgill said, 'What does Derek think?'

'None of your business,' said Lois sharply. 'Now what've you got to tell me?'

'Not much more,' said Cowgill, wishing that Lois was short, fat and ugly, so that he could dislike her, 'except that Edward Abraham has disappeared. There was a court case coming up. Some poor sod trying to get money he was owed. But when Abraham didn't answer any letters, a collector bloke was sent round to try and get something out of him. The father said he wasn't there, and slammed the door. We had a try, and this time it was quiet as the grave, and though we were sure somebody was there – Constable Simpson said he could see a curtain twitching – nobody came to the door. And your Enid Abraham is quite a slippery fish. None of us has been able to talk to her yet. Still, we'll catch up with her. Especially now we know where she's working . . .'

'Lay off!' said Lois. 'If you want my help, it'll be on my terms.'

'As always,' said Cowgill, fractionally bowing his head, and feeling that old *frisson* when she reluctantly half-smiled in acknowledgement. 'But we need to find Edward Abraham. Keep in touch, Lois,' he said, and strode off out of the woods to where he had parked his car. Down Fido, he said to himself as he drove off.

Nine

Sackville's was an old-established property agent with a main office in Tresham, and a small branch in Fletcham covering the villages in that area. They had a reputation for moving property fast, for keeping prices reasonably low, and making sure sales went through with the fewest possible hitches. That way, they wasted no time and little money, and had a considerable edge over their competitors.

Lois parked outside the Fletcham office and went in. A small girl behind a big desk looked up and smiled. 'Can I help you?' she said.

'I'm Mrs Meade, New Brooms. I phoned,' said Lois briskly.

'Ah yes, do sit down, Mrs Meade,' replied the girl. 'There are a few questions I'd like to ask . . . hours and rates of pay and so on.'

After ten minutes, the girl was shaking Lois by the hand, thanking her profusely for dropping by, and wondering who had been interviewing whom. Lois, on the other hand, felt quite content at securing a new client, and drove the two hundred yards up the road to Bill Stockbridge's cottage on the offchance that he might be at home. He wasn't, and Rebecca would be at school, so Lois sat outside their cottage for a while, deciding what to do next.

She had been intrigued by the smartly-dressed woman who had come into Sackville's office a couple of minutes before Lois's interview had ended. She had announced herself as Rosie Charrington, and had wandered about looking at photographs of properties until Lois got up to go. Her opening words, as Lois left the office, had been easily audible: 'I've come about Bell's Farm . . .

you know, I spoke to you earlier . . . I'd like to take a preliminary look.'

Well, it could do no harm to drive round that way. She needed to have a word with Bridie and Hazel in Waltonby, and anyway, Mrs Charrington might be a possible client for the future. She watched until the smart little red car drove off from Sackville's, and then followed at a discreet distance.

The day had not improved. A strong wind had blown away the mist, but great black clouds raced across the sky, chucking down heavy showers of large, cold raindrops. Lois's windscreen wipers were not really up to the job, and she peered through the streams of water at the road ahead. The tunnel of trees approaching Cathanger Mill acted as an umbrella for a few yards, and suddenly she could see more clearly. The red car had disappeared round the corner, and Lois speeded up. Then right in front of her, with no warning, a figure appeared, shrouded from head to foot in dark clothes. It was a man, she was sure of that as she braked heavily. He'd stepped out of the trees and was followed by a big sheepdog, which turned and bared its teeth at her as she squealed to a halt.

'Why the bloody hell don't you look where you're going!' yelled Lois, winding down her window. The man did not turn his head. In fact, he seemed to hunch it even further into his shoulders. He trudged on across the road, and started into a gateway on the other side. The dog, however, stayed on the same spot, facing Lois's car and barking a deep throaty bark that echoed through the trees. Lois beeped, a long impatient beep, and the man, now standing on the grass verge, turned and shouted one word at the dog. Its tail went down and its ears flattened. It slunk away across the road and followed the dark figure down the track. Lois realized her heart was thumping. She'd seen the dog before, in Cathanger Mill, chained to the old gatepost at the entrance, on guard.

A quick glimpse of the man's face as he shouted had been enough to frighten her. It was not an old face, but was pale, unshaven, and had an unmistakable likeness to Miss Enid Abraham.

*   *   *

38

Bell's Farm, although empty for some time, and surrounded by unkempt garden, was a sunlit paradise compared with Cathanger Mill. Lois pulled up a short way past the farm gate, and walked back to where she could see the red car. Two women were opening the front door – Sackville's girl and Rosie Charrington – and, as Lois bent down to remove a non-existent stone from her shoe, they disappeared inside the house. She thought for a moment, and made a quick decision. Turning quickly, she walked up the short path to the farmhouse and knocked at the door.

'Mrs Meade? What are you . . .'

'Sorry to chase you,' said Lois, with an apologetic smile. 'I'm going home this way, and saw the car and you in it. I think I forgot to say we could start next week? Saves me a phone call. And, by the way, we bring our own cleaning materials. All in the price,' she could not resist adding.

Rosie Charrington stood at the foot of the stairs, her hand on a dusty bannister. 'Cleaning?' she said. In her experience, cleaners were gold dust. 'Are you a cleaner?'

'I run a cleaning business,' said Lois cheerfully. 'Looks like you might need us if you move in here!' She reached into her pocket and produced a silvery pen with *New Brooms – we sweep cleaner!* and a telephone number embossed on the side. 'Here – this'll help remind you.' It had been Josie's idea. 'Quality, Mum,' she'd said, 'that's the impression you're out to give.' Lois had been doubtful, but ordered the pens to please Josie. They had been a great success, and everyone on the team flourished them at every opportunity.

'How nice!' said Rosie Charrington, taking the pen with alacrity. 'We've a long way to go yet, of course, but once I've made up my mind, I move fast. Sebastian is the same. If there's not too much to do here, and we could live with it more or less straight away, I might be in touch sooner than you think!'

Sackville's girl was beaming. Things were looking very promising, and she turned to show off the rest of the house, launching into the jargon with practised ease. It occurred to her, as they picked their way through accumulated junk in the big kitchen, that it might be worth getting Lois Meade to clean up the house before they had any more enquiries. First impressions were all important. This Mrs Charrington seemed very keen, but you never knew in this business. She made a note to ring New Brooms when she got back to the office.

'Hi, Lois, what're you doing here?' Bridie Reading had just returned from her job at the vicarage, and was making a cup of tea in the kitchen. 'Got time for one?' she said.

Lois nodded. 'Yep, that'd be good. Make it strong and sweet. Just had a bit of a shock.' She was smiling, but still felt a bit shaky after that encounter in the trees by the mill.

'There's a woman looking over Bell's Farm,' she said conversationally.

'What was shocking about that?' said Bridie, putting a large mug of tea in front of Lois.

'Nothing,' said Lois. 'No, it wasn't her. But I was just telling you that in case you hear anything about it being sold. Could be a new client for us. I put in a word to her, and gave her a pen.' She paused, and Bridie waited.

Finally, she said, 'And the shock? What was that?'

Lois shook her head. 'It wasn't nothing, really. Just that I nearly ran into a bloke who stepped out into the road in front of me. In that tunnel of trees by Cathanger. And a dog, too. Shakes you up, doesn't it?'

'Who was it, then?' said Bridie. She knew Lois so well. There was more to come.

'Not sure,' said Lois casually. 'The dog looked like that brute of Abraham's. I don't think the man was old Abraham. I've seen him in the shop once or twice. Anyway, this bloke was younger. Only caught a quick flash of his face . . . he looked a bit like Enid. You know, Enid who's coming to work for us.'

Bridie's face had darkened. 'Oh my God,' she said. 'I thought he'd gone for good. It'd be Edward, I reckon.'

'Does he look like Enid? I thought he was a lot older?'

'Oh no, Lois. There is a strong resemblance, as you would expect. They're twins,' said Bridie.

Ten

In the semi-darkened room where her mother passed strange, lonely days, Enid Abraham moved about quietly, cleaning and folding her mother's cast-off clothes. In a bizarre routine, each morning Mother would get out of the divan bed against the wall and take all her clothes from the cupboard which Father, on her instructions, had moved from the bedroom upstairs. From the untidy pile on the bed, she would take one dress, or skirt and jumper, and one pair of shoes, and after slowly putting them on, she would stand for a couple of minutes, and then begin taking them off again, ready to pass on to the next outfit. In this way, she would go through all her clothes every morning, and the process would last until it was time for Enid to come in, tidy up and give her a cup of hot chocolate, which, unless it was exactly the right consistency and temperature, would be dumped unceremoniously on the floor.

'What do you mean, Enid?' said Mother now, watching her daughter's every movement like an old parrot. 'What d'you mean, you will leave my chocolate in a flask? Where do you think you are going? You are needed here, my girl. This is your place, make no mistake about that!'

'I shall be out most mornings, I expect,' said Enid mildly. 'I've got a job. Helping out where people need it.' She dare not say cleaning. That would be totally out of the question. No daughter of Mrs Abraham went out cleaning other people's houses.

The hot chocolate hit the wall behind Enid's head. She was used to ducking at the right time, and quickly picked up the empty cup, fetched a bucket and cloth and cleaned up the mess, and then – closing her ears to the invective hurled at her – went calmly out of the room and shut the door. It was some time before the house was quiet, but when she was sure her mother had settled down, Enid put on her coat and wellies, tied a scarf around her head against the cold wind, and went out across the yard to a stone barn where the chickens awaited their usual feed.

'That's the worst bit done,' she confided to a noisy mob of hens, scattering grain in smooth arcs so that all should get their share. 'Now Mother knows, she'll accept it. She'll punish me in her time-honoured fashion, no doubt, but I'm used to that.'

She went to collect the eggs from nest boxes in the corner, and found yet another broken open and the yolk spilled. Her face set, she looked around the milling chickens. She knew which one she was looking for. It had a damaged wing that dragged along the ground. Reaching down, she took it by the neck, ignored its one flapping wing, and neatly pulled the head sharply away from the body. The flapping continued for a few seconds, and its legs pounded away in an automatic effort to escape. Then it was still, and Enid pushed it into the empty grain bucket.

'That sorts out supper for tonight,' she said, this time addressing her Father, who had come into the barn and seen the whole thing.

'Good girl,' he said approvingly. 'Well done. If you get an egg-eater, there's nothing else to be done. Give it here. I'll see to it.'

Enid handed over the bucket and rubbed her hands together. 'I must get off now,' she said. 'Library day. Anything you want, Father?

He shook his head. 'Don't be too long,' he said, with an anxious look back at the house.

Just up the road, in the empty farmhouse, Lois was putting on rubber gloves and collecting cleaning materials together for a major assault on the dust and dirt. Hazel was already there when she arrived, and the pair of them set to work.

'Better tidy up first, don't you think, Mrs M?' said Hazel, pulling out a roll of black rubbish bags.

Lois nodded. 'You start upstairs,' she said, 'and I'll be down here. Give us a shout if there's a problem.'

Hazel picked her way upstairs, noticing that the stairs still had threadbare carpet, but seemed in good repair. The whole house was solid, reassuring, and, unlike some much cleaner but chillier jobs Hazel had been sent to, it had a pleasant, friendly atmosphere. The low sun shining through dusty windows warmed up the rooms, and Hazel set to work with a will. She picked up old newspapers, books with no covers, empty bottles of patent medicines that had never seen a sell-by date, some showing vestiges of dark brown liquid clinging to the sides. She opened one of these, and sniffed. 'Ugh!' she exclaimed. 'Yuk! No wonder they all snuffed it!'

Lois came upstairs. 'What's up?' she said.

'Nothin',' said Hazel, 'it's just these old bottles – here, take a sniff.'

'Ipikek,' said Lois flatly. 'I remember it from my nan. Used to give it us if we had coughs. Kill or cure, I reckon.'

She turned to go back downstairs, and her eye was caught by a pile of curtains in the corner of the room. 'We'd better make a bonfire, Hazel,' she said. 'There's too much rubbish here for us to take away . . . or for the bin men.' She walked over to pick up the curtains, and stopped. There was something organized about them. It looked like a roughly-made bed, with an old cushion where a pillow might be.

'Hey look, Hazel,' she said. 'What d'you think?'

'Down-and-out,' said Hazel with a shiver. 'One of our ever-present homeless,' she added. Hazel knew the homeless scene pretty well, but in Tresham, not out here in the country.

'But how did he get in?' asked Lois, looking round nervously.

'Or she,' said Hazel. She shook her head. 'God knows,' she said, 'but when you're desperate, you'll find a way. Probably a broken window somewhere. Anyway, we'd better dump it all, hadn't we?'

'Yep,' said Lois. 'We got a job to do. I want this place clean and smellin' of roses by the time we've finished.' She bent down and gathered up the curtains and the cushion, and shoved them into a black bag. 'Probably moved on to somewhere else now, anyway,' she said. 'Now the agents are bringin' people round, nobody'll hide out here.'

It took the pair of them hours to get the house into a state that satisfied Lois, and then they piled up the rubbish in the back garden and hunted about for matches. A couple of heavy raindrops hit Lois on the back of the neck. 'Damn!' she said. 'It's goin' to rain again! We'll never get this fire going today. Better find somethin' to cover the heap and come back when it stops.

They found a large plastic sheet, neatly folded, in a disused washhouse at the back of the yard, and stretched it out over the rubbish, weighting it down with bricks to keep out the rain.

'I'll take care of it,' Lois said. 'I'll be round this way again tomorrow.'

'Y'know what,' said Hazel. 'We could ask our Enid Abraham to come up and light it when it dries up. They're only just down the road.'

Lois hesitated. She was well aware that Hazel had reservations about Enid Abraham. This did not worry her, but she had had cause to trust Hazel's judgement in the past, and did not dismiss it out of hand. 'Well, she's not really on our books until Monday,' she said. 'No, I'll do it, Hazel. And by the way, I've told Enid we always have a four-week trial period at New Brooms.'

Hazel nodded. 'Mind-reader, that's what you are, Mrs M,' she said, and touched Lois lightly on the arm. 'Mum said would you like to drop in for coffee if you got time,' she added. 'I'm off to the hall, so you girls can have a gossip together.'

Lois laughed. 'Just watch it, young Hazel,' she said.

It was not until she sat having a late coffee with Bridie, telling her about the junk in the old farmhouse, that Hazel's words came back to her. Down-and-out and homeless, she had said, and a sudden picture of a tall man in dark clothes, with a white, unshaven face, came back to send a shiver down her spine.

*   *   *

'Hello, Bill?' Lois had eaten a delicious savoury pancake, more slowly than usual to please Gran, and now reached across her desk for the notes she had made in Sackville's office. 'Bill, it's Lois here. When did you say you could start? In two weeks' time? Great. I've got just the job for you to start on, and I'll fill in until you can take it on. It's the estate agent's . . . in your village, yes. What?

There were chortles of an unmistakable sort at the other end of the phone, and Lois frowned. 'Never mind about the blonde behind the desk! You won't even see her – we have to be finished in the office before they open up. So you can forget any ideas in that direction. And this is a cleaning agency, not a dating . . . Oh, OK, it was a joke. Yep, well . . .' Lois reached for her mug of tea and took a slurp. Bill continued to apologize, until she said not to worry, she was not totally without a sense of humour. She would see him in two weeks' time at Sackville's office, show him the ropes for the first morning, and then introduce him to the others at the Monday meeting.

Bill put down the phone and turned to Rebecca, who had called in for a swift sandwich break from school. 'Oops,' he said, 'nearly made a mess of it there.'

'She's not a soft touch, not by any means, according to Mrs Stratford,' said Rebecca.

'Who's Mrs Stratford?'

'One of the school grannies,' Rebecca replied. 'Very nice woman, works for Lois Meade. Respects her no end, but says you can't take advantage. So if you really mean to make a go of this cleaning nonsense, you'd better remember that.'

Bill's face fell. 'It's not nonsense,' he said. 'You might give us a chance. You're not ashamed of your bloke being a cleaner, are you? I mean, Rebecca, if that's how you feel, I'll give it up now, before I start. There's bound to be farm work about sooner or later.'

Rebecca looked at his nice open face and relented. She'd been tempted to tell him that Sheila Stratford had more or less said she could get him work on the farm. But who was she to tell him what to do? She wasn't his wife, after all. They had no kids to think of. She thought of all those thickos in the village pub, young sons of local

45

farmers, whose conversation ran out of interest after two sentences. No, Bill was different, and if he wanted to be a char, good luck to him. There must be a euphemism for chars, anyway, like rodent controller instead of ratcatcher. Something like home refreshers? Rebecca looked at Bill, with his hefty rugby-player's shoulders and square jaw, and laughed aloud.

'What's funny?' he said defensively.

'Just wondering what I'll call you,' she said, giving him a peck on the cheek.

'Call a bloody spade a spade,' he said crossly. 'I'll be a cleaner, and that's that.'

'I've got it!' said Rebecca, moving away from him to a safe distance. 'You'll be New Broom Bill, sweeping the world cleaner!' He lunged, but she was out of the room and locked in the lavatory before he could catch her.

Sheila Stratford was a typical grannie, blind to her grandchildren's imperfections, and certain that whatever shortcomings there were, were due entirely to faulty education in the village school. But she had nothing against Rebecca, and said to all and sundry that if anyone asked her, she would stake her life on Bill Stockbridge being a really nice bloke, a hard worker and totally trustworthy.

She looked at husband Sam now over the table. He had just said Bill must be crazy, or a poof, to want to do house cleaning. 'None of our business,' she scolded Sam as he sat back from a satisfactory meal. 'Nowadays,' she challenged him, 'things are different. Women do men's jobs, and men take on women's work in loads of places. Take that son of her up at the manor,' Sheila added, warming to her subject. Sam was trapped, sitting in his socks, whilst Sheila cleared away the dishes.

'That son of her up at the manor,' she'd repeated. 'Got a first at Oxford, whatever that means, but I know it's good. Suddenly decides to be a nurse. A nurse! On skivvy's rates of pay, and dreadful hours!'

'Yeah,' Sam said, getting to his feet and trying to edge past Sheila to the door, 'and now he's got some admin job . . .

good pay and prospects . . . fast track to the top, his dad told me. So your argument don't hold water, Sheila. No, I reckon your Bill's one of them closet blokes. You can't always tell, you know.'

'And what about Rebecca, then?' Sheila replied triumphantly.

'She's his cover, see.' Sam had reached the door, and stood grinning at her. 'I'll be off then. See you later, gel.

'Rubbish!' said Sheila. Sam was just an old-fashioned stick-in-the-mud. Well, she'd do her best to befriend Bill, show him the routines an' that. And there were always jobs that needed a bit o' muscle in New Brooms. Lois knew what she was doing.

Sheila swilled water round the sink, dried her hands and took off her apron. No, she thought, if there were going to be any snags to Bill Stockbridge, it was much more likely to be on the Hazel Reading front. She had an eye for the lads, like any young girl. If Sheila were Lois, she'd make sure not to send them out on a job together. You couldn't be too careful.

Eleven

Rain was still falling relentlessly next morning, and Lois abandoned any ideas of lighting a bonfire at the old farmhouse. Not that there was any rush, but she decided to ring Sackville's and tell them what she had done.

'Thanks very much, Mrs Meade,' said the girl. 'I popped in after you'd gone, and must say it is a complete transformation!'

'It's clean,' said Lois.

'Yes, indeed! And such a good thing, as Mrs Charrington and her husband are coming over again today. She's picking up the key from here – wants them to see it alone, without me rabbiting on! Now you've done such a good job, they'll be sure to buy.'

'Well, we'll see,' said Lois. 'Now, if you were satisfied, I'd like to suggest we get this on a regular footing. What goes for the farmhouse goes for most properties. I do the same thing for another agent in Tresham, and it seems to work well. As you're in this area, perhaps we could have an agreement that you'd call on New Brooms for any properties standing empty and needing a wash and brush-up?'

Gran, who'd come into Lois's office at the start of this conversation, raised her eyebrows. My God, Lois was certainly turning into a real businesswoman! She wished her husband was alive to see it . . . he'd always said she had a good head on her shoulders. And he loved to be proved right.

'So what time is Mrs Charrington expected? I might drop in and see if she's thought any more about a cleaner once they're there.'

'Oh, well, I don't know about that,' said the girl doubtfully. Then, since Lois said nothing, she added, 'Still, if you're just passing and see their car, or something . . . They plan to get there around eleven this morning.'

'Thanks a lot,' said Lois. 'Our invoice on the farmhouse job is on its way. I'll call in soon, and we could maybe see about a discount for quantity!' She made it sound like a joke, but the girl knew for sure that if she played her part, Lois Meade would deliver.

Lois put down the phone, and went back into the kitchen. Jamie had stayed at home today with a sore throat, and she sat down at the table with him to have a game of Scrabble. She looked at his pale face, with its special sweet smile reserved for her, and thanked God that Gran was now living with them. The struggle between motherhood and career would have been overwhelming without her.

Gran put a mug of hot orange juice in front of Jamie, and gave coffee to Lois and herself. It was warm in the kitchen, and with rain lashing the windows Lois felt no inclination to venture out. She allowed Jamie to win the game, and suggested he had a snooze in the old armchair with Melvyn the cat. She tucked a rug around him and waited until his eyes closed. Then she whispered to Gran that she just had to go over to Waltonby for half an hour, but would be back in time for lunch. 'Keep an eye on Jamie, won't you,' she said, and got such a withering look from her mother that she drove off through the downpour with some relief.

It was noon by the time she passed Cathanger Mill and drove on to Bell's Farm. She felt a nervous shiver as she quickened the pace through the dark tunnel of trees, but today she saw nobody. The mill house was shrouded in curtains of rain, and large puddles were forming in the dip by the bridge over the stream. By the time Lois got to the farmhouse, she was wondering whether the Charringtons would brave this awful weather after all.

She reckoned without Rosie's determination. Accustomed to getting her own way, Rosie had dismissed all protests from Sebastian that they'd get marooned, and made use of the opportunity to suggest the need for a four-by-four. She had parked her car just off the road in the farm entrance,

49

and they'd hopped and dodged up the path to the front door of the house.

Sebastian's mood surprisingly improved. 'This is more like it,' he said, scraping his shoes on an old iron bar driven into the ground for just that purpose. 'God, smell that air, Rosie,' he said.

She thought privately that the quicker they got out of the soggy rain-filled air the better, but smiled and nodded. 'This is *real*, isn't it?' she said, and turned the key in the lock.

For a moment she stood and stared, and then, 'Oh, my goodness!' she said. 'This is incredible! It's like the fairies have been in and transformed it!

Sebastian looked at her anxiously. Had she flipped or something? He was used to her going overboard about her enthusiasms, but what was she on about?

'It's so clean!' she explained. 'When I came before – I told you – it was deep in junk and dirt, and really took a feat of imagination to see how it could be restored. Now . . . well, it must be that Mrs Meade – I told you – and her cleaning service.'

They continued round the house, with Rosie exclaiming and Sebastian nodding approval. 'Well done, Rosie,' he said finally. 'This would be ideal, if I get the job. Plenty of room for the family, and –' he peered through the sparkling windows at the rain-soaked garden and the paddock beyond – 'and look out there. We could have a couple of ponies, some chickens . . .'

'And a Labrador . . . a black one, must be a black one.' Rosie's eyes were shining, and she hugged Sebastian in an excess of excitement.

At this favourable moment, Lois knocked at the door. 'I saw your car,' she said, smiling broadly. 'Thought I'd just look in to see how you're getting on . . . Maybe need some information about the area . . . facilities and so on?'

'How very kind,' said Rosie. 'That would be most useful. Why don't you come into the kitchen and tell us about buses and Women's Institutes and things?'

'One thing,' said Sebastian. Lois looked at him. 'What's

that heap in the garden there?' he said. 'Looks like a funeral pyre.'

'Ah,' said Lois. 'Well, it's just a heap of rubbish that we turned out of the house.' She moved across to the window, blocking the view for the Charringtons. 'I'm going to burn it up, as soon as it stops raining.' As she looked out at the heap, she was very glad they could no longer see it. A large rat put its head out from under the plastic cover and sniffed the air, scenting danger. It ran, a black streak through the grass, and disappeared into the old washhouse.

'Farmers are glad, though,' Lois said brightly. 'It's been a dry autumn, and now they need the rain.'

'Farmers,' said Rosie dreamily. 'Of course. We shall be right in the middle of the changing seasons, Sebastian. I'm sure it's wonderful on a crisp, frosty morning, Mrs Meade?'

'Oh, wonderful,' said Lois. They'd learn.

She got a call from Rosie much sooner than she expected, only a matter of weeks after this encounter. Apparently their smart house in Birmingham had sold immediately, and they planned to move into Bell's Farm within days. Sebastian had got the job with the vet's practice, and after Lois's ministrations they could see that the farmhouse was habitable straight away. All the renovations they planned could be done whilst they were resident, and Sebastian had said this would be a good thing, as he could keep an eye on idle workmen. They had decided to give Waltonby village school a chance, and had talked to the headteacher.

'Everything's organized,' Rosie burbled to Lois, 'except the dog! If you know of any Labrador puppies, please let me know.'

Lois pondered on that one. She'd ask at the next Monday meeting. Enid Abraham might know of someone. She had started work several weeks ago, and all was going well. She turned up at her jobs on time, and so far had been reliable. Two or three clients had mentioned how pleased they were with her. So thorough and careful! And quiet as a mouse. One woman, a romantic novelist, who had stressed that the least

51

interruption disturbed her muse, rang Lois specifically to say how wonderful Enid was . . . so sympathetic to the need for a cocoon of silence!

'Good,' Lois had said, and could think of nothing else to say. Blimey, you really saw it all in this job. Now she arranged with Rosie Charrington to send a cleaner in on Wednesday mornings, and said that very possibly it would be Enid Abraham from the mill just down the road. 'I'll have to look at my schedules, but it would make sense,' she said.

Then she remembered that the heap of junk was still there. It had been raining on and off for weeks, and the ground was waterlogged. The farmers had stopped being glad, and were on more familiar ground, happily grumbling that they couldn't get on the land and the seed would be ruined. Lois decided to ask Derek to deal with the heap. He could pour petrol on it, or something, and make it tidy afterwards.

For about a week, the water from the mill stream had filled the ditches either side of the road with swirling, muddy water, and yesterday the banks by the bridge had burst and a deep torrent covered the road itself. Enid had reported that she'd had to go the long way round to get to Long Farnden this afternoon.

'Father's quite worried,' she said to Lois. 'He's never seen the stream so high. And the mill pond's dangerously full. We could be flooded in the house, he says. He's been filling sandbags and piling them up at the ready.'

'Did your family ever work the mill?' Lois said. Gran had asked Enid to stay for a cup of tea and have a chat to Jamie, who was down with another sore throat. Tonsils, the doctor had said. Might have to do something about them, old chap. Jamie had made a face, but Lois was concerned that he was missing school and not his cheeky self at all.

Enid shook her head. 'Oh no,' she said. 'Father's not a miller! Though he did all kinds of jobs in Edinburgh, school caretaker and so on, but really he's happiest with just a few beasts and the hens. Reminds him of his childhood. He was injured, you know, at a factory in Scotland, and gets a small pension . . . just big enough to keep himself and Mother going. And then Edward brought a bit in . . . well, sometimes . . .' She tailed off and looked around the kitchen. 'What a nice cosy room,' she said. 'Are you looking forward to Christmas, Jamie? What's Father Christmas bringing you?' Jamie winced, but obediently said he was hoping for a piano.

Lois stared at him. 'A piano!?' she said. 'Since when? You haven't exactly shone on the violin at school. Why a piano? Which, by the way,' she added, 'there's no chance of your getting. Do you know how much they cost?'

Jamie looked crushed, and nobody said anything for a moment. Then Enid cleared her throat and said in her tentative way, 'I might be able to help. The lady at Farnden Manor – you know, where I go on Tuesdays – said she wanted to get rid of one of their pianos. This one's in the nursery, and never opened now the children are grown.'

'Oh, Enid,' groaned Lois. Why had she mentioned that? Now there'd be a campaign from Jamie until either she or Derek gave way. 'And what about lessons?' she said. 'We can't afford that, Jamie.'

'I could probably help there, too,' Enid said treacherously. 'I used to play a lot. I could give Jamie some lessons – free, of course – and that would be a pleasure, I assure you.'

'There you are!' said Jamie. 'Thanks, Miss Abraham. Can I come to your house for lessons?' Enid's face clouded, and her reply was instant. 'No, dear. I'll come here, if that's convenient. We don't have visitors at the mill.'

'Right,' said Jamie, 'all settled then, Mum?'

Lois looked at the colour returning to his cheeks and sighed. 'It's very kind of you, Enid,' she said. 'I'll discuss it with your father, Jamie.'

Jamie grinned, knowing exactly what Dad would say at first. It was just a case of choosing the right moment, but he could rely on Mum for that.

Twelve

B ill as cleaner had been something of a surprise to Lois. She had been quite prepared for a longish period of training, of polishing up his skills with fine furniture and vulnerable porcelain. When she went with him on his first morning at the estate agent's, he lifted with ease heavy filing cabinets so she could clean behind them, moved wobbly display units of houses for sale without collapsing the lot, and polished with gusto the blonde's desktop, saying cheerfully that she could see herself in all her glory now. So far so good. Strong muscles obviously helpful. Next was a cantankerous old lady, whose drawing-room was like a museum, with a collection of priceless Royal Worcester china.

'Irreplaceable,' the old lady said, looking doubtfully at Bill. Lois crossed her fingers and said everything would be fine. She would see to it herself.

'Trust me, Mrs M,' Bill whispered.

She took a deep breath. 'Right, Bill,' she said, crossing her fingers behind her back. 'I'll just empty the wastepaper basket, and you can make a start on the dresser over there. Be very, very careful.'

It was quiet in the house. The old lady had retreated to her bedroom to sit in an armchair giving her a view of the garden, where she planned to read *The Times* financial pages until Lois made her a cup of coffee mid-morning. Lois returned from the wheelie-bin ready to pick up the broken pieces and offer compensation. But Bill, with an expression of fierce concentration, was taking down one lovely ornament after another and treating each with a confident dexterity that was equal to anything she or the other girls could manage.

She moved about the room quietly, surreptitiously glancing

across to see Bill at work. In the end, she relaxed. It was OK. His big hands were gentle. Well, farmers had to be gentle sometimes, she supposed, delivering lambs and all that. Lucky old Rebecca.

The old lady made a tour of inspection before they left, pronounced herself well satisfied, and came to the door with them as they left. She beamed at Bill and said she would look forward to seeing him next week.

'Well done,' Lois said. 'Bit of a conquest there! I suppose you're used to the effect you have on girls of all ages?'

'Yep,' said Bill cheerfully. 'Can come in very useful.' He looked at Lois as they stood outside the garden gate. No chance of a conquest there. She was a tough one, and had made the boundaries quite clear.

'Where next, Mrs M?' he said.

'Dalling Hall,' she said. 'It's a hotel, and they're expanding, converting stables into more accommodation. That means extra cleaning, and we're off to make sure New Brooms gets the contract. You'd better follow me. Have to go in at the tradesmen's entrance, of course,' she added

Bill shrugged. 'Well, you can't blame them, not wanting that old banger out front . . .' He gestured at Lois's car, and wondered if he'd gone too far.

Lois laughed. 'You wait,' she said. 'When my gleaming white van draws up one day outside Dalling Hall, the guests'll know they're getting a quality service. Anyway,' she added briskly, 'we're wasting time. See you there.'

'Yes, boss,' said Bill, getting into his own car and following meekly behind Lois until they reached Dalling Hall.

The contract was secured, and Lois drove home in a good mood. Then she remembered what she had in her euphoria promised Bill. There was a special school concert at Waltonby tonight, very special, according to Bill, with Rebecca playing the flute, and a popular local singer, as well as wonderful contributions from the children. They were worried the floods might keep people away, and he asked if there was a chance Lois could come? Jamie might enjoy it too, he'd added hopefully.

Lois said the children had too much homework but she would try to be there, and maybe bring Gran. She thought it was not quite Derek's kind of thing . . .

But when she got home and asked Gran, she was reminded that things were very tense in *The Archers*, which could not possibly be missed, and anyway, there was a huge pile of ironing which she planned to do whilst watching a good film on the telly.

'Right,' said Lois. 'It's just me. Never mind about the terrible weather and floods and lightnin' an' thunder and . . .' Jamie looked up from the kitchen table. 'I'll come, Mum,' he said. 'I could help, if you get stuck.

'No, no,' Lois said quickly. 'Only joking, Jamie. I'll set off in a while, and be there and back before you know it. These school concerts are usually quite short. The children can't sit still for too long. No, you get the kettle on for when I get back. That'd be a real help.'

The rising water in the mill stream and pond had alarmed Enid, and she'd gone to bed before tea, saying she had a headache. She buried her head under the covers and willed herself to sleep. Downstairs, Walter sat with his newspaper, and although he rustled pages from time to time, he couldn't read. The storm raged outside, and the sounds of crashing thunder and flapping bits of corrugated iron on the barns were joined by Mother's protests from her room. He'd tried several times to calm her, but only seemed to make her worse.

Walter put down his newspaper and closed his eyes. Poor Enid, she'd had a rotten time, with Mother having got so difficult. He felt ashamed and helpless, and wished he could put it right for them all. Edward had made a life for himself, of a sort, but Enid had tried to do her duty, staying at home and running the house, and had reaped no reward. The fault lay with himself, Walter thought. If he hadn't been so weak and let Mother get away with it, they wouldn't be in this mess. Still, at least my girl's got herself a job that takes her into the outside world most days, he thought. She'd showed a strength over this, in the face of Mother's violent opposition, that he had not seen before. If only he could follow her example.

Now there was another bout of shouting and banging, and he put his hands over his ears. Then he got up, wiping tears from his face, and left the room.

The first half of the concert went on much longer than Lois expected. There was to be an interval, and this went on for half an hour. There were drinks and biscuits and a great deal of shouting and whooping from the children, with animated conversation from proud parents. Just as a bell was rung and they were returning to their seats, Lois felt a hand on her arm. 'Evening, Mrs Meade.' It was Inspector Cowgill, smiling at her, with a sour-faced woman standing close beside him.

'What are you doing here?' Lois said, and realized that was not exactly polite. But she was taken by surprise, seeing him out of context.

'Our grandchildren are performing,' said the woman in an icy voice. She was clearly Mrs Cowgill, though she was not introduced.

'Ah,' said Lois, casting about for something friendly to say. 'That's nice.'

'Oh, look, dear,' said Cowgill, turning his wife round to see a fracas at the other side of the room. 'I think it's our little ones, fighting for supremacy. Better go and sort them out. They take notice of you.' Mrs Cowgill gave him a basilisk stare and moved away.

'Lois, we need to talk. About the Abrahams,' he said quickly. 'I'll ring you tomorrow morning, nine o'clock. Be there, won't you.' Then he was gone, putting on a benign face, leaving her to resume her seat next to a large man who had an appalling cold and no handkerchief.

When she finally found her car in a totally blacked out village street, she was soaked to the skin. The rain fell in sheets, driven by a strong wind, and as Lois stepped into the road to unlock the door, her foot was submerged in an icy puddle. 'Shit!' she said. She climbed into the car and took off her shoe. Halfway along the road to Long Farnden, she saw in front of her what looked like a broad lake, stretching from hedge to hedge. The ditches must have overflowed whilst she'd been in the school. Now what? Maybe they'd drained the swollen mill stream on the Fletcham road. She knew Enid was contacting the council. It was worth a try. She reversed into a gateway, had difficulty with skidding wheels, but finally retraced her way to Waltonby. This time she took the turn to Fletcham, going slowly and peering through the driving rain as she approached the tunnel of trees near Cathanger. Halfway through, her engine spluttered, juddered and finally died. She realized she was stuck in the middle of a rushing flood.

'Oh, no!' Lois yelled to no one at all. 'What the hell am I going to do?'

She squelched her foot back into its shoe, and opened her door. Rain lashed into the car, and she retreated into her seat. Derek would have to come and rescue her. She reached for her bag and took out her mobile. No comforting little screen lit up. Dead as mutton. Then she remembered she'd meant to charge it up last night. She threw it on to the back seat and gritted her teeth. Nothing else for it. She'd have to go and get help. And the nearest habitation was Cathanger Mill, well-known for its warm welcome and ever-open hospitality . . . She could try to get to the Charringtons, but was pretty sure Rosie had said they'd be away all week. Skiing, or something stupid. Lois banged her fists on the steering wheel, heaped abuse on her unresponsive car, and got out into the storm.

Everywhere, on every side, was the fearful sound of rushing water. She kept to the side by the verge, and as she approached the bridge, grabbed the handrail with relief. The flood in the road was deep, and flowing so fast that she felt as if her feet were about to be swept away any minute. She stopped to get her breath back, and turned to look down into the noisy stream. It was a torrent, and in the glimmer of light filtering through the overhanging trees, she could see it about to burst its banks further down stream. A natural dam had formed, made of twigs and detritus washed down from the fields, and in the urgency of finding a new pathway, the stream had divided into two channels.

Something solid in the world of swirling water caught her eye. It appeared from under the bridge, rolling and bobbing in the current. She watched it, trying to see what it was, but in the almost complete darkness, she could make out only a dark shape. But it was big. Moving fast. When it reached the dam, it lurched into the mass of wood and stones and stuck. Lois tried hard to focus on some part of it that might give her a clue. Then, suddenly emerging above the waterline, she saw a white, face-shaped blur.

Lois screamed. Everything swam around her, and she grabbed the rail with both hands, feeling herself falling. She was part of the watery world, her shoes full and heavy, her sodden hair conducting rivulets of water down her neck, her hands slippery and frozen. With a huge effort, she shook herself like an old, wet dog, and began to run as best she could, stumbling, sloshing and sliding, until she reached the entrance to Cathanger Mill.

Halfway up the drive, she turned her ankle in a pothole, and cried out. But the wind carried her voice up and away. She limped on, until the dark outline of the house showed amongst the trees. They must be there, she thought desperately, although no lights showed. Thick curtains, probably, to keep out the draughts. Enid had told her about the difficulties with her mother. Darkness was one of her little ways, no doubt, to repel all boarders.

Just as she approached the door, she saw it open and someone step out into the yard.

'Mr Abraham?' she said loudly, and saw his head whip round and something gun-shaped raised in her direction. 'Please!' she shouted. 'It's me, Lois Meade . . . your Enid works for me. Can you help? Please! There's somebody in the stream!'

After what seemed like hours to Lois, Mr Abraham went back into the house, and then reappeared with a big torch and an old, broken umbrella which he handed to Lois. 'You'd better show me,' he said.

'Too late for that,' Lois said, refusing the umbrella.

'Follow me,' said Mr Abrahams. 'You look as if you've hurt your leg. I know the way to avoid the potholes. Stay close behind.'

Lois was only too pleased. She'd never spoken to him

before, not in the shop or round the village, but he sounded more nervous than angry at being disturbed. The rain was lighter now, and it was easier to see over the bridge and downstream to the dam. Mr Abraham shone his torch, but it was too weak to be much good.

'Looks like it's gone,' said Lois flatly.

'If there was anything,' said Walter Abraham. 'The shadows play funny tricks. Could've been an old sack or something caught in a whirlpool. This water's running so fast it could do that. That's what I reckon – a whirlpool. Shame it frightened you.'

But Lois was not satisfied. She had seen more than a whirlpool. 'Could it've moved on, got taken downstream, round the side of the dam?' she said.

Mr Abraham shook his head. 'Dunno,' he said. 'Most of the water's backing up. That's why it's flooding the road. Better get back now. I'll get out there tomorrow and try to clear it.'

Lois felt frustrated. She was quite sure she had seen a face, and from the helpless way it was tossed about by the water, there was not much life in it. But there was nothing more she could do. 'Could you keep a good lookout for anything that might have been . . . well, you know . . . ?' she said, but was not encouraged by his blank expression.

The sound of a car distracted them. Lights approached the flood, and a Land Rover loomed into sight. The door opened and a tall figure got out. 'Hi! Need any help?'

'Bill!' shouted Lois, and sloshed quickly towards him. She'd seen him at the concert, talking to a pleasant-looking girl by the stage. His Rebecca, no doubt.

'Mrs M? What the . . . ?'

She explained, and asked if he would take a look at the dam.

But Bill came to the same conclusion as Mr Abraham. It must have been a sack, or an old cardboard box in the whirlpool. Between them they pushed her car out of the water and got it going again.

'Lucky I was around,' said Bill. 'Had to take someone

home to Farnden. I'll turn around and follow you,' he added, 'just to make sure.'

Mr Abraham disappeared into the darkness without another word.

Thirteen

'Lois? Good morning, how are you after that stimu-lating theatrical experience at the school?'

'Ha ha,' said Lois. She had finished breakfast, and was sitting in her office staring into space. Last night, when she had appeared, soaked to the skin and dripping pools of icy water on the kitchen floor, they had greeted her with silence.

Finally Derek had spoken. 'I'm not goin' to say nothing,' he said, 'but if you come home looking like that again, I am imposing a curfew. Not allowed out after six thirty on your own. That's all.' He had turned off the alarm clock, and warned Gran to let her sleep in.

Before she'd gone to bed, she had looked in on Jamie. He'd been complaining about a sore throat again, but had insisted on waiting up for her until Derek sent him to bed. He had looked peaceful enough, and she'd bent to kiss his warm cheek. She'd let him down again.

'Lois? Are you there?'

'Yes, Inspector Cowgill,' she sighed. 'I'm here. What d'you want to talk about?'

It would be much better if she'd never heard from Cowgill again, but nagging away at her was that tossing body in the torrent, the white face above the flood. If he needed her, she certainly needed him right now.

'We have to find a new place to meet,' he said firmly. 'The woods are impossible after all the rain. Any ideas?'

Lois was tired, dispirited. 'The police station?' she said.

There was a pause. 'Not feeling too well?' said Cowgill.

'I'm all right,' Lois replied, and applied herself to finding a suitable place for a tryst with a policeman.

'Well,' said Cowgill, after waiting a few seconds, 'I was wondering if you still take the old lady's dog for a walk? You do? Right, well, that would be the perfect cover. At the bottom of the recreation ground, there's a gate and a footpath. It leads through the old allotments down a track to a barn. It's not used at all now, but the track's good. Nobody goes down there. Belongs to the parish council, but they don't use it any more. They asked us to keep an eye on it, in case of vandals, and we locked it up. I've got a key.'

'Who else has got one?' said Lois. She didn't much like the sound of it.

'Nobody,' said Cowgill. 'At least, yes, Constable Simpson has one. The parish council are quite happy about that. Only too pleased to offload the responsibility. They can go to him if they want to get into it, and I've told him not to give anyone the key unless I OK it first.'

'Well, I dunno, I suppose it'd be all right.' Lois hadn't the energy to argue this morning, and she did want to see him urgently.

'Right, then. Twelve o'clock suit you?'

'Sooner,' said Lois. 'When I get back, the old lady likes to chat, so make it ten, and I'll be there.'

Cowgill was waiting for her. She peered into the dusty window of the barn, and he immediately opened the door. She slipped inside, dragging the dog, whose every instinct told him not to enter an unknown, dark interior. Cowgill locked the door behind her.

'For goodness sake!' Lois felt irritation rising. This cloak and dagger stuff could not possibly be necessary. Sometimes she thought Cowgill enjoyed it, playing the great detective.

'Security,' he said now, 'in your interest, Lois. Trust me.'

'Just as well I do,' she replied tartly. 'Shut up in a mouldy old barn with a strange man, with only this flea-bitten old dog for protection.'

Cowgill smiled his chilly smile, and said mildly, 'Hardly a strange man, Lois.'

'Well, anyway, get on with it,' she said. 'What's new with the Abrahams?'

'It's the brother. We need to find him. Something's come up . . . One of his creditors over the other side of Tresham has taken his own life. Wife says he was very depressed about money, and desperately needed what Abraham owed him. Seems our Edward turned up last week and threatened him to keep quiet, or else. She has no idea where he came from, or where he's holed up. But it's very serious now, Lois, and we need to find him.'

'Oh, my God,' said Lois. 'Poor Enid. I suppose you'll be searching the mill?'

'We did that last week,' said Cowgill. 'We found nothing, except Enid, her father, and a reclusive old mother who shouted at us to clear out. Nothing in the barns or anywhere else.'

Time to tell him about last night, thought Lois, and gave him as lucid account as she could manage whilst the dog tried desperately to escape.

'Are you sure it was a body?' said Cowgill. He was all attention, willing her to remember. 'Not a hundred per cent,' said Lois, shaking her head. 'It was so dark, and there were shadows and noises everywhere. But I could swear that I saw a face. So yes, I suppose I am sure. And it certainly wasn't there when old Abraham and I went back, and Bill couldn't see it either. Mind you, the rate the water was flowing, it could easily have been swept on downstream.'

Cowgill asked her a few more questions, and then Lois said she was leaving. 'Got to get this dog back,' she said. 'Old Polly will worry. Let me know if you find anything.'

Cowgill nodded and put out his hand to touch her shoulder. 'Thanks, Lois,' he said. 'Take care. I shan't be happy until we've got that Abraham. Nastier customer than I thought.'

Huh, thought Lois, as she trudged back up the playing field, the dog pulling at the lead and straining her arm, much he cares about my safety. And then she knew she was being unfair. He had a job to do, and because she had always refused payment, saying she was no snout, she was perfectly free to get out of her involvement any time she liked.

'So on we go,' she said to the dog. 'You'll get your biscuit, and I'll get a rocket from your mistress.'

*   *   *

64

There was a message waiting for Lois when she returned home. Enid Abraham had left her glasses at Farnden Manor, where she had been cleaning this morning. Should they drop them in to Lois in the village? It would be no trouble, and they didn't like to think of Enid having problems without them. She was such a good soul, such a reliable help. They had found them in an upstairs bedroom, on the windowsill, and were quite sure they were Enid's.

Farnden Manor was a ancient house, and historic for two reasons. One was its age. It had been built halfway up a hill outside Long Farnden, overlooking the village, in a peaceful, bosky position, and had stood there for four hundred years, until twentieth-century demands had caused a motorway to be built uncomfortably close. The other was that its owner, a man of extraordinary imagination and engineering skill, had some years ago arranged for the house to be moved, in its entirety, uphill, with a better view of the village. This had been an epic feat, and for a while had achieved international status in the media. All this was now largely forgotten, and Long Farnden had spread itself to meet the manor, with its new community hall, the playing fields and discreet housing velopment.

Lois said if the client was coming in to the village anyway, that would be very kind, and put down the phone. She quickly settled in to a morning round of telephone calls and adjustment of schedules. Sheila Stratford was off sick – only a nasty cough, she said – and Lois was juggling with Sheila's jobs, giving Hazel extra hours and doing some herself.

Light snow was falling outside the window, reminding Lois that it would be Christmas in a couple of weeks. She'd left much of the shopping to Gran this year, but planned this afternoon to go into Tresham to buy Derek a present, and clinch the decision on what to get for Josie. She had given them a list of unsuitable clothes, and Douglas's consisted entirely of obscene rap discs. 'Don't see any harm in them meself,' said Derek, when Lois exploded. 'The lad's goin' to listen to his friends' if he don't have his own, so we might as well give him what he wants. At least it's not a piano!' he added darkly. He had not taken Jamie's request at all well. No son of his was goin' to have piano lessons . . . bloody Fairy Snowflakes and Off We Go To Bloody Market . . . He couldn't stand it!

Derek seldom swore, and Lois could see it was going to be a battle. Still, this was only round one, and Derek was such a softie at heart that he almost always gave way in the end. 'Best thing,' said Lois, when he had calmed down, 'is to see how much they want for the piano, and then think again. Enid's offer to teach him for nothing is quite a bonus, Derek,' she added, but he said nothing and slammed out of the kitchen.

When Enid called in at lunchtime for her glasses, Lois asked her about the piano. 'Did you have a chance to mention it? I forgot when I talked to them.'

Enid nodded. 'They said if you could arrange to move it, you could have it for nothing.' She smiled proudly. 'It's a good piano, Mrs Meade,' she said, 'better than mine.'

'Right,' said Lois, 'then you can tell them I'll be in touch. Derek and his mates can handle the move. Just got to get the OK from him, and then we're in business.'

'Oh, I don't want anything!' said Enid, looking alarmed.

'No, no,' said Lois, wondering where Enid had been for the last thirty years. 'Just a thing people say.' Then she remembered the Abrahams had no television and weren't allowed to listen to the radio. That would account for Enid's old-fashioned – though some would say correct – mode of speech. 'Anyway, Enid, I'll let you know what happens.' She handed her the glasses, and said, 'Didn't know you needed these? I've never seen you wearing them.'

'Only for distance,' said Enid. 'Considering my age,' she added modestly, 'my sight's pretty good. I can even do my lace work without specs. No, I only need them occasionally, thank goodness. Funny really, Edward's the same. Just needs glasses for distance . . .'

Her voice tailed away, and Lois said, 'Probably because you're twins.'

Enid's reaction was sharp. 'Of course we're not twins. Wherever did you get that idea from, Mrs Meade?'

Lois shrugged. Bridie must have been mistaken. 'Sorry,' she said. 'Mixing you up with somebody else. And by the way,' she added, 'I'd be very happy for you to call me Lois.'

Enid shook her head. 'Thank you, but no,' she said. 'I was brought up to respect my superiors.'

Blimey, thought Lois. Am I superior? Must tell Derek.

'But if you don't mind,' Enid continued, 'I'd like to call you Mrs M, like the others do. Would that be all right?' She tucked her glasses into her handbag, and turned to leave. 'Oh, yes,' she said, 'I nearly forgot. The police were round at the mill this morning. Something about a mysterious object floating in the stream? I just wanted to reassure you, Mrs M. Father was out there at the crack of dawn this morning, checking again and making sure nothing was there. A trick of the shadows, I expect. Cathanger Mill is full of shadows . . .'

She left then, closing the door quietly behind her as usual. Lois watched as Enid slipped neatly into her car and drove off. From her office, Lois could hardly hear the sound of engine noise, and marvelled at Enid's ability to cope. Something strong about Enid. A survivor, maybe. Funny about the twin thing, though. She would check with Bridie.

Fourteen

Three days of snow did not hold up the post in Long Farnden. The post lady was small, plump and easy with her favours, so the gossips had it. Snow was nothing to her. She was reputed to pedal at speed round the village, delivering the post before breakfast with tireless efficiency, and would end up at the house of whoever took her fancy that week. Lois didn't care. As long as the post came in good time, the postie could do exactly as she liked.

'What about me being her last port of call, then?' Derek had said with a smile. He didn't see why Lois should automatically leave him off the list. Mind you, with Lois's office being in a front room of the house, and Gran always around, there wasn't much chance of a spot of the other with Miss Postie.

It was a surprise to Derek, then, when he called back to the house to pick up a forgotten tool box mid-morning, and saw a white envelope lying on the door mat. Gran was busy in the kitchen and called out, asking if Derek wanted coffee. He bent to pick up the letter. It was addressed to him, in capital letters, and had no stamp. That explained it. It must have been delivered by hand. He did not recognize the handwriting, which was old-fashioned and distinctive. The hall clock struck ten twanging notes, and Derek shoved the letter in his pocket. He was late now, and the client was already complaining about delay. He would read it later. 'Got no time, thanks, Gran!' he shouted, and was gone.

He was working over in Waltonby, and decided to get a quick bite for lunch in the pub, rather than go home again. He sat down with a half of bitter and a plough-man's, and began to read the paper. The pub was not crowded, and the only other customers were strangers to Derek. Halfway through a story about a postal strike, he remembered the letter. Quickly slitting it open with a cheesy knife, he pulled out a single sheet of paper. The writing, as on the envelope, was in even capitals, and the message was short:

YOU WANT TO WATCH YOUR WIFE WITH THAT COP. I SEEN THEM, DIRTY SODS. A WELL-WISHER.

Derek stared at it. The pub was quiet, and Betty behind the bar glanced over at him. 'You all right, Derek?' she said. 'You've gone all pale. Nothing wrong with the food, is there?'

With an effort, Derek folded the paper and put it back in the envelope. 'No, nuthin' wrong,' he said. 'Not really hungry,' he added, and struggled to his feet. Like a blind man, he made his way across the bar holding on to chairs, and left, tottering down the steps unsteadily to his van.

'Blimey! What's wrong with him?' said Betty, looking worried.

'Too much of the old infuriator,' said a stranger with a chuckle.

Betty glared at him. 'That's a decent working man,' she said. 'And a regular. So I'll thank you to keep your remarks to yourself.'

The stranger shrugged. Plenty of pubs around. He made a mental note to give this one a miss next time he was in Waltonby.

'Hello? Is that Lois? It's Betty at the pub. Yes . . . no, nothing wrong. At least, I don't think so. No, no, not another accident.' There had been a dreadful accident, when Derek had been injured by a hit-and-run driver, and both Betty and Lois had been deeply involved.

'It's just that Derek's just left . . . hasn't finished his ploughman's, and looked a bit shaky. I thought I'd give you a ring, in case you want to find him. He's probably on his way home, anyway. Don't want to alarm you! Rest of the family well? Good . . . see you, Lois.'

Derek was not on his way home. He had returned to work, and sat in a freezing cold bedroom of the house he was rewiring. He had the letter in his hand, held between thumb and forefinger as if it was contaminated – which it surely was, by spite, revenge and who knew what else? – and read it over and over again. He realized that it touched him on a raw spot, and was more painful than anyone could have known. Or did they know? Did they know that ever since Lois had been mixed up with that Cowgill, playing at cops and robbers, Derek had had a nagging suspicion that Lois fancied the tall, grim-looking inspector? He had never said as much, of course. Never would, unless he had concrete proof. Didn't believe in checking on Lois, any more than she would on him . . .

A faint smile crossed Derek's face, and he sighed deeply. None of them had led blameless lives. He supposed there were very few who did. No, he thought, standing up and getting back to work. This was a nasty, vindictive piece of rubbish from some poor sod who probably got his kicks from sending poison pen letters. He started to crush it in his hand, and then stopped. He smoothed it out, and put it back in its envelope. Better keep it for a day or two, just in case. He put in his jacket pocket, and tried to forget about it.

Lois had a very uncomfortable afternoon. Derek was not answering his mobile, but this was nothing new. He often switched it off if he was in the middle of something tricky. Couldn't be too careful with electricity, he'd say. Interruptions could be fatal. For this reason he did not encourage her to phone him at work. But the message from Betty had frightened her, and although she had to go out, working with Bill at a job he usually did with Sheila, her mind was not on it, and he noticed she was not her thorough, particular self.

'Feeling all right, Mrs M?' he said. She nodded. 'You seem to be somewhere else,' he added, moving a large chest of drawers as if it were a coffee table. A mouse ran swiftly across the floor, disturbed from its hiding place which had been safe

70

for years. 'Cor, look at the dust!' said Bill. 'Nobody's been behind here for a while.'

Lois hated mice. She tried to hide her phobia, but would freeze and sometimes scream uncharacteristically if one appeared. But today, she watched it vanish with apparent indifference. 'Bill,' she said. 'We're nearly done. Would you mind finishing by yourself? I really need to get home – the children . . .' she added lamely. This hearty young man would not understand her increasing panic. Her work with Cowgill had made her a number of enemies, and Derek had been the victim before. If anything had happened . . .

''Course,' said Bill. 'You look a bit peaky, as my mum would say. Go home and have a nice cuppa. Put your feet up.

Lois smiled wanly. 'You're a good lad,' she said. 'Thanks, Bill. See you tomorrow.'

There was no van in the drive. Derek was not at home, and Lois grilled her mother to see if she'd noticed anything odd about him at breakfast.

'Nothing,' Gran said. 'And when he popped in later for some tools he seemed fine. Just came in and went off again – wouldn't stop for coffee. Didn't even open his letter.'

'What letter?' said Lois sharply. She had picked up the post this morning, and there'd been nothing for Derek.

'On the mat,' said Gran. 'I'd noticed it ten minutes before Derek came in. Addressed to him. My arms were full of dirty sheets, so I meant to go back later. Then it was gone, so I knew he'd taken it.'

A letter delivered by hand. Derek acting strangely in the pub. Lois tried to see a possible connection, and then heard the van crunching up the drive. She rushed out and wrenched open Derek's door. 'Are you all right?' she said, staring at his face. It looked the same as usual.

His hands on the steering wheel were steady, and he looked her straight in the eye. 'Fine, o'course,' he said. 'Why shouldn't I be?' And then he felt it, the stab of doubt, of suspicion, that was to be his uncomfortable companion for weeks.

71

'It was Betty, at the Waltonby pub,' Lois said, subsiding with relief. 'She rang and said you'd left in a hurry, looked shaky and sick. I bin worried all afternoon. Anyway, you're back now.' She leaned in and kissed him on the cheek. He didn't respond in the usual way, but she put that down to surprise at his curious homecoming.

'Let's get in then,' she said. 'Gran's made a cake, chocolate, specially for you. If you feel like it?' she added anxiously.

'Righto,' he said. 'And don't worry, gel. There was somethin' a bit off about the ploughman's,' he lied. 'Didn't like to say so to Betty. You know how she is. Thought it'd be better to let her think I'd come over a bit dizzy. Anyway, a piece of Gran's cake'll go down a treat.'

As he took off his work jacket and hung it up in the back porch, he heard the envelope crackle. He should burn it. That would be best. Burn it, and forget it'd ever existed. But he didn't. He left it there, and went into the warm kitchen to his mother-in-law's comforting chocolate cake.

Fifteen

'If it's not too late,' said Lois to the manager at Dalling Hall, 'I've bin thinking I'd like to have a Christmas dinner for New Brooms. Hope you're not booked up.'

'Didder?' said the manager, who talked as if he'd accidentally stuffed an olive up his nose. 'Fully booked for didder until Christmas, I'm afraid, Lois, but I could fit you in for lunch, I'm sure. How many would there be?'

Berk, said Lois to herself, not in the least discomforted. Dinner, lunch, whatever you like to call it, matey. 'There's me, and Bridie and Hazel . . . and Bill and Sheila . . . and there's Enid, of course. So that's six.'

The manager smiled. 'One man amongst the girls! Sure you wouldn't like hubbie to come too?'

Oh God, sighed Lois silently. 'No, quite sure, thanks,' she said. 'Can you do it?'

It was all settled. They would have lunch on Wednesday, mid-week being quieter at the Hall. Six could be accommodated with ease. They were all delighted at the meeting, excited as children at the prospect of lunch at Dalling Hall. Sheila Stratford asked anxiously what she should wear.

'Ball gown, o'course,' said Hazel, and Bridie nudged her to be quiet. Bill did not seem in the least bothered about being a 'thorn among the roses', as he gallantly said. Hazel raised her eyebrows at Lois, who ignored her and said Bill should count himself lucky.

If that manager shoves us in a corner, thought Lois, I shall make a scene, and he'll be sorry. She grinned as she vacuumed the big dining-room where they'd be guests themselves.

When Derek was told, he shrugged. 'If that's where

you want your profits to go, no business of mine, gel,'
he said.

Lois was for the moment downcast. It was so unlike Derek
not to encourage her, whatever she did, so long as it was not
dangerous. Perhaps he really wasn't feeling too well. She'd
have to keep an eye on him when he wasn't looking. Derek
never admitted to illness, but soldiered on through colds and
flu, stomach upsets and occasional bursts of the runs.

A couple of days later, as he drove carefully along the narrow
Dalling Hall road, Derek felt the wheels sliding on black ice
and slowed down to a crawl. Rounding a bend where high
hedges concealed a view of the road ahead, he was just able
to stop safely as a car suddenly appeared in front of him. He
backed to the nearest field entrance, and pulled off to one side.
The car passed, and Derek drove on, looking at his watch and
frowning. What was he doing coming this way, anyway? He
was still working in Waltonby, and this was nothing like the
shortest route.

He'd been into Tresham for supplies, and now it was
nearly lunchtime. Lois had said it would be best for him
to get something at the Waltonby pub, as they were all
livin' it up at the hall. None of the others had mentioned
the celebration to him, some embarrassed that Lois had told
them she'd not asked Derek to come because he was sure to
mock. But Derek did not know that, and wondered. Lois had
said he could reach her on her mobile, or leave a message at
the hall reception if something urgent came up.

So she was definitely at the hall. But doing what? And
who with? Was it really a New Brooms lunch? Or was she
up in one of them luxury bedrooms, naked and lovely, in the
arms of . . . In the arms of who, Derek? He felt the envelope
crackle in his jacket pocket, and faced his suspicion. In the
arms of Inspector Hunter bloody Cowgill, that's who.

It would be easy enough to check. All he had to do was
go in and ask for her. Pretend there was something up with
one of the kids. He'd see then. They'd either go off to the
dining-room, or get on the blower to one of the luxury
bedrooms . . .

Derek stopped the van a couple of hundred yards from the entrance to Dalling Hall. He put his head in his hands and groaned. This was bloody awful. He should just go on to Waltonby and get on with his work. Lois was still Lois, tough, loyal and truthful . . . more or less. He gritted his teeth, let out the clutch and drove forward. When he came to the tradesmen's entrance to the hall he slowed down and turned in, parking the van out of sight of the rear windows of the hall. He looked at his watch. It was half past one. They'd certainly be in the dining-room now. If they were there at all.

He got out of the van and locked it. He walked like a zombie into reception, and asked if he could speak to Mrs Lois Meade. It wouldn't take long, just a message that couldn't wait. The receptionist smiled at him. 'Yes, of course,' she said. 'I'll fetch her. They all went in to lunch about half an hour ago. A very jolly party! Aren't you joining them?

Derek mumbled something about having to earn a crust, and when the girl had disappeared to fetch Lois, he retreated as rapidly as he could. Half-running to the car park, his head down for concealment, he bumped into a tall figure walking purposefully towards the hall. 'Sorry, mate,' said Derek, and looked up. It was Detective Inspector Hunter bloody Cowgill, clutching his stomach where he had been mildly winded. Derek rushed to the van, and was out of the gates, grating gears, and on his way to Waltonby before Cowgill could recover his breath.

The road and passing hedges were a blur, and Derek had no idea how he got to the pub yard. He sat down in front of a pint, shook his head when offered food, and did not hear Betty saying he still looked a bit peaky, and was he sure he was fit for work?

So, it could still have been a cover story. The same dreadful possibility went round and round in Derek's head. They could have had the meal, then the others go back to work and Lois skipped up to the luxury bedroom, laughing and bouncing around with Cowgill in her wonderful way. Derek drank down the pint, and asked for another.

'Are you sure, Derek? On an empty stomach?' asked Betty,

now very concerned. He didn't answer her, just waved his hand towards the pump. She drew him another pint, and went to fetch Geoff, the landlord.

Lois walked into reception and looked around. 'Where is he, then?' she said.

The girl looked surprised. 'Well, he was here. That's odd . . .'

They looked around in the various conference rooms, and sent the barman into the gents in case Derek had been taken short. But no Derek. 'Are you sure it was him?

The girl frowned, and nodded. 'Pretty sure. I just assumed . . . Still, now you mention it, he didn't say his name. Maybe it was somebody else. Anyway, it couldn't have been very important.'

Lois shrugged and turned to go. She'd ring Derek after lunch and check. As she was going back into the dining-room, a voice behind her pulled her up.

'Afternoon, Lois,' said Cowgill.

'Blimey, are you following me?' said Lois crossly. 'We're having our Christmas dinner, and this is not the place for a chat with you.'

He smiled. 'Just coincidence,' he said mildly. 'I'm meeting the wife. But all the best for the festive season,' he added. As she turned away from him, he said, 'Oh, and by the way, your husband just headbutted me on his way out to the car park. I do hope it wasn't intentional.'

Lois returned to the others, and Bill said, 'Penny for 'em, Mrs M. You're miles away. Come on, you've got some catching up to do. We're on the third bottle, and have ordered pud. What're you having?'

Lois sat down and tried to concentrate. No doubt there was a perfectly good explanation. She looked around the table. They were all relaxed and enjoying themselves, and even Enid lifted her glass to Lois, a lock of her neatly permed hair fallen over one eye. With a huge effort, she ignored the table in the corner where Cowgill sat with his steely-faced wife, and did her best to be the life and soul of the party.

'A toast,' said Bill loudly, when they'd finished coffee and all the etceteras. 'To our gorgeous boss . . . Mrs M!' They all raised their glasses, and Enid sang a quavery line of 'For she's a jolly good fellow'.

'I'll drink to that,' said a voice *sotto voce* in Lois's ear, as she stood up to reply. It was Hunter Cowgill, threading his way through the tables with his wife leading the way towards the exit.

'Oy, oy!' said Bill, looking round at a now empty dining-room. 'D'you know him, Mrs M, or shall I punch him on the nose?'

'Neither,' said Hazel, butting in. She had drunk only water, and had noticed Lois's worried look. Lois smiled at her now, mute thanks. Hazel was sitting next to Bill, and the pair had been getting on famously, as far as Lois could see.

Sheila, on the other side of Bill, had had only Enid to talk to, but seemed content. She came over to Lois and said her thanks. 'It was very nice of you,' she said. 'I've enjoyed talking to Miss Abraham . . . Enid . . . She was quite forthcoming, actually. Anything you need to know about the Abrahams, you just ask me,' she added. 'Except the whereabouts of her rotten brother! She seemed a bit bothered about that. Concerned for him, though I'm blessed if I would be! Yes, we had a good old gossip. I don't think she's used to the drink!' Sheila smothered a hiccup, laughed and said she didn't know what Sam would say, and left with others in a merry group.

Only Lois and Enid were left. 'Will you be all right, Enid?' said Lois. 'Where are you working this afternoon . . . it's the Charringtons, isn't it?'

Enid nodded, now suddenly perfectly respectful and sober as a judge. 'That's right,' she said. 'I've got my things in the car, and shall go straight there. It has been a most enjoyable interlude, Mrs M. Thank you so much. It was a pity I didn't have a chance to catch Mrs Cowgill . . . I haven't seen her for such a long time. Used to teach piano to her little girl, you know. That was before . . .'

Enid's voice had tailed away as usual, and she stood quietly staring straight at Lois, seeming to expect an answer or comment of some kind. She didn't get it. At that moment,

Lois's mobile rang. It was Betty at the Waltonby pub, asking Lois if she could pop over as soon as possible. Not urgent, not to worry. Just Derek, needing a bit of help.

Lois left Enid without a word, and was on her way to Waltonby in seconds.

Sixteen

Enid Abraham took a packet of Polo mints out of her handbag. She was sure Mrs Charrington wouldn't like her to arrive for work smelling of alcohol, though she had told her about the Christmas lunch. She liked working at Bell's Farm. It had all been smartened up, with a Victorian-style conservatory built out into the garden from the sitting-room. Everywhere was freshly painted, and Rosie had hung cheerful curtains in every room. The children had all the latest toy crazes, and Rosie allocated for herself a little room she called her sewing-room, where she made clothes for Maria, and worked tapestry seats for the dining chairs she had picked up for a song at a junk shop in Tresham. To Enid, this clean and colourful family home was paradise, and if anyone had suggested the Charringtons had sinned in destroying most of the original farmhouse, she would have considered them crazy.

The only snag was Anna, the au pair. Enid could see straight away that the girl was not happy. In a rare moment of friendliness, she confided in Enid that she had always lived in towns and hated the country. 'It is so cold always, and dirty, and nobody to be my friend,' she had said, and there were tears in her eyes. Rosie Charrington seemed not to notice, and Anna's unhappiness caused her to take it out on the children, and especially on Enid. If she could find fault with any of Enid's work, she would grin in triumph and mention it to Rosie with glee.

'I find a dirty tissue behind the laundry basket in children's bathroom,' she said lightly one morning to Rosie, well within Enid's hearing. 'Do you think Enid overlooks it?'

Fortunately, Rosie was only too well aware that cleaners

were hard to come by, and dismissed Anna's remark with a laugh. 'It was me,' she said, 'I missed the rubbish bin; and it was after Enid had done the bathroom anyway. Do put the kettle on, Anna, and make us all a nice cup of coffee.'

Confident that her breath now smelled sweetly of peppermint, Enid cheerfully began work. When she took a short break for coffee, she noticed Rosie taking something from the drawer in the kitchen table. 'Look, Enid,' Rosie said. 'We finally managed to tidy up that pile of rubbish left in the garden when it was so wet. Sebastian made a start on getting it straight, and when he raked the ashes he found this.' She held out her hand, and Enid saw a blackened penknife. 'Perhaps Mrs Meade might know whose it is?'

Enid took it from her. She looked at it more closely, and saw what she suspected at first sight. The initials 'E.A.' showed up clearly. She felt dizzy, and grabbed the back of a chair. Hoping Rosie had not noticed – and she hadn't – she collected herself, and shook her head. 'Doesn't mean anything to me,' she said quickly, 'but if I can take it, I'll ask Mrs M. She might know. If not, do you want it back?'

Rosie said no, they didn't approve of having knives around the house, except those needed in the kitchen. 'Knives and guns, even toy ones, are absolutely forbidden,' she said. Enid did not mention she'd seen six-year-old Felix conducting a fierce battle with his sister, both of them wielding gun-shaped twigs with great expertise.

'No, you take it, Enid. I am sure you can find a home for it.'

I am sure I can, said Enid to herself, and slipped it into her overall pocket. She did not show it to Lois, Lois especially, as she knew perfectly well whose it was, and intended to keep it to herself.

Lois was, meanwhile, concerned with more important matters than penknives. She arrived at the pub and rushed into the bar. No Derek in sight, but Betty had seen her coming and beckoned her into the room at the back.

'Um, he's there,' she said, pointing to a slumbering figure, head back and snoring, in a comfortable armchair.

'Is he . . . ?'

Betty nodded. 'Sleepin' it off,' she said. 'I asked Geoff what to do, and he said to serve him four pints and on no account let him out of the door. That's why I rang you. I hope it was all right, Lois?' she added anxiously.

Lois frowned. 'Stupid bugger,' she said. And then she sat down opposite Derek and stared hard at him. 'There's something up with him, Betty,' she said. 'He's not been right for a while. Not himself at all.' Derek stirred in his sleep, and Lois caught a word in a slurred voice . . . It sounded like her name, and she put her hand on his arm.

'Derek?'

He stirred again, and his eyes opened a fraction. Then he groaned, turned his head away, and seemed to go back to sleep. But Lois knew him only too well, and reached for a glass of cold water that Betty had placed on a nearby table. Her aim was deadly.

Derek sat up, spluttering and shouting. 'Bloody hell, what d'you think you're doin', Lois?!'

'Taking you home,' she said bluntly, and dragged him to his feet.

'Geoff and me'll follow and bring the van,' said Betty, trying not to laugh. 'Time to close up, anyway.'

Lois got Derek into her car, and they made their way back to Long Farnden in a silence broken only by heavy sighs from Derek and the occasional 'Huh!' from Lois.

When Betty and Geoff had gone, Lois and Gran made another mug of black coffee and got it into an unwilling Derek. Lois had telephoned the house where he should have been working, and made an excuse that he'd had to go out on an emergency call in Tresham. The customer wasn't very pleased, but said he hoped Derek would be at work at the crack of dawn tomorrow as it was time the job was finished.

By the time the kids came home from school, their father was more or less sober, but feeling very fragile. He grumbled that the telly was too loud, that the smell of Gran's cooking was making him feel sick, and that he thought he'd be better putting his feet up for a bit.

Lois put a stop to that. 'There's that washer needs replacing in the cloakroom,' she said. 'Might as well do it now, while you've got the time.'

'Oh, Lois,' said Gran, 'you're a hard-hearted one. Probably only having a festive drink with his mates in the pub.'

'Not according to Betty,' said Lois shortly. 'And anyway, I can smell burning in the kitchen. Hadn't you better see to it?'

Gran knew that with Lois in this mood, it was best to keep out of the way. She retreated, telling herself it was none of her business, and never to come between man and wife.

Next morning, Derek was up and away to work before Gran had had time to cook him breakfast. 'Looked a bit green, Lois,' she said tentatively.

'I'll give him green,' said Lois. 'He'll be black and blue if he comes that trick again. He's got a family to look after and his own business to run, and if he gets a reputation for bein' unreliable the work'll dry up and then where shall we be?'

'Not like him, though, is it, Lois?' Gran persisted. 'Is he worried about anything? Has he said anything?

Lois shook her head. 'No, nothing. I suppose everything hots up this time of the year. Everybody wants things done yesterday. Still, it's never bothered him before.'

'You've not had a business before,' said Gran quietly.

'What d'you mean by that?' Lois's voice was sharp.

'Well, perhaps he relies on you more than you think. You know, to talk about his work, an' that. P'raps you haven't given him so much time lately.' Gran knew she was running the risk of an explosion here, but was determined now to have her say.

Lois did not explode, but stalked off to her office, slamming the door behind her without a word.

The day passed routinely, with no more calls for a rescue party. The only call Lois had was from Derek's football mate from Tresham ringing to say he could bring the piano over on a trailer late on Christmas Eve, if that was OK with Lois. She agreed, and thanked him profusely. He was a family man, she knew, and was doing them a big favour.

She rang the manor to check that it was all right with them, and they asked if she'd like to pop over and have a quick look at it, to make sure. They'd be happier if she saw it before the move was made. She protested she wouldn't know one piano from another, but they said she'd surely know whether she liked the general appearance, and were insistent. After all, she was putting it in her sitting-room. So she agreed to be there around half past five, just for a quick look.

It was dark when she set off, and raining again. She had some supplies to drop in on Bill in Fletcham, and Sheila in Waltonby, and so decided to go round the triangle and call in at the manor on the way back.

Bell's Farm was ablaze with light, and Lois smiled. It had certainly brightened up this stretch of road. Before the Charringtons came, it had been the gloomiest half-mile in the county, with the neglected farmhouse and Cathanger Mill with its overhanging trees shutting out all except the smallest glimmers of moonlight.

She slowed down to round the bend before coming to the bridge. No floods now, thank goodness. Her headlights were weak, but picked up a moving shadow by the entrance to the mill. As she approached, the shadow divided, and she could see it was two people, one tall and stooping, bending down towards a smaller figure. Was it Enid?

Better not stop. Probably that old father of Enid's trying to persuade her to do something or other. But suppose she was in trouble? Lois made a rapid decision, and put on her brakes. Two faces turned sharply towards her, and she could see one of them was indeed Enid, frowning and angry. The other was pale and familiar. This was all she had time to see, before the pair of them turned away from her, moving quickly down the rutted track towards the mill.

Lois sighed. 'And a Merry Christmas to you too, Miss Abraham,' she muttered, and moved off. It took her only fifteen minutes to see the piano, approve it, and be on her way again.

By the time she reached home, Derek had come back from work, the job completed. He was holding a great bunch of flowers, which he handed to her at the door, pecked her on the cheek, and said, 'Sorry, gel.'

She breathed in the flowery scents and thanked him with a forgiving smile. It had been a nice thought, but on reflection, she'd rather have had one of his lovely bear hugs and done without the flowers.

Seventeen

'Did your lot do a really good search?' Lois looked closely at Hunter Cowgill. It was very dim in the old barn, with only a thin beam of daylight filtering through the dirty window. She thought he looked shifty. 'Did you get the helicopter out, an' that?' she persisted.

He shook his head. 'They were busy that night, with people trapped in floods all over the county. Not too impressed with a glimpse of a white face and a tumbling shape in the mill stream.' His voice was apologetic. The truth was that Constable Keith Simpson and another young recruit had tramped through the muddy fields either side of the stream for about two hundred yards, then returned to the mill and had a cursory look around, and given up until next morning. Then they'd asked old Abraham a few questions, got some very dusty answers, and gone back to report nothing amiss.

Lois was cross and frustrated. She was certain she had seen something – no, more than something, she had seen a body, unless it was still alive, in which case it was a very inert human being – being tossed about in the torrential stream. 'I didn't imagine a face,' she said, glaring at him. 'Maybe I might've taken an old cardboard box for a body, with my heated imagination . . .'

'No need to be sarcastic, Lois,' said Cowgill mildly. 'We do our best under very difficult circumstances.'

'As I was saying,' continued Lois, 'I might have mistook a biggish shape for a body, but not a face! Blimey, I know a face when I see one! An' that was a face. Still, if you're not interested . . .' She turned towards the door. It had not been convenient for her this morning. The dog was off-colour and was allowed to stay in his basket, and there was no reason why she should be walking in the playing field without him. She'd felt a thousand eyes on her as she tramped down and across the footpath to meet Cowgill. When he'd phoned, she had tried to get out of it, but he'd said it was urgent.

'Just a minute, Lois,' Cowgill said now. 'We are still looking for Edward Abraham, and it is important we find him.

'Couldn't it have been him in the stream?' said Lois, speaking as if to a three-year-old.

'Yes,' said Cowgill flatly. 'It could. And you'd have been right to be angry with me. But there's been a sighting since.'

Lois thought of what she had seen in the shadowy entrance to the mill. It had definitely been Enid, but the other? She had thought it must be the old man, but she wasn't sure. Perhaps she'd not tell Cowgill about that. The more she knew of Enid, the more she liked her. If it was possible to guard her against painful police questioning, she would try to do what she could.

'Where has he bin seen?' she said.

'Outside Fletcham, crossing the railway line,' he replied. 'He was seen by someone who knows him fairly well, but only from a distance. Not conclusive, but a reasonable chance.'

'He could have hitched a ride,' said Lois. 'The road runs along by the rail track there for about a mile.'

'True,' said Cowgill seriously. 'But he doubled back, apparently, and disappeared into the woods.'

'Our woods?' said Lois.

Cowgill nodded. 'Alibone Woods,' he confirmed. 'So that's why I would like you to ask Enid Abraham if they ever picnicked there . . . You know, ask her casually, in conversation. It is possible she knows where he is, and would warn him. I know you'll do it right, Lois. Would you mind?'

'Of course I mind! She's one of my staff,' snapped Lois. 'In any case, I'm sure your brave boys have searched the woods?'

Cowgill sighed. 'Yes, we have,' he said patiently. 'And found nothing. But there might be some hidden place they found, she and Edward. They used to go everywhere together, apparently. Anyway,' he continued, 'we can't do the full bloodhound bit. He's not committed murder or abducted a child, so far as we know. Only fraud and intimidation are on his sheet at the moment, so I need some way of getting information from Enid without her knowing she's giving it. That's where you come in.' He put out a hand and touched her arm lightly. She backed away and he laughed. 'Oh, for God's sake, Lois!' he said.

She smiled faintly. 'Sorry,' she said, and then added hesitantly, 'Well, if it would really help, I could get around to it somehow. She's offered to teach piano to Jamie, so there might be an opportunity. I'll try, and give you a ring. Can I go now?'

He smiled at her, an unusually broad smile. 'Don't know why I bother with you, Lois Meade,' he said.

'I do,' she answered, and added that she thought it would be best if they went back to meeting in the woods, whatever the weather. She didn't feel safe from prying eyes in the barn.

He replied that in that case he'd get some new wellingtons, and they parted on more reasonable terms than usual.

Derek was working on a new job, rewiring an old house being restored to life twenty miles the other side of Waltonby. Restoration jobs were a big part of Derek's work these days. Young couples, with big salaries and even bigger expectations, were roaming the villages looking for old, decrepit properties to convert. It was a mystery to Derek why anyone would want to drive for a couple of hours each day before getting to work, but this is what a lot of the men did. It wasn't like that with the new lot at Bell's Farm, he knew that. Mr Charrington was the new vet, and, Derek had heard, was popular with the farmers.

This house had been empty for five years, but before that no money had been spent on it for fifty years. Derek took out his sandwiches and a flask of coffee. Too far to go home to dinner, and anyway, he quite liked to sit quietly and read the paper for half an hour or so. But today he couldn't concentrate. He'd heard the telephone ringing in

Lois's office after breakfast, and she'd rushed to answer it, carefully shutting the door behind her. He had loitered around outside, pretending he was looking for a needle Gran had dropped and couldn't find.

'Leave it, Derek,' Gran had said, passing by on her way upstairs. 'It'll turn up.'

But he'd continued to peer down at the floor, moving backwards and forwards outside Lois's door. He had heard her voice, but not the words, until she said, louder, 'Oh, all right, then, give me an hour and I'll be there. But for God's sake make sure we're not seen.'

He'd gone cold all over, and felt sick again. Before she came out of her office, he was off in the van, going too fast on his way to work. Now he sat staring blindly at fuzzy newsprint in a cold, dismal house, and wondered what the hell he was going to do.

Enid Abraham also sat miserably in a cold, dismal house, but now it was early evening, and the only light came from a dim overhead lamp in a frosted glass shade, a cold, unfriendly light. She looked around the dingy room, and said sadly to her father, 'It's years since we did any decorating, Dad. Do you think we could have this room freshened up? I'd be happy to contribute, now I'm earning.'

Walter Abraham had come in his old, darned socks, stamping his feet on the worn rug to warm them up. He looked across at his neat, pleasant-looking daughter and felt the familiar pang of guilt. Poor Enid. She'd have made somebody such a good wife . . . and mother . . . maybe given them some grandchildren . . . had a happy, normal life. But then, he thought, excusing himself, how was he to know that Mother was going to turn so difficult. It was an illness, he knew, an illness of the mind, and there were doctors for that sort of thing. But she would never see anybody, not even when she'd got bronchitis that time. Enid had looked after her so well that she'd recovered without needing medical help. No wonder Enid had been upset when she too was shut out.

The morning after the flood and storm, he'd had to tell Enid that Mother didn't want anyone, not even Enid, to go in her room any more. They could leave her food and necessaries outside, and she'd pick them up them when they'd gone away. And her washing and contents of the commode . . . that was to be put out in the same way.

'But Father!' Enid had said. 'How will she manage? And what have I done? I thought she'd got used to me going out to work. It hasn't made any difference to the way I look after her. She's not gone without, not at all.'

Walter had nodded and tried his best to placate Enid. 'Let's try it, dear,' he'd said, 'just to keep her happy. Last night's terrible storm seems to have made her worse. Give her time and she might forget about it, and we can get back to normal.'

Normal! That was a joke, thought Enid now, as she waited for her father to answer her plea for brightening up the place. Normal at Cathanger Mill was getting through the day without storms and tantrums from her mother – though it was true she'd been better under her new regime – and coping with household tasks with an ancient old vacuum cleaner and an even older Calor gas cooker. None of this would have mattered so much to Enid if there'd been occasional cheerfulness, a few jokes and maybe even a visitor or two, well chosen, who would dispel the awful gloom for an hour or two.

'We can think about it, Enid,' her father said now. 'Perhaps in the spring, when the lighter evenings come. I could get some paint and have a go. Wouldn't take much. And maybe you could make some new curtains.' His heart twisted as he saw her face lighten. Such a small thing needed to cheer her up. And worst of all, he knew he'd never do it. If only things had been different, Edward could've helped them such a lot . . .

'Come on, Father,' said Enid, drawing him nearer to the fire. 'I'll get you some dry socks, and we can have a game of crib when you've warmed up.' He had taught her to play when she was a little girl, and she had always loved the game. They had an old pottery cribbage board, and used sharpened matches to peg up the scores. The dog-eared cards were familiar old friends, and when they found time to play their worries retreated and were kept at bay for a hour or so.

'Any news from Edward?' said Enid, taking a chance on her father being mellow enough to discuss the usually taboo subject. He certainly seemed to have changed lately, more inclined to listen. Sometimes, she thought, he even appeared . . . well, not exactly frightened, but wary of her.

He shook his head. 'Heard nothing,' he said. 'Best to forget him, Enid. I suppose he was never any good, but your mother couldn't see it. If we'd been harder on him when he was a lad, he might've made something of his life. Now then,' he added, visibly shrugging off thoughts of his only son, 'I'll change m' socks, and then we'll have a game.'

Eighteen

Christmas Eve, and excitement in the Meade household was mounting. The kids had been on holiday for several days, and were plunged into a frenzy of shopping, wrapping and squabbling. Josie and Douglas claimed to be too old and mature for squabbling, but had frequent spats with Jamie to keep him happy. Or so they said. On the subject of the piano, both were sceptical.

'Don't be ridiculous, Jamie, of course you're not getting a piano. D'you think Mum and Dad are made of money?' Josie was merciless. She knew Jamie had a sneaking hope that a piano would miraculously appear, and though she quite fancied having a go on the keyboard herself, she thought it her duty to save him from disappointment.

Gran knew, of course, that late that evening men would arrive and somehow hump a piano into the sitting-room without anyone waking up. She was to stand guard at the top of the stairs and steer any night-walkers back to bed with a well-rehearsed excuse for the noise. She had been looking forward to it, to being part of the fun and seeing Jamie's face next morning. But she was increasingly aware that things were not right between Lois and Derek. There was a palpable chilliness in their conversations, which were not frequent, and she had noticed that Derek hadn't once given Lois one of his usually frequent cuddles.

'Shall we keep the telly on?' Lois said now, as Derek brought his mates into the room to show them where to put the piano. 'It would cover the bumps and bangs.'

'What bumps and bangs?' said the chief remover indignantly. 'We've borrowed a proper trolley, and you'll be amazed at our skill.'

He winked at the others, and Derek patted him on the back. 'Very good of you, boy,' he said. 'Let's get movin', then.'

A piano is a cumbersome and weighty thing, and the two steps up to the front door nearly defeated the removers. In the end, Derek improvised a strong ramp, and finally the piano was in place. 'Looks really good there,' said Lois. 'That was where the Rixes had theirs.

The chief remover remembered the village scandal causing the doctor to move away. 'How do you know where they had the piano?' he said. 'Andrew Rix was a doctor wasn't he? Did you know them?'

'I used to clean for them,' replied Lois. 'I thought everybody knew that.'

''Course you did. I remember now . . . and you helped them a lot in other ways, so I heard.'

Lois frowned. 'There's not much the network doesn't know, is there?' she said. Derek hurriedly butted in. 'Now then, lads,' he said. 'What're you going to have? Gran's got some eats ready in the kitchen, and there's every form of alcohol known to man. So come on, let's get stuck in.'

Lois lingered behind. She lifted the lid of the piano and put her fingers on the keys. She wouldn't play any notes, in case the kids heard, but in her head she could hear music, the piece that Mary Rix used to play when she was feeling happy. She had her troubles, but she sorted them out in the end. Perhaps Lois could do the same with Derek.

An hour or so later, when it was after midnight and Christmas Day had officially arrived, the men kissed Gran and Lois enthusiastically under the mistletoe and, leaving them clearing up in the kitchen, tiptoed with exaggerated stealth out into the night.

The last to go paused briefly in the hall. 'Here, Derek,' he said. 'Looks like a letter caught up in the door curtain.' He handed it over, and Derek forced himself to take it. He had glimpsed the handwriting, and recognized it.

Nineteen

Anna, the au pair, had finally stopped crying, and Rosie Charrington heaved a sigh of relief. It was all so silly and unnecessary. They had said she could go home for Christmas, had aired the subject thoroughly weeks ago, and the girl had been insistent that she wanted to see an English Christmas. She'd obviously had snow and robins, carol singers and jingle-bells in mind. But at the farmhouse, surrounded by mud and raw weather, Christmas Day for Anna was clearly a sore disappointment. Added to that, her parents had telephoned early that morning, but the line had been so bad she could hardly hear them. She'd started crying then, and hadn't really stopped until after the big family lunch.

'She's spoiling it for the children, Sebastian,' whispered Rosie. 'What more can we do?'

The sun was shining weakly over the sodden garden, and Sebastian had an idea. 'Send her out for a walk,' he said. 'She could take the dog, commune with nature in Cathanger woods, that sort of thing. Cheer her up no end. These Swedes are a gloomy lot.'

'She's not Swed—' But Sebastian had drifted off to sleep in the armchair once more. Rosie decided his idea was worth a try. She went up to Anna's room and knocked on the door.

Anna picked her way in borrowed wellingtons, dragged along by the Labrador impatient to reach the woods where he could be taken off the lead. What a dreadful day! She had now reached a philosophical state where, realizing things could get no worse, she was storing up details to relay the utter awfulness of it to her parents when she went home. When the dog, released at the edge of the wood, tore off after a rabbit and disappeared, she smiled. Things could get worse, after all. She plunged into the thicket, calling out fruitlessly for the dog to return.

At the other side of Cathanger wood, a tall, thin figure in a long black coat, shrouded in a thick scarf, crossed one of the rides and pushed through the undergrowth, shunning the footpaths and tracks where ramblers and locals walked in summer. Today he was more or less safe. Nobody in their right mind would attempt to penetrate the wood on Christmas Day. Water stood in deep puddles everywhere, and even the grassy dells, which looked dry, proved to be boggy and treacherous. Still, the air was fresh – extremely fresh – and he decided to turn back soon, just in case.

The wood was familiar to him, and he had just reached an open space where he planned to stop and retreat, when a large black dog came crashing out of the trees. He froze, and so did the dog. Seconds passed, and neither moved. Then the dog inched forward, lowering its body and flattening its ears. The man stayed absolutely still. Only when he heard a voice, a girl's voice, calling loudly and getting nearer, did he move. Then he crouched down and said quietly, 'Here, boy. Come on, here. That's it, nothing to worry about. Here, there's a good dog . . .'

The dog relaxed. It was a family dog, used to children, and nobody had ever been unkind to it. It moved slowly towards the man, and its tail began to wag imperceptibly. The man saw the signal of friendship, and brought his hand out of his pocket. He was holding something hard and bright, and when the dog was within reach, just as the girl emerged from the trees, he raised his arm and brought it down with such force that the dog was felled instantly. Then he moved towards the girl. But she was younger, fitter and very frightened. She turned and ran, screaming.

He almost caught up with her when she tripped over an exposed root, but she managed to regain her balance and pick up speed in time to leave him still a couple of yards behind her. Finally she drew ahead, and as the brightening light showed they were approaching the Bell's Farm edge of the wood, the man stopped. It would be better to go back, get out of sight before the girl raised the alarm. As he passed the prone body of the dog, he bent down, then straightened up with difficulty and disappeared quickly into the dark interior of the wood.

Rosie filled the kettle and glanced out of the window to see if there was any sign of Anna. She should be back very soon, and Rosie prayed that the walk had been as therapeutic as Sebastian had predicted. Emotional au pairs were a frequent source of conversation between the more affluent young mothers, but Rosie considered Anna had topped the lot in creating such a disturbance on Christmas Day. It would be something to tell the others at the school gates!

She was turning away to prepare tea, when a movement at the edge of the wood caught her eye. Was it Anna? Rosie frowned. Whoever it was, the figure looked in trouble, stumbling and sliding about in the mud. Then she could see that it was indeed Anna, and she rushed out of the back door, into the garden and across the field at top speed, not bothering to grab a coat, but yelling as she went, 'Seb! Come quickly! Anna's hurt!'

It was several minutes before they could establish that Anna was not physically hurt, just exhausted and distressed beyond speech.

'Where's Rick?' Sebastian had looked around for the dog, but he was nowhere.

'Never mind about him,' said Rosie.

'But he might be lost. It might be why she's so upset,' said Sebastian practically.

At this, Anna's hysteria reached a critical point, and Rosie amazed herself by slapping the girl firmly on the cheek.

'Mummy!' chorused the children, standing open-mouthed by the door.

'Hey, come on you two,' said Sebastian. 'Mummy knows what she's doing. Let us go and have a look around for Rick. Breath of fresh air will do us good.'

Suddenly Anna found her voice. 'No,' she croaked urgently. 'No, don't take the children! I must speak with Rosie alone. But don't take the children, *please!*'

Sebastian was now confused, but Rosie nodded at him. 'Why don't you all get the new game out and read the rules. Then we can play after tea, when Anna's better.'

Left alone, Rosie led Anna to the sofa and pulled her down beside her. She put what she hoped was a motherly arm around the thin shoulders, and waited. The pitiful story came out in fits and starts, but was clear enough. By the time Anna had reached the point where the man finally abandoned the chase and disappeared, Rosie was thoroughly alarmed. 'I think we must tell Sebastian,' she said quietly. Anna nodded, meek and quiet now.

'My God!' said Sebastian, called in by Rosie and now sitting on the floor in front of Anna. 'Did you get sight of his face?'

Anna shook her head. 'He was covered, except for his eyes. When he ran, I could hear him . . . er . . . panting. I don't think he was very good. The little bit of face around the eyes was very . . . how do you say . . . pale?'

'Right,' said Sebastian, getting to his feet. 'You telephone the police, Rosie, and I'll go and find Rick. Don't like to think of him out there . . . It's getting dark now, and you never know, he might not be quite . . . well . . . you know . . .'

'He is,' said Anna flatly. 'He is dead. But I think you should not touch him. The police should see him first, I think.'

Rosie blew her nose hard and nodded. 'She's right, Seb. Best not to touch him for the moment.' Then she left the room, and Sebastian could hear her choking back tears before she lifted the telephone and dialled the police.

He made a decision. He was a vet, after all, and he could not leave an animal possibly in pain. 'I'm going to look for him,' he said, passing Rosie in the hall. 'I won't touch him, unless there's something I can do for him. If there is, then bugger the police.'

Enid Abraham woke up and saw that it had grown dark. Christmas Day had not been a very festive affair. She'd done her best, cooking a chicken her father had killed, and heating up the pudding she'd bought from the shop. It was all good, and even the plates put outside her mother's door were completely empty. Every bit of both courses had been eaten, and Enid had felt gratified.

'Why don't you have a rest, Enid, after all that cooking,' her father had suggested, even proposing to do the washing-up.

'I shall fall asleep for sure,' said Enid.

'Good thing too,' said her father. 'You've been looking tired lately, doing all that housework for other people.' She ignored the jibe, but agreed that a snooze would be quite a pleasant prospect. She'd gone up to her room and been asleep in minutes.

Now she could hear her father out in the yard, banging the chicken shed door and clattering pails in the barn. Time to get up, Enid, she told herself. There wasn't much to get up for. Another dimly lit evening by a smouldering fire. The wind had got up, and moaned around the old mill. Perhaps I'll just stay here in bed, she thought. At that, she stood up swiftly and began to tidy her hair. That was probably how Mother's long retreat into reclusion had started. Giving in once to temptation, and then the next time things had been bad with Father and Edward, finding it easier to shut herself away again . . . and then for longer periods of time, until she reached her present hermit-like existence.

Enid went downstairs as her father came into the kitchen. 'Ah, there you are,' he said. 'Time for a surprise.' Her heart stopped. Surprises at the mill were always bad ones. What was Father up to?

Walter walked over to the cupboard where he kept his gun, unlocked it and opened the door. He reached inside and then turned around, a broad smile crossing his lined face. 'Happy Christmas, Enid,' he said.

It was a small cake, iced, and with holly berries stuck into the top. She had seen them in the shop, but had thought them too expensive. She blinked. 'My goodness, Father,' she said. 'You've certainly been slaving over a hot stove while I was asleep!'

In the warmth of the shared joke they sat down at the table, and Enid poured tea and cut cake. 'If only Mother would . . .' Enid's voice tailed away as usual, and her father nodded.

'Maybe one day,' he said, and wiped his hands across his eyes.

Twenty

N ext morning, Rosie and Sebastian Charrington awoke
to a specially clear, cold light that could mean only
one thing. Snow. In the night, unexpectedly, snow had fallen
heavily. The children rushed into their parents' bedroom
whooping with excitement, demanding that everybody must
be up and dressed and outside before it all melted away.

Rosie surfaced with difficulty. It had been such a dreadful
day yesterday, and for one blissful moment before properly
awake, it had gone from her mind. But then, as she sat up to
drink the cup of tea Sebastian brought, the whole appalling
business rushed back.

Constable Keith Simpson had finally arrived, clearly
resentful at being called out on Christmas Day. Anna, now
more or less recovered, and beginning to feel quite important
and the centre of attention, had led the way in the twilight
into Cathanger wood, saying she remembered exactly where
Rick had been done to death.

They had met Sebastian on the way, and he'd frowned at
Anna. 'Where did you say he was?' he'd asked her, and she
had guided them to the clearing where she'd seen the blow
falling on the unsuspecting dog's head.

She was shivering again, and Constable Simpson had
put his hand on her arm. 'All right, gel?' he'd asked, and
Sebastian had reluctantly taken her hand.

Then the embarrassment had begun. No dog, dead or alive.
The clearing was quiet and empty. The soggy grass stretched
away from them, undisturbed, and though they'd hunted
around for a long time, thinking he might not have been quite
dead but crawled away to die, as animals will, they had found
nothing. In the end, they had returned to the house and Anna

made a statement for the records. After profuse apologies for getting Keith Simpson out on such a day, they had made a great effort to return the family to normality, doing their best to ignore Anna's frequent lapses into tears.

Now, pulling on some old clothes, Sebastian took the children away to get dressed. 'We'll get Anna up,' he said to Rosie. 'She was keen to see snow at Christmas. And there'll be some talking to do later,' he added grimly. Late the previous night, when he and Rosie had exhausted all the possibilities of what might have happened, he had been very definitely sceptical. 'Made it all up, that's what I reckon,' he'd said finally.

'But why?' Rosie had asked.

'I expect she just lost him, and was scared,' he'd replied. 'Invented the whole thing, knowing we'd go and look and find nothing, but not thinking much beyond that. Perhaps she thought when we couldn't find him, we'd just wait for him to come back. I don't suppose she really cared much whether he did or not. She's never seemed particularly fond of him.'

He was not a great fan of Anna, but kept quiet because she undoubtedly made life easier for Rosie. Up to now . . . Rosie did not agree with him, but had been too tired to argue. Now it was Boxing Day, and they were all due to go to the pantomime in Tresham this afternoon. She slid out of bed feeling unrested and depressed.

In the garden, building a giant snowman with the children and a subdued and wan-looking Anna, Sebastian evolved a plan. He felt very strongly that the whole family relied on him to find their dog, and the children seemed to think because he was a vet, he could, if necessary, magic him back to life. He was going to need help.

Young Bill Stockbridge, one of Lois Meade's cleaners, had approached him several weeks ago. He'd explained who he was, and said although he enjoyed the New Brooms' work, he was missing his dad's farm. 'Mostly the animals,' he'd said. He had wondered if he could help Sebastian at the weekends. 'Money's not important,' he had said confidently, though Rebecca had thought otherwise.

'If you're disappearing to work for hours over the week-end,' she'd said, 'I shall expect big treats in compensation.' 'Treats don't need to cost money,' he'd replied, with a lascivious look. He had gone out once or twice with Sebastian, and been very helpful.

Now his services would be required for something different: a big trawl through the woods, an exhaustive search for Rick, as soon as the snow disappeared. Sebastian noticed the temperature rising, and the snow on the house roof was melting at the edges already. Soon it would slide down, turn into slush, and be gone in hours. Sebastian returned to the house and rang Bill's number.

Rebecca had said she must go home for Christmas and had invited Bill, but he had found good excuses for declining. His own family did not expect him, regarding him and Rebecca as being more or less married, and saying he should stay with her at such a time. But Bill felt uncomfortable with Rebecca's family. He knew they did not really approve, and she became a different person in their midst. So in the end it was agreed that he would stay and mind the cottage, be on Lois's emergency list, and have a good time in the pub on Christmas Eve.

When the telephone rang, Bill was sure it would be Rebecca. She had rung twice yesterday, and sounded miserable. Well, that was no bad thing. But when he heard Sebastian's voice, he was pleased. He had begun to feel lonely, though he wouldn't admit it, and when the idea of a search through the woods was put to him, he agreed gladly. 'This afternoon then?' he said.

He and Sebastian set off from the farmhouse soon after lunch, to make the most of the light. The snow had almost disappeared in the bright sun and rising temperature, and when they plunged into the deeper part of the wood the canopy of trees had protected the ground beneath. They did not talk, concentrating on the job. When they came to the place Anna had pointed out, a thin layer of snow had drifted into the clearing.

'Nothing here, Bill. You can see that,' Sebastian said, stopping and looking all around.

101

'Well, there's no dog, that's for sure.' Bill wandered off through the trees and halted suddenly. He bent down, looking at the melting snow. 'There is something here, though,' he called. Sebastian joined him, and they looked at what was clearly a footprint in the snow.

'That's odd,' said Sebastian. 'The snow came during the night, long after any of us had been in the woods. Someone else has been here.' He frowned. It didn't seem likely that walkers would be out in the woods today, and anyway, these prints – there was a small trail – led up to where Bill stood, and then turned around and went back the same way.

'She spoke of a man, did you say?' Bill measured the print with the span of his big hand. Sebastian nodded. Bill straightened up and said, 'Well, this'd be a very small man, more like a child or a woman.'

'Very odd,' said Sebastian. He looked away through the trees, and suddenly stiffened. 'Hey! Stop! You there, stop!' Bill looked in the same direction and saw a figure, a small figure, disappearing fast. They both took off at speed, crashing through the underbrush and yelling as they went. They were faster, especially Bill, who was used to charging through human obstacles on the rugby field. Bushes were nothing to him.

'Stop! Stop!' he yelled, as he closed in on the fleeing figure. Sebastian followed close behind and saw that their quarry had finally come to a halt and was leaning against a tree. Bill was there first, and saw arms and hands stretched out against him, as if to stop any violent approach he might make.

'It's all right, Miss Abraham,' he said, seeing a terrified Enid struggling for breath, pushing her muddy hands into her pockets. 'Why on earth didn't you stop? I'm really sorry if we frightened you.'

Sebastian had caught them up and stared at her. 'Enid!' he said. 'What on earth are you doing here? And why did you run . . . surely you could see it was us?'

Enid Abraham shook her head. Making an obvious effort to keep back tears, she said in a small voice, 'I wasn't sure . . . It's so dark in the woods . . .'

Sebastian looked at her white face and said, 'Let us walk

you back home. Do you know the way?' Enid nodded dumbly, and he took her arm. 'I was just out for a breath of fresh air,' she muttered after a while.

Bill said, 'But why were you frightened?

She did not reply, and they walked on in silence. Then she said, 'I've always been frightened of the woods. The locals say there's a big old cat in there, a wild one, that attacks people . . . and somebody had a dog badly scratched once.'

Sebastian told her about Rick's disappearance at once, of course, and she sympathized, saying she did hope he would return of his own accord. Dogs often did that. But Bill thought privately that it was all a bit much of a coincidence. Seb's dog going missing, and then Enid comes along with her cock-and-bull story of a big bloody cat! He'd worked alongside Enid, of course, and had no fault to find with her. There was nothing to dislike, and yet he disliked her. She never gave anything away, never relaxed or told him anything about herself, except to make it clear that visitors to the mill were not encouraged.

They reached the Abrahams' track, and Enid stopped. 'Thank you both very much,' she said. 'I would invite you to come and have a cup of tea, but you know how it is. Mother would never . . .' Her voice trailed away in its usual fashion, and the men stood and watched as she picked her way carefully through the ruts and potholes.

'That's that, then,' said Sebastian. 'Better get on with our search.'

'And watch out for the Big Bad Cat,' said Bill, with a caustic look at Seb. 'Never heard such rubbish,' he continued, after she'd gone.

'Oh, I don't know,' said Sebastian, reluctant to mock Enid. 'There are such things as feral cats, and they can be vicious. It is possible.'

Bill said nothing, but thought that he would like to know more about Miss Enid Abraham's habit of taking walks in dark woods that frightened her out of her wits. He would have a word with Lois.

*　　*　　*

103

'Where've you been?' said Walter Abraham, as Enid came into the kitchen and took off her coat. 'It'll soon be dark out there. I suppose I'd better do the chickens for you . . .'

'Thanks, Father,' Enid said. 'I just went for a walk. The snow's all gone, thank goodness. All very well for children and people who don't have to tend animals, but I'm glad to see the back of it.'

She watched her father put on his boots and when he had gone out she felt in her coat pocket, bringing out a note on a dirty piece of paper. Yesterday, even though it was Christmas Day, she had hoped for a last minute card to swell their meagre collection and went to check their improvised letter box, a broken drainpipe at the end of the track. No card, but she had found the note. It had been a shock to see it was unmistakably Edward's handwriting, so like her own. It instructed her to go and look for a dead dog he'd come across in the woods. He'd moved it to a suitable place, and she was to take something to dig with, and bury it. That was all. No clue to his whereabouts, no explanation of his disappearance, no message of affection or concern.

She had collected a trowel and gone reluctantly to do as she was bidden. After wandering about for a while, she'd found the dog and was horrified to see it was the Charringtons'. She'd dug as well as she could with the trowel. It took a long time, and the dog was heavy. She'd wept as she spread loamy soil over him and a thick layer of leaves, and then, not really satisfied that all trace had gone, she'd heard a rustle in the undergrowth and panicked, running back home and planning to complete the job next day.

At the second attempt, she had concealed the grave to her satisfaction, and was returning to the mill when she'd caught sight of Bill and Sebastian. Panicking again, she had fled, but when she was finally out of breath, they'd caught her. Long experience of Edward's lying explanations warned her not mention the dog. 'Found a dead dog' could mean much more. Still, they had seemed satisfied with her explanation, though it sounded thin, even to her. She threw the note on the fire. It had been best to do as she was told, even though she had no idea why. Edward had always been like this, giving her orders, never explaining, skipping off when there was trouble and leaving her to face the music. Then he would laugh away her anger and she would forgive him. Always that bond between them. And now, not once did it occur to her that she should tell the police.

Twenty-One

Jamie had woken early on Christmas morning and spent an hour reminding himself that there was no chance Mum and Dad had got him a piano. Too expensive, taking up too much space, and anyway he wouldn't stick to it. He'd heard this so often that he had believed it himself – almost. But he'd still had a sneaking hope that Mum would know how keen he was, would work on Dad and come up with the impossible. She was good at that. He had tried to stop thinking about it at all, and had fallen asleep again, only to be woken again by shouts from downstairs.

'Hey! Jamie!' Josie had shouted, and then the whole family had gathered while Jamie tore off the paper and discovered his piano. For a couple of seconds he couldn't believe it, and just stood and stared.

'Go on then,' Derek had said. 'Give us a tune.'

Gran had wiped away a tear, and Lois smiled. 'Give him time, Dad,' she'd said. 'Wait till Enid's given him some lessons, and then we'll be hiring Tresham Town Hall for a concert!'

Now it was Monday again, with Christmas and New Year behind them, and New Brooms staff were sitting in Lois's office, chatting about the holiday and waiting for the meeting to start. Enid Abraham had been last to arrive, and Bill noticed that she avoided looking at him. She was very pale, with dark shadows under her eyes. But everything else about her was as usual, neat and inconspicuous.

Lois came in with coffee, and the meeting started. Bill began to wonder if there was trouble afoot. Lois seemed to be giving them only half her attention. Sheila had had to say something twice, and Bridie looked puzzled when

Lois's answer to her question made no sense. Finally, when Hazel Reading said, 'You feeling OK, Mrs M?' Bill knew he was right. He heard Derek's van drive off and saw Lois watch it go, and her expression told him something was wrong between the two of them. But what? They had always seemed to him an example of how successful a marriage could be, in spite of three stroppy kids and a live-in Gran. Ah well, none of his business. He was hoping to have a quiet word with Lois about Enid, but hadn't quite decided how to put it. He was sure the old thing was up to something, possibly to do with the Charringtons, her neighbours. And that dreary mill, with its overhanging trees and loony mother! He couldn't think why Lois had hired the woman, when there must have been plenty of normal, cheery candidates for the job.

'All set, then,' Lois was saying. 'Let's get off to a good start for the New Year. Any problems, anyone?' She didn't give them much chance to answer, and made it clear that the meeting had ended. All except Bill left the house and went their ways, but he hung back, hoping that inspiration would come if he could delay Lois for a few minutes.

'Something to say, Bill?' she asked, hovering by the door.

He nodded. 'It's private, really,' he said. He knew that Enid and Gran had struck up a friendship, and this was for Lois's ears only.

'Sit down, then,' said Lois, shutting the door. 'I'm in a bit of a dash,' she added, 'so make it quick, if you can.'

'It's about Enid,' he said.

'Enid?'

'Yep.'

'What about her?'

Bill was good at keeping to the point. He noticed that Lois suddenly snapped to attention when he mentioned Anna's dog story. 'In the woods, did you say? Near the mill stream? And the body of the dog disappeared?'

'Yep. Seb thinks Anna made it up. But there were these footprints, and then we found Enid and she was in a great old fluster.'

'You're not suggesting Enid killed the dog!' Lois stared at him. Thoughts were whirling round in her head. A body seen,

107

and then disappeared. She remembered with a shiver that night of the storm, the tumbling shape in the stream, the white face against the dam. A body seen, and then disappeared.

'Dunno,' said Bill. 'I just know she was very upset. Shifty, really. Very anxious to get rid of Seb and me.'

'Well, she's always nervous about people going down to the mill,' said Lois. 'Batty old mum an' that. I pity her, in a lot of ways. Funny old life, with not much fun. But I'd trust her . . . wouldn't you?' Lois looked at Bill's wide face, with its open, straightforward expression, and felt a moment's doubt. Perhaps there was more to Enid than she knew. That brother, Edward, for a start. Why had she denied so quickly that they were twins? She still hadn't asked Bridie, and must remember to do so. She knew what Derek would say. Keep to a business relationship and leave personal things out of it. But this was impossible in New Brooms. They were all close, good friends. That was the way it worked.

'You've seen a bit of Enid at jobs,' she said. 'There's never been any difficulty, has there?' None of the others had ever complained. The reverse, really. Enid got on with everybody. But, now she thought of it, Enid's way of getting on was to keep quiet, make no impression. None of her colleagues had ever said anything against her, but no words of praise, either. Clients, yes, had often said how pleased they were with Enid. Her fellow cleaners accepted her well enough, but kept their distance. Perhaps were *made* to keep their distance.

Bill got to his feet. 'No, Mrs M. It's not about work, I suppose. Perhaps I shouldn't have said anything. Just a feeling I had, and wanted you to know about. I don't even know why. Sorry if I've wasted your time.'

Before Lois could get up from her chair, he had opened the door and gone. She sat and thought about Enid for a while, then made a note to remind herself about piano lessons.

After lunch, Lois telephoned Bridie. Hazel answered the phone, and repeated her question. 'You OK, Mrs M?' she said. Lois, aware that Hazel was still very much in touch with Cowgill, said that she was fine, and was Bridie there?

'Hi, did you forget something?' Bridie sounded concerned. For a second only, Lois had an impulse to tell Bridie all about her worries with Derek. They were old school friends, after all. But they were also employer and employee, and Lois stifled the impulse at once.

'I'm fine,' Lois said. 'It's just a small thing. You said a while ago that Enid and her brother were twins. I think a birthday's coming up, and I don't want to put my foot in it . . . you know, with Edward being a villain an' that. She might not want reminding.'

It sounded lame, but Bridie answered cheerfully. 'Not sure about twins, really. I know they were very close. There were rumours about them bein' involved in dodgy deals. Him, mostly, though. Anyway, it was all a long time ago.'

Oh, my God, poor Enid, thought Lois, as she dialled the mill number. No wonder she's so buttoned up. Plenty to keep quiet about, I reckon.

'Hello?' It was a gruff voice, and Lois said, 'Is that Mr Abraham? Mrs Meade here. Is Enid there, please?' Piano lessons were on Lois's list, but she had also not forgotten her task of finding out what Enid remembered of Alibone Woods. An uphill task, more than likely. Still, she had half-promised Cowgill, and she didn't want him pestering. It was something to do with him that had made Derek so odd, she was sure of that. Inspector Cowgill, and Lois's work for him, had been the only really big thing to come between them for years.

'Hold on, I'll get her.' She heard footsteps receding on the stone floor. There was never any hope of a conversation with Walter Abraham, and Lois doubted whether it would be much use anyway. If Enid was buttoned up, he was doubly zipped.

'Yes? Can I help . . . did you forget something?' Enid sounded sympathetic, and Lois frowned. So they'd all noticed.

'No, it's the piano lessons,' she said. 'Did you mean what you said about Jamie? He's really keen. Hasn't stopped going on about it since Christmas! O'course, we'd pay you. Derek insists.'

'Goodness, yes, I always mean what I say!' Enid's voice

had brightened. 'I'd love to teach him. Such a nice lad. When shall I start?'

All Lois's suspicions, raised mostly by Bill, that Enid might not be what she seemed, were dispersed. She was surely a good woman, and had so much to cope with at home. 'How about tomorrow afternoon? Now the Browns in Fletching have moved away, you've got a free hour. The kids get home about half past four. Could you come then?'

'Yes, indeed, I shall look forward to it.' Enid sounded as excited as if someone had invited her to a party, and added that she'd bring some piano books. 'We've still got the ones we had when we were children,' she said. 'Edward was always ahead of me, of course. Quicker at everything, really. But he wasn't a sticker, and gave up after grade two! He could probably have . . . well, no point in that now . . .'

The collapse of Enid's euphoria was very apparent to Lois, and she said quickly, 'Good, I'll tell Jamie when he comes home and he'll be over the moon. Thanks a lot, Enid. See you tomorrow.'

Gran came into the room as she put down the phone, and her expression was serious. 'Lois, I want a word with you,' she said.

'No, Mum,' said Lois. 'I know what you're going to say, and it's none of your business. Derek and me will sort it out.'

Gran looked astonished. 'What on earth are you talking about?' she said. She knew perfectly well, of course, but wasn't going to admit it. 'I wanted to tell you there's a letter been shoved through the door, not by the postie. By hand. It's the same handwriting as last time. Here,' she added, and held out a white envelope.

Lois took it gingerly. 'Sorry, Mum,' she said. 'Hey, you don't think it's a bomb, do you?'

'Not the kind you mean,' said Gran, and she wasn't smiling. 'There's different sorts of bombs, if you ask me.' She was a sharp woman, in full possession of her marbles, and had noticed that it was after that first letter that Derek had turned against Lois.

'What d'you mean?' Lois knew her mother well enough to see that there was more to come.

Gran explained. She wondered if there had been others, ones that Derek had picked up without them knowing. 'I reckon they're poison pen letters, Lois,' she said. 'You should open that one.'

'Open it! What – steam it open over the kettle? Oh, come on, Mum . . . you've bin watching too much telly!'

Gran shrugged. 'All right, then,' she said. 'Give it here. I'll open it. Somethin's got to be done. You and Derek can't go on like you are.'

'I told you . . . it's none of your—'

Gran interrupted sharply. 'Now look here, Lois. I'm still your mother, an' if I see you making a mess of things, I shall tell you. You can chuck me out after, if you want.'

Lois was silent, thinking rapidly. Mum was right. They couldn't go on without it being sorted out. 'But that letter might have nothing to do with me and Derek,' she said weakly.

They prised open the envelope with great care. It was poor quality, and the glue did not hold for long. As they unfolded the sheet of grubby, lined paper, Lois saw the anonymous capitals. 'Is it the same as that one you saw on . . .' she began, and then stopped in horror. 'WATCH THE COUNCIL BARN, MISTER. SEE THE SHOW. THE COP AND YOUR WIFE AT IT. WORTH A LOOK.' The words swam in front of her eyes, and she reached out to grab the back of a chair.

'Lois! Lois!' Gran rushed round the table and caught Lois as she collapsed. She managed to get her to a chair, and then swiftly fetched a glass of cold water.

An hour later, Gran looked anxiously out of the window as Lois slammed her car door and drove off with grating gears. There was nothing she could do to stop her. It had taken only a few minutes for Lois to get herself together and telephone Cowgill. 'Usual place,' Gran heard her say, 'and no, for God's sake, no, not the barn. Alibone. And yes, now!' Then the back door had slammed, and Lois started her car.

111

There was, after all, something Gran could do, and she did not hesitate. She found the number in Lois's address book and dialled Derek on his mobile, praying that he would answer.

Twenty-Two

It began to rain as Lois parked off the road in the entrance to Alibone Woods. In her hurry to get away she had forgotten her boots, and now squelched along the muddy path towards the meeting place. She couldn't see Cowgill's car, and was working up a good fury when she saw the tall figure of the inspector standing by the usual tree.

'How did you get here?' she said unceremoniously, and Cowgill saw that she was shaking. 'Calm down, Lois,' he said. 'I found another place to park, not so obvious. Don't forget Edward Abraham might know these woods.

Lois stared at him. She had forgotten Abraham. Of course, Cowgill would think it was about him she'd phoned. Some urgent revelation. Well, hard luck. She pulled the letter out of her pocket and handed it over to him without a word.

He took it carefully, holding it by one corner. 'Ah,' he said. 'So that's it.'

'Yes, that bloody well is it!' said Lois. 'That's the end of it. No more playing detectives for me. I'm in deep trouble with Derek, and you've got to put it right. I don't want to see you any more, ever again, and don't get in touch. No phone calls, no lyin' in wait round corners. Just leave us alone!'

She stared at Cowgill, but he wasn't even listening to her. Not looking at her, either. His eyes were on the track behind them, and she turned around. 'Oh, God,' she said quietly.

Along the track, head down against the driving rain, trudged Derek. His head was bare, and the rain had soaked his hair so that it flattened to his scalp. Lois and Cowgill did not move. When Derek reached them, Lois could not be sure that the water coursing down Derek's cheeks was rain. The misery in his eyes made it more likely that they were tears. He stopped and looked at Cowgill.

'Well,' he said, 'get talking. You first, then Lois.'

High up in a tall fir, yards away from the three, a hunched figure crouched in the branches. Approaching footsteps crunching the bracken had warned him. He had always been good at climbing trees, and he felt quite safe, hidden from view. As he heard the voices, one measured and calm, one loud and angry, he smiled. The woman was silent, and that was satisfactory. All going to plan then. He reached into his pocket and took out a mint. He brushed off the grey fluff, and popped it into his mouth. He'd missed lunch, and was hungry. Soon be time to be getting back, as soon as the coast was clear. They were moving away now, and he could no longer hear their voices.

'Now, just a minute,' said Cowgill. 'This is getting us nowhere.

Derek turned on Lois. 'I'd have said you two've bin getting quite a long way lately,' he accused, 'so why've you got nothin' to say, Lois?'

Lois narrowed her eyes and stared angrily at him. When she spoke, her voice was dangerously quiet. 'I've got plenty to say to you, Derek Meade,' she said, 'and most of it in private. But this is for now. What bloody right have you got accusing me of having it off on the quiet with someone else? Have you forgotten that tart, Gloria Hathaway? Because I haven't. Forgiven but not forgotten, Derek. Never would have brought it up again if you hadn't put your stupid great foot in it here.'

Derek flushed. He was beginning to feel a fool, but would not back down until he'd got the truth.

'Anyway,' continued Lois, 'I'm not walking round here in the rain another minute. We got to sort this out, and the best place for it is in your office, Inspector Cowgill. And,' she added, seeing his expression, 'it'll not be a waste of time. Because if you don't convince this idiot that there's absolutely bloody nothing going on between us, then I'll blow everything you've told me about the Abrahams, an' I'll warn Enid and she can warn her brother, and you'll never sodding well catch him!'

Derek stared at her. 'What's all this?' he said.

'Come on, then,' said Cowgill, 'I'll meet you there. You can park in the public car park opposite, then come round the back of the station and I'll let you in. Don't want you being spotted.'

'No thanks,' said Derek. 'We'll come in the front door, not the bloody tradesman's entrance. If Lois wants to sneak round the back, well, fine. You'll find me in reception.'

They drove in convoy – a ridiculous convoy, comical under other circumstances – into Tresham and duly found their way to Cowgill's office. He had had time to work out his strategy, and began by ordering coffee for them all.

'Now then, Derek,' he said.

'Who said you could call me "Derek"?' The tone was belligerent, and Cowgill sighed.

'Oh, don't be stupid, Derek,' Lois said.

'Well, shall I call him "Hunter"?' replied Derek, rounding on her.

'Now, now, it is unimportant what anybody calls anybody,' Cowgill said. 'As far as I'm concerned, there is one big issue. Derek has had anonymous letters suggesting Lois and I are having an affair. It is my responsibility – since I persuaded Lois to work for me – to convince Derek that this is rubbish of the first order.'

'Go on, then,' said Derek.

Cowgill had marshalled his thoughts, and spoke at length. He didn't know that Derek had already made up his mind. Lois's reaction in the woods, her outburst and threat to warn Enid . . .

Bloody hell, said Derek to himself as Cowgill droned on, hadn't he lived with her all these years? . . .

He knew when she was telling the truth, and that snipe about Gloria Hathaway had brought him up short. Still, he'd never liked the sound of this Cowgill bloke, and he might as well let him go through his paces. He also thought Lois should suffer a bit, like he had for the last weeks. If she hadn't started this daft business of playing private eye, they'd not be sitting here listening to a top cop talking to them about their marriage.

Hunter Cowgill finally stopped and looked at Lois and Derek, sitting yards apart. They stared back at him and said nothing at all. What more could he say?

Then Derek stood up. He walked across to Lois and held out his hand. 'Right then,' he said. 'Best be gettin' home.' There was a fractional pause, and then Lois took his hand. 'Silly bugger,' she said, and they both left the room without a backward glance.

Cowgill was left with three cooling cups of coffee and a feeling of desolation. It would have been much easier if he'd never met Lois. Crimes would have been solved without her, and his dull, respectable marriage been enough. But the sight of her, trouble as she was, lifted his day. He hated to think he might never speak to her again. Also, on a more professional level, he realized that he now had no undertaking from Lois that she would keep to herself what he had told her, nor did he know whether she would continue to work with him. He sighed again, and leaned back in his chair, his eyes shut. He had work to do. Thinking work. Time passed, and he was following a convoluted train of thought when he heard his door open and a voice addressing him.

'Shall I take these away, sir?'

He nodded, without opening his eyes. If he concentrated hard, the girl would go away without the usual exchange of pleasantries. He heard cups rattling, but no footsteps leaving his room. It was no good, his concentration had gone, and he opened his eyes. Lois stood there, with a tray in her hands, and she was smiling broadly.

'Oh, no,' groaned Cowgill, but he was smiling too. 'Don't tell me he's chucked you out.'

Lois shook her head. 'Derek's no fool,' she said. 'We came to a compromise. He says I'm to go on doin' what I do for you – getting information, an' that – because he knows I'll give him hell if he tries to stop me. But I got to tell him what's goin' on. And you got to find out who wrote those poisonous letters.'

Cowgill stood up. 'It would be a more sensible arrangement if you'd take money, Lois,' he said, but she shook her head. 'Oh, all right then,' he continued. 'I agree to your – or is it Derek's? – terms. And of course I'll find out who wrote those letters. That's our job. Now go away, before I—'

'I'm gone,' said Lois, and disappeared. Two minutes later she was back.

'I forgot,' she said. 'There was something to report. That Edward . . . he's a nastier piece of work than we thought. I've still got to talk to Enid about Alibone Woods, but I reckon we got to tread carefully. There's a funny old set-up there, between him and her, and I don't really know which way she'll jump.'

'Right,' said Cowgill, the wise, senior policeman once more. 'I leave it in your hands, Lois. Thanks. Now, *please* go home.'

Twenty-Three

Gran awoke next morning feeling that a great weight had been lifted from her. Then she remembered why. Derek and Lois had returned home from Tresham, in separate cars, but somehow together again. She had said nothing, but cooked Derek's favourite steak and kidney pie for supper.

The kids, too, had seemed to sense a return to normality, and had teased Jamie about his promised piano lesson. 'You don't need lessons,' Douglas had said loftily. 'I can teach you all you need to know,' and he'd picked out chopsticks with no trouble at all.

'Go on then,' Jamie had protested, 'what else can you play?

'Too busy, too much homework.' Douglas had disappeared before he could be challenged.

Now it was nearly time for the school bus to deliver them back for tea, and Enid Abraham was at the door, early and apologetic. 'Doesn't matter, dear,' said Gran, ushering her in. 'Come on in. They're not back yet, so we've got time for a chat. It's really nice of you to teach Jamie piano. He's so excited!'

'It'll be a pleasure,' said Enid quietly. 'It is so long since I played myself . . . lost heart, really, when Mother got so agitated every time I sat down to play. Now I have a reason to take it up again, and I've looked out some music. Most of it is Edward's . . . he forged ahead of me. So clever at everything . . .'

Gran nodded. 'Lois told me. But Jamie is only a beginner, so he'll just need someone with patience, mostly!'

Enid smiled. 'Ah, well, that's a commodity I have in

plenty,' she said. 'Did you know Patience is my middle name? I mean, really . . . I was christened Enid Patience . . .'

'Well I never!' said Gran. 'There's a coincidence.'

'And Edward's second name is Justice . . . that was my mother's idea. I sometimes wonder if it was a good one.'

'Perhaps justice is what he'll get in the end, with any luck,' said Lois, coming in behind Gran and smiling at Enid to show she was joking.

With Edward in the forefront of their minds, Lois and Enid went through to look at the piano. Enid sat down and played a few bars. She had a light touch, and Lois could see at once that she was good.

'It's a very nice instrument, Mrs M,' Enid said. 'You did well . . . Oh, is that the children coming back?'

Lois had been hoping to bring Edward back into the conversation, but now there was the usual turmoil of grumbles and quarrels, and desperate hunger, and the need for help with homework; in general a settling back into the nest.

Jamie rushed in, having seen Enid's car. 'Hi, Miss Abraham,' he said. 'Can we start?'

Enid smiled. 'If Mother says it's all right,' she said. 'Might as well not lose any time.'

Lois shut the door quietly on the pair of them, their heads already together over the first piano primer. She heard a few tentative notes, then Jamie's fruity laugh, and knew that all would be well.

An hour later, Lois heard Jamie calling. 'Mum! Come and listen!'

He had mastered the first scale, and stumbled through it with pride. 'You got to get the right fingers, Mum,' he said knowledgeably, and Enid nodded.

'An apt pupil, Mrs M,' she said, 'and now, Jamie, we've done more than enough for today. Run along and have your tea, and we'll have another lesson next week.'

'Not 'til next week!' Jamie was exaggeratedly horrified. 'But what do I do 'til then?'

'Learn the notes. Practice that little tune, and your scale, until it's easy. Learn it off by heart, and play it to the others. You'll be surprised how much time that takes!'

'Now Enid,' said Lois. 'You and I are going to have a cup of tea, and you can tell me how we can help Jamie.'

'That would be very nice,' Enid said politely. 'The only thing you need to do is give him time. Don't try to force him. Children are very easily discouraged in the early days. I remember when Edward started, Father was very stern with him, and it caused endless trouble. It was why he gave it up in the end, I think. I was dogged, though less talented, and . . .'

She dried up, as usual, and Lois began talk. At first it was about anything and everything: New Brooms, the weather, the garden. Then, had Enid seen the bluebells in Alibone Woods? They weren't out yet, of course, but a little later on they'd be spectacular.

'Oh yes,' she replied. 'I've been there many times in the spring. We all used to go, even Mother in her good days, and if it was warm we'd take a picnic. Weekends were busy of course, but during the week we'd be the only people there. Edward would disappear, hunting for rabbits, he'd say, but I think it was to get away from Father. He was often at home, never seemed to be able to keep a job. They got on one another's nerves. I was often the only one who could handle Edward. Father used to say he never knew what he would get up to next. I felt the same, and sometimes it frightened me . . . One day,' she continued, and now she was gazing out of the window at the darkening garden, 'one lovely day, when the sun was shining through the leaves and the birds were singing at the tops of their voices, Edward disappeared and didn't come back.'

Enid was silent, lost in memory. Lois shifted in her chair. She didn't want to break the spell, but she could hear raised voices in the kitchen, and wasn't sure Gran could cope. 'Did he eventually come back?' she said, after a minute or so.

'No.' Enid's voice was so quiet, Lois could hardly hear her. 'At least, not that day. We had to go home without him. There was a terrible row. Then he turned up next morning, chirpy as a cricket. Father started at him, and then Mother collapsed, so he had to stop. It was horrible. Father went off to the barn, and Mother shut herself away.'

'And Edward?'

'He laughed,' said Enid, turning to look at Lois. 'He laughed, and said he'd had a very peaceful night. Said if he ever decided to become a hermit, he'd found just the place. And then he made himself a huge breakfast and ate it.'

The din from the kitchen had subsided, and Lois refilled Enid's cup.

'I'm sorry, I don't know why I've told you all this,' Enid said. 'How did we get on to Alibone Woods? Oh yes,' she added, with a shaky smile, 'it was the bluebells. Wonderful colour, Mrs M, but it never comes out on photos. Something to do with the light.'

As she left, she turned to Lois and said again, 'I'm so sorry I went on a bit. It won't happen again. I so much enjoyed my time with Jamie. Lovely boy. Goodbye for now.'

She was gone quickly, and Lois watched the rear lights of her car vanish down the village street. Poor woman, poor, poor Enid. She thought again about the Alibone Woods story, and could imagine it all. A lovely day spoilt by a wayward son. Was he just wayward, or was it worse than that? Enid had said she was frightened of what he might do. Anyway, he'd certainly discovered a hiding place of some sort, and this piece of information she would pass on to Cowgill. For the rest, it was Enid's personal life, and Lois would keep it to herself.

Wednesday, and Enid was due at the Charringtons' at nine o'clock. She had her own key now, in case everybody was out. Rosie took the children to school, and often went on with Anna into Tresham to shop. Sebastian was always off early on his errands of mercy to the livestock of the area. Today, however, he had a day off, and retreated to the small room that had once been old Bell's farm office to do some paperwork. He was the only person at home, and heard Enid come into the kitchen.

'Morning!' he yelled, in case she should be frightened, thinking the house empty.

She appeared at his door. 'Good morning, Mr Charrington,' she said quietly, neat as ever. 'Is it all right if I carry on as usual?'

'Yes, of course, why not?'

'Um, well, you are not usually at home . . .'

'Catching up,' he said, already back into his work. Her silence interrupted him. He looked up, and saw that she was still standing in the doorway. 'Was there something else, Enid?' he said. He was never sure about calling her by her Christian name. She was so dignified, so unlike a char, that he felt impertinent. But Enid smiled slightly, and nodded.

'I was wondering,' she said, 'if you ever heard any more about poor Rick? Was he found anywhere?'

Her question nudged Sebastian uncomfortably. He repeatedly promised the children that he would go into the woods and have another look for their lost dog. He had little hope of finding him, and he would certainly be as dead as mutton if he did, but he supposed he should do as he promised.

'No, no trace of him. I'm going out to have one more look, just to satisfy the children. They haven't forgotten, of course, and Rosie has said they can have another puppy once we're sure Rick's not coming back.'

'Ah,' said Enid, turning to go, 'you might as well just get another puppy straight away. I know dogs, and once they're gone they seldom return.'

This was so patently untrue that Sebastian stared at her. How many times had relieved dog owners turned up at his surgery with thin, filthy skeleton dogs that had been God knows where for weeks, and then turned up again on the doorstep looking hungry and contrite?

'Not sure you're right there, Enid,' he said mildly. 'Anyway, I promised the children. Might go this afternoon, if it stops raining.'

She nodded seriously and went off. He heard the vacuum cleaner going in the sitting-room, and wondered why he felt as if he had been reproved for not doing as he was told. That was it, he realized. Enid always made him feel as if Nanny was cross with him. He grinned to himself, and got on with his work.

At coffee time, Enid set a steaming mug and a couple of biscuits on his desk. 'Still raining, I'm afraid,' she said. 'The forecast said it would last all day. February fill-dyke! A bit early, but the seasons are not at all how they used to be.'

'Very true,' said Sebastian absently. He was reading a report on the aftermath of the foot-and-mouth outbreak, about farmers driven into bankruptcy, depression, and one or two to suicide. He was not really listening to Enid.

'Um, I was wondering . . . ?'

'Yes, Enid?' Sebastian looked up, irritated at the interruption.

'Um, I was thinking . . . Father knows this dog breeder over the other side of Tresham . . . black Labradors . . . they always have puppies. Would you like me to get details? I'm sure the children would be excited to have a puppy again.'

Oh dear, thought Sebastian. Nanny does not give up. 'Well,' he said, 'that would be very useful, once I'm sure we've lost poor Rick for good. If you could leave the details with Rosie, that would be most helpful. And thanks for the coffee,' he added. That was a clear dismissal, surely? But Enid was still there, hands neatly folded in front of her.

'So there'll be little point in trudging through wet woods this afternoon!' she said, almost merrily. 'There's a country house sale viewing day over at Fletching, with some good stuff. Wealthy family moved away. Mrs Charrington was looking for a display cabinet, I know, and you'd more than likely find one there. I used to love going to auction sales . . .'

Sebastian knew she was expecting a reply, and gave her the one she clearly wanted. 'Good idea, Enid,' he said, but added stubbornly, 'we can go over straight after I've had my sortie in the woods.' So there, Nanny. I'm the boss here. Sebastian smiled at how much disapproval could be expressed by a retreating back. He did not think to wonder why on earth she should be so keen to prevent him blundering about in the woods.

Rosie was delighted at the prospect of snooping round a large country house. She loved to sniff the air and imagine how the family had lived. Servants, gardeners, tennis on summer evenings and impromptu dancing in large drawing-rooms in winter. She would stare at faded photographs of shingled women and doggy-looking gentlemen with large moustaches. Poor things had come to this. Nosy hoards of commoners strolling around private bedrooms, picking up personal possessions, poking into cupboards that had nothing to do with them. Rosie would feel deliciously sad, and when it came to bidding for this or that, she felt she was rescuing a loved item and giving it a home.

'We'll go as soon as I get back,' said Sebastian, pulling on his boots.

'I'll come with you,' Rosie said. 'I need some air. Anna's in her room . . . I'll tell her we're out for a bit.'

They set off across the field towards the woods, and Rosie pulled up the hood of her Barbour. 'Enid was right,' Sebastian said. 'She said it would rain all day.'

'Was she OK today?' Rosie negotiated the gap in the fence where they plunged into the woods. 'Fine,' said Sebastian. 'Bit stern with me, but fine.'

'Stern?'

'Yep, you know how she is. Bit nannyish. Said I'd be wasting my time looking for Rick again. Tried hard to stop me! Hey, look out, Rosie . . . it's very boggy there.'

They had come to a place in the woods where the mill stream ran through on its way to join the river. Sometimes it was a torrent – as now again – and in summer it trickled amiably through grassy banks dotted with wild flowers.

Rosie struggled through the waterlogged ground, and put out a hand to save herself from falling as she stepped over an exposed root. Almost prone, she gasped. 'Oops! Give us a hand up,' she said. Sebastian leaned across to help her, and his eye was caught by a patch of freshly turned earth. Moss covered the ground around, but here it was bare.

'Look at that, Rosie,' he said.

'Somebody's been digging,' she replied, and her heart began to beat fast. 'Seb! You don't think . . .'

He pulled her free of the bog, and told her to go and sit on a tree stump a few yards away. 'Better take a look,' he said, and with a sinking feeling he found a strong stick and began to root around in the loose earth. The stick struck something hard almost straight away.

'Rosie!' he shouted.

'What? What is it?'

'You'd better go back home now.'

'Why? Have you found something?'

'Just go on back, there's a love. I shan't be long.'

He watched until she was out of sight, then began to move the loose leaf mould with his bare hands. He continued to scrape gently, his hands covered in wet earth. Finally he sat back on his haunches and stared down. Well, he knew the remains of a black Labrador when he saw one. He eased the rotting collar round so that he could see the metal tag. '*Rick – Bell's Farm*'. Sebastian choked, and pushed back the earth, stamping it down. He marked the spot with the stick, and chipped at the root until he could recognize it again, just in case.

Twenty-Four

Rosie and Sebastian sat at the kitchen table, silently staring at each other. They were shocked and grieving. For an hour, they had talked about Sebastian's grisly discovery, speculated on who could have done it, and – most of all – why? The most likely explanation, Sebastian decided, was a tramp in the woods, an unhinged tramp who was scared by the sudden appearance of Anna and the dog. Tramps often carried knives for cutting up food, or opening tins, and he could have used a heavy handle to finish off poor Rick. Maybe he hadn't meant to kill him, but just stun him to stop him barking, so that he could get away quickly.

'Get away from the frightening sight of a defenceless young girl?' countered Rosie, who was not impressed by this theory.

'But a tramp out in the woods in that wintry weather would not be a rational human being, Rosie,' Sebastian explained patiently. 'Panic probably took over. Then after Anna had gone, the tramp buried Rick to cover his tracks.' He was trying hard to convince himself, as well as Rosie. He had a recurring mental picture of a neat, middle-aged woman hoofing it through the trees next day . . . In other words, Enid Abraham, with muddy hands.

Rosie, who could read her husband's thoughts, said, 'Well, what about that time you and Bill found Enid in the woods? She's not a tramp, and is a perfectly rational human being. So far as we know . . .'

'That was another occasion entirely,' Sebastian said. 'And she lives right by the woods, just like us, and would naturally go in there for a walk. We do, all the time.'

'Mm.' Rosie got up from the table. 'Might as well make

a cup of tea. I've gone off the idea of the auction. What are you going to do, anyway? I suppose we should tell the police? After all, now we know Anna wasn't making it up, we should do something to show we believe her. Are you going to tell her you've found Rick?'

Sebastian was silent for a minute. 'Oh, I dunno, Rosie,' he said finally. 'I don't want to alarm the girl, or make her too nervous to go out with the kids. Perhaps it would be best to keep it to ourselves for a bit, until I've done some thinking. I shall go back and collect him. Take him to the surgery and see if I can get a better idea of what killed him.'

'I'd be happier if you told the police.' The thought of their beloved Rick reduced to a decomposing corpse, being taken to bits – even if it was by Seb – like a laboratory specimen, set her off weeping again.

'Oh, come on, love, pull yourself together,' Sebastian said. He was only too familiar with grown men and women sobbing their hearts out in the surgery as he prepared to ease their pets into whatever animal heaven awaited them. He had always respected this raw emotion, and sometimes felt tears prick his own eyes. Dogs, particularly, were heartrending in the way they looked at their owners, trusting that they wouldn't let them down. And, in a way, they didn't. Sebastian often thought it would be a good thing if human beings, lingering on in great pain and with no possibility of recovery, could be 'put to sleep'. It was a daily event in the surgery, and he'd never had a moment's doubt.

Rosie scrubbed at her face with a tissue, and gave him a watery smile. 'Seb,' she said, 'I think there's only one thing to do now.'

'What's that then?' said Sebastian, dreading that Rosie would demand an emergency call to Tresham Police Station asking for the Chief Inspector to come out to the scene of the crime immediately. He misjudged her.

'We'll go to the view day of the auction after all,' she said. 'I saw the catalogue the other day . . . one of the mums had it outside the school. There was this rather nice-sounding display cabinet . . . just what I'm looking for. D'you think it would be all right to go . . . not heartless?'

Sebastian sighed with relief. 'Good girl,' he said. 'I'll sort things out while you tell Anna we're going.'

He disappeared out into the yard and Rosie turned off the kettle. She quickly tidied things away and picked up a scrap of paper from the table. About to screw it up and bin it, she saw handwriting. Ah, yes, Seb had said Enid mentioned a Labrador breeder who'd be sure to have puppies. Well, now they could go ahead, absolutely sure that Rick was not coming back. She smoothed out the paper and tucked it into the kitchen drawer, noticing with mild surprise that Enid's script was all in spiky capitals.

By the time they reached the grand country house, they had about an hour before the view day closed. 'Let's go straight to the display cabinet,' said Rosie, and looked up the lot number in her catalogue.

'Oh, Seb! It's just what I've been looking for!' Rosie was ecstatic, and Sebastian shushed her, saying they didn't want everyone to spot it.

'No chance of that one going at a bargain price,' said a voice at his elbow. It was Bill Stockbridge, grinning at them and holding hands with a good-looking girl he introduced as 'my Rebecca'.

'We've already marked it down,' she said. 'Got just the place for it in the cottage.' She and Rosie eyed each other competitively. Their smiles had a definite edge. It was a cut-throat business buying at auction.

'Seen anything else you like?' said Sebastian, changing the subject tactfully. Bill and Rebecca had made a short list. Furniture in the cottage was still a bit sparse, and they'd spotted a sofa and a couple of bookcases they hoped to get.

'Coming tomorrow, then?' said Rosie lightly. Rebecca nodded. 'My head teacher has very kindly given me time off . . . she'll cover for me for the time it takes. All the lots I'm interested in are coming up before lunch.'

'Well, then,' said Rosie, 'I shall see you here. I expect the dealers will push up the prices. They usually do, at quality sales like this.'

Bill and Sebastian had wandered off to look at an old bag of golf clubs. 'Look at this – hickory shafts!' Bill said. He pulled one out and tried a few practice swings, narrowly missing a small woman coming suddenly round the corner.

'Enid!' Bill was mortified and apologetic. 'I thought you were working this afternoon?'

'I am, just on my way,' she said. 'I was just having a quick look around. I love auction sales, as I said to Mr Charrington.' She turned to smile at Sebastian, who had difficulty returning the smile. 'Glad to see you took my advice,' she said. 'Did Mrs Charrington find a cabinet?' Sebastian nodded mutely. All he could think of was the rotting body of his dog in a rough grave in the woods.

'Well, I must be off,' Enid said happily, looking at her watch. 'Mustn't be late, or I shall be getting New Brooms a bad name,' she added. 'And that won't do, will it, Bill?'

After she'd gone, Bill looked at Sebastian and said, 'You all right, mate?'

Sebastian nodded. 'Yes, I'm fine,' he said, 'but I think there's something I should tell you. Remember that day we went looking for Rick in the woods, and we didn't find him? Well . . .'

Rebecca was subdued that evening, and in the middle of a television programme that neither of them was really watching, Bill switched off.

'All right,' he said, 'come on, let's have it. What's bothering you?'

'Nothing.'

'Rebecca!'

'OK then, there is something. But you'll be cross.'

'Try me,' said Bill.

Rebecca pushed her hair back from her face and twisted it at the nape of her neck. 'Well, it's those people we met today. The Charringtons.'

'What about them?'

'Didn't you say Enid worked for them?'

'Yes, she does. She'd been there today, as a matter of fact. Why?'

'Well, she went to Uncle Christopher the other day, filling

in for Bridie Reading – is that her name? – and he told me something really odd. Seems Rosie Charrington told one of uncle's young mums . . . he's started a family service in church, and she's a regular . . .'

Bill shook his head as if to clear it. 'Could you stick to the point, Rebecca duckie,' he said. 'Now, your uncle told you something that his young mum told him, about Enid Abraham, and it was really odd. That right?'

'No need to be so patronising, William Stockbridge! You're only a old char, don't forget!

Bill began to get up, offended, and then saw her laughing and thought better of it.

'Sorry,' he said. 'Go on.'

'Well, the young mum had called at the vicarage about the next family service, and Enid answered the door. Uncle had talked to the mum in the hall, which, as you know, is big enough to accommodate this entire cottage, and she had asked if he'd heard any more about that Edward Abraham who'd gone missing. Seems Rosie Charrington and some of the other mums are scared, wondering if he'd attack a child on its own, maybe. They've all got extra careful, apparently.'

'Really,' said Bill, with mock patience.

'And then, after she'd gone, Enid had asked to speak to him. He said it was very embarrassing, though he's used to hearing all sorts of things. But he's a nice old bloke, as you know, and he felt sorry for Enid. Seems she'd overheard what the mum said, and was really upset that her brother should be thought of as a child molester. Said the worst he'd ever done was get into debt and try to evade the money men.'

'What did he say?' Bill didn't see what was odd about all this. Perfectly natural for a sister to stick up for her brother, he thought.

'He tried to cheer her up. Then the odd thing happened.' Rebecca fell silent.

'You'd make a good mystery writer,' said Bill. 'Go on, for God's sake.'

'Uncle heard a door slam at the back of the house. And then he swears he heard footsteps running down the gravel path that leads to Glebe Close behind the kitchen garden.

130

Enid had opened all the windows while she was cleaning – one of her less appealing habits, as far as Uncle is concerned – and he could hear clearly, he says.'

'And?'

'So he asked Enid if anyone had called at the back door, and she said no. When he suggested she should go and look, she wouldn't, said it was not necessary, it must be the draught had blown the door shut.'

'And the footsteps?'

'She laughed, and said Uncle's hearing must be play-ing tricks on him. Annoyed him, actually. He hates being reminded of his age. Anyway, they didn't say any more about it, but Uncle went out after she'd gone, and said he could swear some of the gooseberry bushes that hung over the gravel path had been broken off, little twiggy bits that stuck out.'

'Ah,' said Bill. 'Now that is odd. What's she up to, old Enid?' Time for another word with Lois, he reckoned. If Enid was upsetting the clients, that was serious.

'You don't like her, do you, Bill?' Rebecca said, coming over to sit beside him on the floor.

He took her face in his hands. 'Yum,' he said. 'I like you best, my little duckie. Come on, let's go to bed.' His conversation with Sebastian was still circling in his mind, and he hoped he wouldn't dream of dead dogs. Still, dreaming wasn't what he had in mind at the moment.

'If we get that long sofa at the sale,' said Rebecca, never one to miss an opportunity, 'we'll not need to go to bed, will we?' She kissed him long and sweetly, and he would at that moment have forked out for anything, three sofas if necessary.

Twenty-Five

'I don't see any point in living in a village if you don't join in things,' Gran said. A taste of spring had warmed up the village for a day or two, and Lois and Gran were strolling round the garden, looking at bulbs coming up and a drift of snowdrops under the silver birch.

'The doctor planted that tree. He told me. Very proud of it, he was,' Lois said.

'I expect he was sad to leave this place.' Gran spoke quietly, remembering the tragic circumstances. 'Still, I bet he was pleased you lot were moving in. It's a good family house.'

Lois nodded. 'Funny, isn't it though, how soon Derek has put his stamp on this garden,' she said. 'It always used to be neat and tidy, o'course. Mrs Rix was like that. A place for everything and everything in its place. But there was never much in the garden, if you know what I mean. Now Derek's got loads of veg and fruit, and rows of chrysanths for us to cut in autumn, and he's got the greenhouse going again. It's Derek's garden now, isn't it.'

Gran agreed. 'He's put his roots down here,' she said, and then laughed her hearty laugh.

'Very witty,' said Lois.

'I try,' said Gran. 'Anyway, Lois, as I was saying' – Lois knew what was coming, and sighed – 'Maybe you should come and join the Women's Institute with me. I'm going along tonight. They're a new branch, and trying to recruit members. Especially young ones . . .'

'No thanks!' said Lois. 'I've got a few years yet before it comes to that!'

'Just showing your ignorance,' said Gran, unmoved. 'They've

got several young women, younger than you, actually. It's not what it used to be.'

'Jam and Jerusalem, that's all I know,' said Lois. 'But anyway, I don't want to put you off. Sounds just up your street.'

They were outside the kitchen door now, and Lois said she would nip down to the shop for a couple of things. 'I might have a wander round,' she added, 'see what's happening. They're putting a new mobile classroom in the school . . . might take a look.'

Lois was interested in the village school. She'd been a parent governor of the kids school in Tresham when they lived there, and enjoyed the contact with little ones. Sometimes she looked wistfully at five-year-olds going past the gate in their scarlet and grey uniforms. But Derek soon put a stop to any thoughts in that direction.

She would walk past and have a look, maybe have a chat to whoever was in the playground. Must be break time about now. She walked briskly down the street, collected a few purchases and items of gossip from the shop – nothing useful about the Abrahams – and strolled more slowly round to Farnden school. It was playtime, as she'd hoped, and the long-serving headmistress was in the playground, cup of coffee in hand, doing duty. She was rare among head teachers in wanting to watch the children at play as well as in the classroom. She was also wise, seeing useful pointers to the way they progressed in their schoolwork in the constantly shifting patterns of friendship and gang-warfare amongst the children in the playground. 'Concentration on the whole child is not a philosophy invented yesterday,' she would say gently to her young staff.

'Morning, Miss Clitheroe!' Lois called, and the head teacher walked over to the school railings.

'How are you, my dear?'

'Very well thanks,' said Lois.

Miss Clitheroe was an old pro at public relations and said, 'How's your mother? Such a nice helpful person at our jumble sale!'

'Yeah, well, she likes nothing better,' said Lois. 'Works

in the Oxfam shop . . . a regular rag-and-bone-lady, we tell her.'

'Did I hear that you've acquired a piano? I'm sure that didn't come from the Oxfam shop!'

Lois laughed. 'News gets around pretty quickly, doesn't it,' she said.

'Certainly does to me,' said Miss Clitheroe. 'Some parents would be horrified if they knew what their offspring write in their newsbooks! Anyway, is the piano for your mother?'

'No, no, it's for Jamie, my youngest,' Lois said, and then happily saw a way to get to the subject she'd had in mind all along. 'He's having lessons from Miss Abraham from Cathanger Mill. I expect you know her?'

'Oh, goodness, yes. We know Miss Abraham . . . Enid. She used to teach recorder – and piano, if required – round all the schools in the county. Very popular, too. Used to give little concerts with the children, singing and playing, for parents and friends. She was much missed when she had to give up.'

'Why did she stop?' Lois prayed that the end-of-break bell would not go yet.

'Family problems. Her mother became a recluse, and began to work on Enid to stay at home with her. Then there was the brother . . .'

'The brother? Edward?'

Miss Clitheroe gazed across the playground, where an impromptu game of Creeping Jinnie had got going with much screaming and shouting. 'That man was one of the nastiest pieces of work I've come across,' she said flatly. 'Enid was scared of him, you know, frightened of what he might do next.' she added. 'He and his mother ruled the whole family. Sponged off his father, and wound Enid round his little finger. They were close, in a funny way. Sometimes I thought she hated him, but then she'd turn and defend him. I've heard they're twins, though she denied it when I asked her. He resented her having friends, or anyone visiting her. In the end, it was easier for Enid to give up. She braved it out as long as she could, but they won in the end. Poor Enid.'

'Do you know where he might have gone?' said Lois

quickly, seeing the playground monitor approaching the rope that pulled the old bell.

'To hell, I hope,' said Miss Clitheroe vehemently, and walked off to shepherd her flock back into school.

Nothing new there then, thought Lois, setting off for home. The twins thing again, though. She stopped on hearing a voice calling her name. 'Mrs Meade! Just a minute!'

It was Miss Clitheroe. Must be something urgent for her to leave her class. Lois turned and walked back towards the hurrying figure. 'There is something,' Miss Clitheroe gasped. 'Must tell you now, in case I forget.' Lois waited. 'That Edward Abraham – you asked me if I knew where he might be. I saw on television that he'd done a runner.' Miss Clitheroe was more or less up to date with jargon, even if she was close to retirement.

'Well?' Lois smiled at her encouragingly.

'Alibone Woods. I remember Enid telling me he sometimes vanished for two or three days, living rough in some hiding place he'd found. She laughed when I asked if it coincided with the full moon. But seriously, Mrs Meade, I think he is a bit mad. Whether dangerously mad, I don't know. But I hope the police find him soon. Do you think they've looked in Alibone Woods? And in other woods around?'

'I think they have, but maybe not well enough,' said Lois. 'Do you remember anything else she said about the hiding place?'

Miss Clitheroe thought hard. 'There was . . . oh, now what was it . . . Ah, now wait a minute. She said there was some sort of cave where there'd been a landslide . . . something to do with an old quarry. It was completely grown over with trees and bushes. I remember she said he came home with snagged jerseys and even ripped trousers. And, of course, Enid had to mend them. Yes, that was it.'

At this point they heard a shout from the school direction, and looked round. 'Oh lor,' said Miss Clitheroe, 'that's my deputy waving her arms about! Better dash . . .'

'Damn,' said Lois. 'Still, thanks very much, Miss Clitheroe.' Time for a report to the top cop.

*   *   *

Cowgill was waiting for her. She noticed he was dressed entirely in a kind of khaki-green, and smiled.

'Camouflaged, are we?' she said.

'Ever been birdwatching, Lois?' he replied, without an answering smile.

She shook her head. 'The likes of me don't go bird-watching,' she said.

'Rubbish,' said Cowgill, and continued, 'and anyway, if you had, you'd know that if you want to be invisible you don't wear a scarlet anorak.' Then he smiled, and she didn't. The anorak had been her Christmas present from Derek, and she was very fond of it.

'I could be mistaken for a robin,' she said. 'You know, Robin Redbreast?'

'Shall we get down to business?' he said. 'I presume you've got something to tell me, and this isn't a trap where I shall be attacked by a revengeful husband?'

'Yes, I have,' said Lois frostily, 'but first you can tell me where you've got to in finding the writer of those shitty letters.'

'We're making progress,' Cowgill said. 'And may I suggest we call a truce? At least for this morning? I wish you both nothing but well, Lois, you know that.'

She wasn't so sure about the 'both', but began to tell him the latest on Edward Abraham. 'Miss Clitheroe said the cave was somewhere in these woods, near to where an old quarry used to be.' She went on to fill him in on the impossible situation for Enid at Cathanger Mill, and ended up, 'So the sooner we catch the bugger the better.'

'Right,' he said. 'Most useful. But there is one small thing I have to point out to you. I know you're Enid's employer, and feel sorry for her, and like her. But we cannot ignore the possibility that there is collusion there. If he had that much hold over the family, he may still be exercising it. He's been missing for longer than we'd usually expect in such circumstances, and this probably means someone's helping him.'

'You're not suggesting Enid is . . .' Lois bristled, and Cowgill retreated a step or two.

136

'Steady now,' he said. 'Just try to think it out clearly, Lois. In this business the head must always rule the heart, and there's nothing wrong with your head.'

'So what do you want me to do?' Lois said grudgingly.

'Talk to her. The piano lessons should give you the opportunity. Does she trust you?'

Lois nodded. 'I think so. And that's why I don't want to . . .'

'Well, it's up to you,' said Cowgill, straightening his khaki cap and turning away. 'But don't forget, Lois,' he added, 'you could be helping Enid Abraham in the long run. Maybe changing her life. Think about it.'

Twenty-Six

'Staff meeting this morning,' Lois said, climbing out of bed and helping Derek zip up his trousers. The zip had stuck, and he was losing patience.

'Hey! Watch it!'

Lois began to laugh. 'You'll be puttin' our marriage in danger if you don't go careful. Here, let me do it.'

And then, of course, one thing led to another, the zip was fixed, and some time elapsed before both of them went downstairs and into the kitchen for breakfast.

'You're late,' said Gran. 'I've got some black puddin' spoiling here in the pan. The kids have refused to eat it, so I'm relying on you two.' She was surprised at the way they wolfed it down, especially Lois, who normally nibbled a piece of toast.

'Nothing like a spot of exercise,' said Derek, 'to give you a good appetite.' Since neither had been outside the back door, Gran merely raised her eyebrows.

'Bill phoned,' she said. 'He might be a bit late for the meeting. His client asked him to do an extra hour – got people coming to stay – so he said unless he heard from you, he'd go ahead and do it.'

'Fine,' said Lois. 'Thanks, Mum.'

'Hope he remembers his apron,' said Derek, carefully distancing himself from Lois, 'specially if they got guests.' Lois stood up, but she was not quick enough, and he had gone, Douglas holding the back door open to aid his escape.

'Hi, everybody.' Lois noticed that Bill had not yet arrived, but all the others were there. Bridie and daughter Hazel were sitting at opposite ends of the room, and Lois wondered what

138

was up. Sheila Stratford had brought her knitting, and was triumphantly casting off the final sleeve of a vast jersey for her husband. Enid Abraham sat neatly as ever, smiling gently at her colleagues, but as remote as if merely an onlooker.

They had the usual discussion on schedules, and then Lois asked if there were any problems. Silence. This was also usual. It took a few minutes before anything personal emerged. Then Bridie spoke. 'There is something,' she said, 'but it's about Bill's girlfriend, so I'm not sure . . .'

'Do you want to tell me privately?' Lois said.

'Not really. It affects us all, so if it's OK?' Lois nodded, and Bridie continued. 'Well, you know she works at Waltonby school? Apparently someone's been gossiping there, and saying New Brooms is rubbish. The most likely person is Rebecca, though she seems nice enough to me.'

There was a shocked hush, and then Sheila Stratford spoke. 'I've not heard anything,' she said. 'And I often stand at the school gates talking to the mums. I meet my grandchildren, and they haven't said nothing, either.'

Bridie looked across at Hazel. 'Well,' she said, 'go on, Hazel, tell what you heard.'

Hazel sighed. She had told her mother to keep quiet about it, but she wouldn't listen. They'd had words before coming to the meeting. Hazel had said the best thing to do with gossip was to ignore it, but Bridie was incensed. Lois, her oldest friend, was being criticized, and she intended to get to the bottom of it.

'Well, Hazel?' Lois was curious, though not particularly worried. Gossip was meat and drink to some, and she always listened. But it hadn't been about her lately, and could mean something. Something to do with Enid?

Hazel glared at her mother, and said, 'It's probably nothing much . . . just one of those big-mouths at the school gates. I happened to be talking to a friend, and heard this woman say she'd heard things about New Brooms. Rotten job, cleaning, she reckoned. Only fit for people who couldn't do anything else. Like that woman from the mill. Nobody else'd employ her, they said.' Lois looked up sharply, worrying that Hazel had gone too far, but Enid's face was as calm as ever. 'Then

139

they started laughing,' Hazel continued, 'and Bill's name was mentioned. I suppose they think a bloke doin' cleaning is a real joke. Anyway, I just turned round and told them to mind their own bloody business, and they went off to get their precious darlings from the playground.' She shrugged. 'Sorry, Lois,' she added. 'I don't think there's anything to worry about. You know what they're like.'

'Yes,' said Lois, remembering the unpleasant buzz that went round Long Farnden when she, a cleaner, and her family moved into the doctor's house. 'Yes, I know. Thanks anyway, both of you. And don't *any* of you think any more about it. Could be one of them didn't get the job when I was recruiting. But the gossip's not likely to come from Rebecca, not when her Bill is one of us. Still, I'll mention it. He's coming later.'

Bill came about ten minutes later, and Lois said nothing, planning to keep him back after the meeting. As it happened, he wanted a private chat too, so after the others had gone the two sat down again and Lois opened the conversation. She told him what Hazel had said, and he exploded. When he had calmed down, Lois gave him the possible explanation, and he agreed that probably the best thing was to do nothing. 'But if it gets around that Rebecca is gossiping, then that's serious,' he said. 'Could prejudice her job.'

Lois smiled. 'Not with her uncle bein' chairman of the governors,' she said.

'Ah, well, p'raps not,' he answered, and added, 'anyway, can I just tell you something funny that happened? Something to do with Enid Abraham? I know you think I've got it in for her, but I haven't, an' it's something you ought to know.'

He told her what the Rev Rogers had relayed to Rebecca. 'Enid was really upset about that woman saying her brother was a danger to children. And then there was that odd business with slamming doors and running footsteps, and her denying hearing anything.'

He added what Seb Charrington had told him about Enid and the dog, and her trying to stop Seb going into the woods. 'She's up to something, I reckon,' he said finally. 'Hazel thinks so, too. You could say it's none of our business, but

140

this is more than gossip.' He got up then, and looked down at Lois.

He's an attractive bloke, she thought objectively. She had noted Hazel's name included in his judgement, and wondered when those two had got together. It wasn't on any cleaning job. She had instinctively avoided that. She didn't want to lose him. He was a big strong lad, and might come in useful if she ever got herself into another tight corner working for Cowgill.

She thanked him and said she'd be on the watch, but that Enid had proved satisfactory in every way as an employee of New Brooms. 'Still, I'll certainly keep my eyes and ears open,' she said, and saw him to the door.

Gran and Lois sat at the kitchen table. There were just the two of them for lunch, and silence had fallen.

'Meeting go all right?' said Gran. She could see that Lois was distracted.

'Yeah, fine, except for Hazel telling us a nasty piece of gossip from Waltonby.' Lois did not elaborate.

'Villages are rife with it.'

'Yep.'

'Don't you want to know why I said that?' Gran was irritated by the monosyllabic Lois.

'Oh, all right. Why did you say that?'

'Well,' said Gran, settling in her chair, 'at the WI meeting last night I heard a little tit-bit that might interest you. It was a group meeting, with other WIs in the district.' Suddenly Lois was concentrating.

Gran warmed to her task. 'There was this woman, secretary of the Round Ringford lot. Miss Beasley, or Beastly, or something. I heard her talking to our president . . .'

'Ooh la!' interrupted Lois, smiling, 'it's "*our* president" already?'

'Be quiet, Lois,' said Gran. 'Let me finish. There was this Miss Whatever, and she was asking about the cleaning service in our village. Said she'd heard about it, and was it true that Enid Abraham was working for it?'

Lois's heart sank. Snippets of suspicion about Enid were

piling up. But suspicion of what? Most of it seemed to be about brother Edward. She'd heard nothing bad about Enid herself. There was that hint from Cowgill that she might be involved in Edward's disappearance, but he'd had nothing to go on. 'What did she say about Enid?'

'I couldn't hear much, as I was being introduced to some other woman, but I did catch Miss Beastly's voice saying, "If you ask me, they should put them both behind bars, unpleasant pair. That's twins for you". That was a surprise, Lois. Enid's never mentioned she's a twin.' Gran got up then, and began to clear the table.

'She's not,' said Lois, 'she told me. But it's odd that I heard that from Bridie, too.'

'Well, twin or not, she's a very nice woman, and I count her as a friend.' Gran began to stack plates in the dishwasher with a clatter, as if to bring an end to the subject, and Lois took herself off to her office to make some notes. She'd better have a word with Hazel this afternoon. And Enid would be coming to give Jamie his piano lesson tomorrow. There should be an opportunity then to see what else she could discover.

Bridie was at home when Lois arrived, but Hazel was still over at Mrs Jordan's on the new estate.

'That job's a doddle,' Bridie said. 'House as clean as a new pin, and nothing out of place, before Hazel starts! Not like our muddly old vicar . . . Have you got time for a cup of tea, Lois?'

As the purpose of Lois's visit was to see Hazel, she said yes and sat down to wait.

'You know you said Enid was a twin,' she said to Bridie, who was busying herself with mugs and tea bags, pleased that Lois was staying for a gossip. They had been good friends ever since school, but now Lois was her boss, there was a slight reserve between them.

Bridie never knew quite how much she could, or should, say. Like the others, she was puzzled by Enid Abraham. She did not exactly dislike her, but found her distant . . . though always pleasant. Bridie supposed it was because she seemed so superior, with her previous jobs and her piano playing. None of them could quite work out why Enid had taken to cleaning. But then, come to that, why had Bill? Because he wanted to, he said frequently, and that was good enough, surely.

'Yep, I know I said it, but I'm not sure. They were just very close, like I told you.' Bridie handed Lois her mug of tea and sat down opposite her. 'Why? Is it important?'

'Dunno,' said Lois. 'Enid seems to be a bit of a mystery. Mum heard someone at the WI last night saying she and her brother should be locked up . . . Well, for God's sake, why?'

'Ah,' said Bridie, and then stopped.

'Go on,' Lois said.

'Well, um, you know you always say New Brooms shouldn't gossip, so I'm not sure if I should say . . .'

'I'm sure,' said Lois firmly. 'It could be important, Bridie. Was it something that happened in the past?'

Bridie nodded. 'There was a kind of scandal, about ten years ago. Something to do with swindling a shop in Tresham. It was him, the brother. He used Enid's name somehow. I don't quite know how it worked, but he juggled payments until he'd run up a huge bill. The police were involved eventually, but it was all hushed up at Cathanger. Now it looks as if the bugger is at it again. Gone missing, hasn't he?'

'Who's gone missing?' said Hazel, coming in breezily after a very untaxing afternoon's work.

'Oh, you know, that chap from Cathanger,' said her mother, disappointed that her cosy chat with Lois had been interrupted. Once Hazel was back, no one got much of a chance of a quiet conversation.

'Oh, him,' said Hazel, 'brother of our Enid. Yes, well, the longer he stays missing the better, from what I hear.'

'What have you heard, Hazel?' said Lois.

'He's a villain. A small-time crook, according to the locals. And you'd do well to keep an eye on Enid. Me and Bill were talking, and agreed it's just as well you don't keep a lot of cash in your office.'

Lois stood up, furious. 'Hazel! You deserve your cards for that! How dare you talk like that about one of your

143

colleagues? It's all just bloody gossip and tittle-tattle! Enid, poor sod, has enough to put up with, without people she thinks are her friends putting the boot in. If you or any of the others have got something to say about her, please say it to me. And, by the way, when have you and Bill been getting together to stir it up?'

Hazel stared at her. 'What d'you mean?' she said. 'Bill and me? That's rubbish! He's got Rebecca, and they're really good together. If you really want to know, and I don't see it's any of your business, we had a drink when we met in the pub – and Rebecca was there too – and talked a bit about Enid, because we all think she's a bit weird!'

'I'll be the judge of that,' said Lois. 'As an employee of New Brooms, she's excellent, can't be faulted. I get good reports all the time.'

'Bully for her,' said Hazel mutinously.

'And now I'm going. Thanks for the tea, Bridie. You can ring me when you've thought a bit, Hazel. I'm not sure an apology will be enough, but you can try.'

The door slammed behind her, and Bridie began to speak, but Hazel interrupted. 'Leave it, Mum. I've got things to do.'

Bridie, left alone, sighed. Since her husband Dick died, she had found it a comfort having Hazel still at home. But if she left New Brooms she'd probably be off somewhere else, to college or to find another job. It would be lonely without her.

Lois was still steaming when she arrived home. The kids were back from school, and Jamie had gone straight to the piano to do his daily practice. As well as the exercises Enid had given him, he picked out familiar tunes, getting them right first time. Derek had listened and reluctantly agreed with Lois that the boy had a good ear. If he had the stamina to keep it up, maybe he'd go somewhere with it.

'Jamie! Tea's ready!' Gran could see Lois was in a rage, and decided diplomatically to take over the children until she calmed down.

Jamie closed the piano lid and ran out to the kitchen, bumping straight into his mother in the doorway.

'For God's sake, Jamie!' Lois said. 'Look where you're going!'

He grinned at her. 'Sorry . . . but you want me to practise, don't you? And it's my lesson tomorrow. Miss Abraham'll be cross if I haven't practised. 'Cept she's not like that, is she. Really cool, for an old woman.'

His grin had its usual effect on Lois, and she ruffled his hair. 'Good lad,' she said. 'I'm glad Enid has one fan, at least.'

Twenty-Seven

J amie was ready for Enid Abraham ten minutes before she was due, and he sat playing his scale, up and down, over and over again. He heard the telephone, but didn't get up. It'd be one of Mum's cleaners. He began to pick out his favourite tune, and attempted a few notes that sounded OK in the left hand.

The door opened, and Lois came in. 'Jamie, that was Enid. Seems she's stuck. A tyre's blown, and her dad's gone out in the truck. He'll see to the tyre when he gets back, but it won't be until later. She's really sorry, and says she'll give you a lesson another day. We'll fix it tomorrow. Sorry, love.'

Jamie's face fell. 'Oh, Mum! I was all ready for her . . .' He followed Lois into the kitchen.

'Never mind,' she said. 'Have something to eat, then you can get on with your homework.'

'Great! Just what I was hoping for . . . an early start on my homework . . .'

'No need to be cheeky,' said Gran quietly. 'Here, I made this cake this afternoon. Try it . . . might sweeten you up.'

Jamie finished his homework and sat staring out of the window at the road, where the light was slowly going. He was fed up. All week he'd been looking forward to another piano lesson. Couldn't Miss Abraham change the tyre herself? He thought of her small, clean hands and thought probably not. Come to that, why hadn't she said he could go to Cathanger instead? He could easily bike over, and would be no trouble. That dopey old mother of Miss Abraham wouldn't object to one boy playing the piano very quietly, surely? He looked at his watch. Not much time before it got dark, but he'd got lights on his bike. He could be back before anyone noticed.

He stood up, tidied his homework and went quietly downstairs into the living-room to collect his piano book. He opened the front door gently and slipped out. No one saw him go. Josie and Douglas were buried in homework, Derek was not home yet, and Lois and Gran were busy in the kitchen.

There was very little traffic on the country road to Waltonby, and Jamie went fast, happy to be released and sure that, after all, he'd get his lesson and be able to get on to the next stage. Just before he reached the tunnel of trees by Cathanger Mill, he realized it was nearly dark, and got off to switch on his lights. Before he remounted, he heard a voice and saw a girl coming towards him, leading a Labrador puppy. It hadn't quite got the hang of going for a walk, and was jumping about all over the place.

'That's a nice dog,' he said, and the girl smiled.

'Yes, isn't he sweet one?' she said, and Jamie realized she was foreign.

Must be that au pair girl Mum had mentioned. Anna, was that her name? 'I'm Jamie Meade,' he said. 'I think my mum's lady comes to clean your house?'

'Of course,' said Anna. 'Miss Abraham comes. Rosie – Mrs Charrington – thinks she's so good, but I think she is a . . . a . . .'

'I like her,' said Jamie stoutly. 'I'm goin' there to have a piano lesson. She usually comes to us, but her car got a flat tyre, so I've biked over.'

'To the mill?' Anna seemed surprised.

'Yep,' said Jamie, getting back on his bike. 'Better get goin', else it'll be too late. Bye!'

Anna stared at his retreating back and shrugged. She knew nobody went inside the mill except the Abraham family. Ah well, maybe the old woman had changed her mind. She untangled the puppy's lead and went on her way, dreaming about a student she'd met at her English classes. She forgot all about Jamie Meade.

The track down to the mill nearly threw Jamie off his bike several times, but finally he came to the yard. It was almost empty and silent except for the occasional lowing from the cow shed. He couldn't see any life in the house, and two of the windows had curtains drawn tightly already. Right, fine, he'd knock at the door and Enid would be pleased to see him.

Several minutes passed, and he saw a curtain drawn back a fraction. Another shiver caused Jamie to step back. Better give up and go home, he thought. As he turned to go, he heard the door creak open.

'What do you want?' a gruff voice said.

'Is Miss Abraham there?' said Jamie, and heard his own voice tremble.

'Not sure,' said the man. 'What do you want her for? We don't like kids coming down here . . .'

He began to close the door, and Jamie said quickly, 'She teaches me piano. I've come for a lesson . . . she had a flat tyre and couldn't come to us in Farnden . . .'

Then he heard Enid's voice calling out from behind the man. 'Who is it, Father?'

'Some kid says he's come for a piano lesson. Must've got the wrong house. Best be off now,' he added to Jamie, and the door once more began to close.

'It's Jamie!' said Enid's voice, and then she was there at the door, pushing past her father. 'Who told you to come here? You know we don't have visitors, Jamie,' she said, and her voice was kind, trying to be normal and pleasant.

'Nobody told me. I decided,' said Jamie. 'I was fed up you couldn't make it, so I biked over. I've got lights,' he added helpfully.

'Get rid of him, Enid,' her father said, 'else you know there'll be big trouble.'

But Enid shook her head. She smiled crookedly, not her usual smile, and put out her hand. 'Never mind, Jamie,' she said, 'now you're here, you'd better come in. Come along, follow me.' She took his hand and drew him inside. The door shut behind them, and he heard bolts being pushed into place. Suddenly, he wished he hadn't come. He wished he was back home with Mum and Gran in the warm kitchen, where there was plenty of light and the smell of supper cooking, and he was safe.

Twenty-Eight

'D oes your mother know you've come?' It was the first thing Enid had said to Jamie since leading him through a silent kitchen, where cats were curled up on the rag rug in front of the fire, closed-up balls of fur, and a sheep dog growled and bared its teeth at him.

'Um, yes,' he said. 'But perhaps I'd better not stay. That man said—'

'Oh, don't take any notice of him,' said Enid. 'That's my father, and his bark's much worse than his bite.' She led him through into a dark hallway, and he almost tripped over a tray of dirty dishes left on the floor outside a closed door. 'Oops!' said Enid gaily. 'That's my mother's. She likes to eat on her own . . . well, do everything on her own, really. She puts her tray out for us to collect.' She bent down, picked it up and put it on a side table. Then she opened another door on the opposite side of the hallway and said, 'Come on in, Jamie, we can make a start.'

It was the dining-room, Jamie supposed. A harsh overhead light shone on a large oval table, highly polished, with a vase of artificial flowers set on a lace mat, exactly in the centre. Six chairs were neatly placed around it, and at the side were silver candlesticks and covered dishes on a massive carved sideboard.

'What're they for?' Jamie walked over and touched the ornate lids.

'Oh, vegetables and things,' said Enid casually. 'Never used now, of course, but I keep them cleaned. They came from Father's family, and I don't like to get rid of them. Who knows when we might need them?'

Jamie accepted this without question, and looked around.

'Cool!' he said, seeing the piano in the corner. It was very large and solid, plain in a good way. He could read the word *Bluthner* on the front, and *Dale, Forty & Co.* in gilt lettering.

'It came from Cheltenham, many years ago. It was my great-grandmother's,' Enid said.

'Will I be able to play it?' said Jamie apprehensively.

'The keyboard's exactly the same as yours,' said Enid reassuringly, opening up the lid and setting a piano primer on the music rest. He sat down, and Enid showed him how to adjust the height of the stool, spinning round and round, until it was right for him. Then she drew up one of the big dining-chairs beside him. 'Right,' she said, 'off you go. Let's have the scale of C major.'

He began to play, and could hear at once that the piano was out of tune. It bothered him, but he said nothing. Everything Enid told him was like a magic way into a different world. He was totally absorbed, and at first didn't hear the noise coming from the other side of the hall. Finally he stopped playing, and looked at Enid. 'What's that?' he said, as the rapping became savage and sharp.

Her expression had changed, her shoulders drooped and she looked down at her hands. 'It's Mother,' she said. 'She doesn't like us playing the piano. I'm so sorry, Jamie, but I'm afraid we'll have to stop. But never mind,' she continued, 'I'll give you some exercises to do for next week, and then you can get back home. It's dark now, and I expect your mother will be glad to see you back.'

They left the dining-room, and Enid switched off the light, pulling the door shut. In the dim, narrow passageway, Jamie followed close behind. As Enid picked up the tray from the side table, Jamie froze in terror at a loud hail of raps and shouts coming from very close to him.

'Give Jamie a shout,' said Lois to Douglas. They were all relaxed in front of the television, and the scent of freesias brought home by Derek filled the room. 'It's his favourite programme,' she added. 'Must have done his homework by now.'

'Unlike him to be s'keen on maths homework,' said Derek, his feet propped up on the stone fireplace. 'Cold tonight,' he added. 'Clear sky later, and no wind.'

'Just as well you didn't put out them plants,' said Lois comfortably. 'Douglas, please do as you're asked,' she added. 'Go and call Jamie to come down. You bet he's stuck to that computer again.'

Gran sighed. 'I think he's sulking a bit, about missing his piano lesson. He's really keen, that lad.'

'Yes, well,' said Derek. 'He'll have to learn that life's full o'little disappointments. *Douglas!* Do as your mother said, and do it now!'

Douglas got up from his chair reluctantly and sloped off to the foot of the stairs to call his brother. When Jamie did not appear, Derek stirred. 'No, you stay there, Lois,' he said, as she also began to rise. 'I'll go. Do me heavy father act. That should bring him . . .'

Lois heard Derek padding upstairs, and then silence for a few seconds. Then she heard doors opening and shutting, and finally Derek's rapid descent.

'He's not there!' he said.

'What d'you mean, "not there"?' Lois frowned, but Douglas shrugged.

'Probably in the bog,' he said.

'No, I've looked. I've looked everywhere, and he's not in the house.'

Sudden fear shot through Lois. She ran out into the hall and began to call. 'Jamie? Jamie! Come here at once!' Old memories of enemies she had made through working for Cowgill came rushing back. Revenge for her part in nobbling villains had already struck at her family.

'Hold on, Lois,' Derek said. 'Let's think.'

'Ring the police,' said Gran. 'You can't muck about when a lad's gone missing. In the dark and cold . . .' There was a break in her voice, and she disappeared into the kitchen.

'Not for the minute,' said Derek, switching off the television. 'Sit down, all of you. Now, where might he have gone. Douglas?'

'His friend Sam,' said Douglas. 'Just down the road. We could ring.'

'OK – you do that,' said Lois, holding on, as Derek had said. 'Josie? You got any ideas?'

'You could look in the garage, or the shed,' she replied. 'Start close to home. If the daft little sod's hiding, it could be there.'

'Language,' said Derek automatically. 'Go and look, Josie.' He said it without much hope. Why should a boy hide away in a freezing cold shed for no reason at all? Douglas came back from the telephone, shaking his head. 'Sam hasn't sin him since they got off the school bus. Didn't know where he could've gone. He said he'd help look, but I said we were OK.'

Lois clenched her fists to keep the panic down. 'He wouldn't go with them kids round the back of the village hall, would he?' Nobody wanted to think about that. It was well known as the local meeting place for having a smoke, exchanging tabs, Long Farnden's very own drug scene.

Josie came in from the garden. 'Nope, he's nowhere there. But his bike's gone, Mum.' Not good news, she knew. The village hall kids always had their bikes for a quick getaway. Lois pulled on her anorak, and turned to Derek. 'You stay here for a few minutes,' she said. 'I'll be back. If I don't find him, we ring Keith Simpson.'

Derek nodded, but thought privately that they could do a better search themselves than bring in Constable Plod. He felt reasonably calm. Jamie was a sensible lad, and would not normally do anything stupid. But was this a normal thing? He'd never run away before, or anything like that. Always been a bit spoilt, perhaps, being the youngest. But not wilful or disobedient. Sometimes Derek thought he could be a bit more independent, not so close to his mother and Gran.

In the kitchen, Gran sat at the table, eyes closed, thinking.

Lois walked quickly. She had a torch, but did not switch it on. Long Farnden had no street lights, but she knew her way like a cat, avoiding potholes and broken pavements. She intended to come round the corner of the village hall very quietly, and hoped to surprise them. She knew most of them. They were not all deprived kids from broken homes, not by any means. Good, middle-class backgrounds, most of them. Working mothers, though. She felt a pang of guilt.

As she expected, the small huddle of teenagers broke up quickly, peeling off on their bikes and disappearing into the night. Only one figure remained, and it was not Jamie. 'Mrs M? What are you . . .?' Lois knew the voice at once.

'Hazel?'

'Yes, it's me, in case you're wondering. I'm working. For our mutual friend. Spy, informer, grass . . . What shall we call ourselves? This is my patch . . . but I s'pose you're not here to help?'

In the anxiety of the moment, Lois had forgotten her row with Hazel. 'I'm looking for Jamie,' she said. 'He's gone missing. He could have been here.'

Hazel shook her head. 'Not a chance, thank God,' she said. 'This lot are regulars. Not your Jamie. When'd he go?'

'Not sure.' Lois explained the details briefly to Hazel, then said she must be getting back.

By the time she returned to the house, Derek had made a plan. 'I'll get the van,' he said, 'and you take your car, Lois. We'll go slowly round the villages and see if we spot him. Josie and Douglas can go round likely friends in the village. And stick together, you two. Gran can stay here, in case Jamie comes back, or there are any phone calls or messages.'

'An' if we don't find him, we ring Keith Simpson,' repeated Lois. She looked at the clock. It was half past eight. Time was passing, and they still had no idea where Jamie had gone. 'Where's Gran?' she said.

'In the kitchen,' Josie said, putting on her coat. 'Tell her to stay here and wait.' Lois fished in her pocket for car keys.

Josie went into the kitchen, and saw Gran sitting there, eyes closed. 'Gran?' Poor old thing. Must be upset.

'Yes?'

Eyes still closed.

'Um, we're all goin' out looking. Mum says will you stay here and hold the fort?'

Gran nodded. 'I'm thinking, dear,' she said. 'Off you go.'

153

Twenty-Nine

Jamie sat in the Abraham's kitchen, a mug of hot milk in his hand, and a cat curled up on his lap.

'Drink that all down,' said Enid. 'Then we'll get you home.'

Walter Abraham had said he was sorry Mother had made such a scene. 'Not a good idea, you coming down here,' he added wearily. In a voice Jamie had not heard before, Enid retorted that Mother'd soon get used to it if they didn't pander to her so much. Walter raised his eyebrows and said when Jamie had finished his milk he'd load the bike into the back of the truck and run him home. 'Shouldn't be out at this hour on your own, anyway,' he said. 'I don't know what your parents are thinking of.'

'Shouldn't we ring them?' said Enid. 'Just to tell them you're on the way home?'

'No, they won't worry,' lied Jamie. 'I often go out at night on my bike. I got lights. I'll be OK – no need for you to take me in the truck.' He was not at all keen on arriving home in the care of Mr Abraham. He was planning to say he'd been for a ride around, and hadn't noticed it was getting dark. Perhaps he'd say Sam had asked him to go round to his house. They wouldn't mind that. Apart from a bollocking for not telling them, he'd probably get off lightly. But not if he arrived home in Mr Abraham's truck.

Enid had made light of the storm from inside the locked room. Ushering Jamie back into the kitchen, she had confronted her father's angry face with a joke about Mother being so stupid that she didn't know when she was listening to a budding genius. Then she'd insisted on giving him this milk, in spite of him saying he didn't much like hot milk. 'It'll warm you up,' she said, 'before you go home.'

He was certainly warm now. The fire was in a kind of basket in an old black range, and the other cats were as near to it as they could get. The one on his lap was purring loudly, and he felt quite at ease. If he had to go home in the truck, he'd get Mr Abraham to drop him outside the gate, and then wait until he'd gone before he went inside. Yes, that'd do. He downed the last of the milk and carefully set the cat down on the floor. 'We got a cat,' he said to Mr Abraham. 'He's called Melvyn, after Josie's boyfriend. He's in prison now . . . well, some sort of prison. You probably heard about it.'

The silence was electric. 'Prison?' said Walter finally. 'No, we've heard nothing about prison in this house.' He was making a great effort to remain normal, pleasant. He had to get this boy out of the house and back home without causing any more upset. 'Get his coat, Enid,' he said. 'I'll put the bike in the truck, and we'll go.'

The yard was very dark, and Jamie could just see the outline of the old truck over by the barn. 'Why don't you have an outside light, Mr Abraham?' he said. 'My dad could fix you one of those that comes on if anybody goes by. Warns you of intruders!' Jamie laughed, completely at ease now. He couldn't see in the darkness that there was no answering smile from Walter Abraham. Jamie climbed into the truck cab, and glanced back through the dusty window. His bike was safely in the back. And so was something else, some*one* else, hunched into the corner. Jamie looked harder. It wasn't Mr Abraham, who was fiddling about at the front of the truck. All Jamie could see was a whitish face, and it was looking straight at him. His new-found confidence evaporated at once. Who was it? And why was it staring at him like that?

Walter climbed into the driving seat and turned the key. The engine spluttered and died. 'Damn!' he said. He tried again, with the same result.

'There's a man in the back,' Jamie said, and his voice wobbled.

'Nonsense,' said Walter impatiently. 'It's only shadows.

Now let me get this engine started and we'll be off.' He tried again, but still with no success. 'Damn,' he said again. 'I'll have to go and get some stuff . . . engine's probably damp. Wait here, boy, I shan't be long.'

'Don't leave me!' said Jamie, now very frightened. 'There *is* a man in the back! I can see him!'

'You got a good imagination,' said Walter, and climbed out of the cab, disappearing into the darkness.

Lois and Derek arrived back at the house more or less at the same time. 'Did you . . .?' Lois could see that Derek's van was empty. No Jamie. She had had no luck, either, although she'd knocked up Bill and Rebecca to ask them. Bill had immediately pulled on his jacket and set off to get his bike.

'I'll be able to use my ears as well as eyes,' he said. 'The more of us looking, the quicker we'll find him.' He was gone before Lois could protest. And anyway, she was glad. There was something so reassuring about Bill.

They went into the kitchen and found Josie and Douglas sitting with Gran at the table. Their faces dropped when they saw that Lois and Derek had no Jamie with them.

'Right,' said Lois. 'Time to get Keith Simpson. I'll go and phone.'

Gran looked up. 'Wait a minute, Lois,' she said. 'I bin thinking, and I've got a suggestion. It's probably no good, but worth a try.'

'What?' said Lois baldly. She was feeling increasingly panicked, and had a hard job to remain calm in front of the others.

'Well, you know he was upset about missing his piano lesson . . .'

'So?' Lois was over by the door now, on her way to the telephone.

'Suppose he went to see Enid? He often goes over to fish in that stream with other kids in summer. He knows the way. He might've thought she'd be pleased to see him . . .' Her voice broke. 'We'd all be pleased to see him right now,' said Lois, and burst into tears.

'Hey, Gran,' said Douglas. 'That's a good idea! Just the

156

sort of stupid thing he would do. I know!' he said, with
sudden inspiration. 'Let's look and see if his piano book's
still there!' He got up quickly and went to the door.

'Wait, Douglas,' said Gran. 'I looked. It's gone.'

Lois collected herself rapidly. 'Oh my God,' she said.
'Cathanger bloody Mill. Why didn't I think of that?'

'Because you think your precious Enid Abraham could do
no wrong!' snapped Derek. 'Come on, let's get going.'

'Mum, why don't you phone?' said Josie practically. 'We'd
know straight away, then, and not worry any more . . . if he *is*
there . . .'

Lois shot out and they were all silent, listening. After a
few minutes, she returned, white-faced.

'There's no reply,' she said. 'D'you think they've abducted
him . . . gone off somewhere?'

'Course not,' said Douglas stoutly. 'Probably can't hear
the phone with Jamie playin' the piano the way he does. Go
on, Mum, get goin',' he added, patting her reassuringly on the
arm. 'Sooner he's back here the better.'

Gran got up from the table and, much to his embarrassment,
hugged Douglas tight. 'Good lad,' she whispered. Josie
sniffed, and Lois and Derek went out again into the night
without saying another word.

In the now total darkness, Jamie sat in the truck cab, frozen
with fear. He daren't look behind to see if the man was still
there. He couldn't hear any sounds of Mr Abraham, who had
vanished. He thought of getting out and running off, running
anywhere, so long as it was away from this dreadful place.
Then he remembered the staring man. He'd be out of the
back of the truck in no time, and could catch him with no
trouble.

Walter Abraham was searching in the old barn for stuff to
dry out condensation on the spark plugs. He was sure there
some somewhere. Bloody truck! Trust it to seize up just when
he needed it most! The boy had been quite cheerful, up until
the time he claimed there was a man in the back. He could've
got him home, apologized to his parents, and no more would
have been said. He stood back and surveyed the shelves. Not

there, then. Perhaps it was in the house, in the back scullery. He probably left it there when he'd last used it.

He came out of the barn, needing no light to see his way. But as he approached the truck, the clouds parted and suddenly, like the moment of Creation, there was light. The moon shone into the yard, casting long shadows, but illuminating clearly the truck and Jamie's bike in the back. And – Walter peered closer – the hunched figure of a man. He recognized him at once. It was his son, Edward, crouching like a hunted animal waiting to spring.

Jamie, surprised by the blessed moonlight, turned once more to look through the dusty window. He saw the man stand up, and then, horrified, watched him leap out of the back of the truck, straight on to the bent figure of Mr Abraham. Both men went down to the ground, and he heard muffled shouts and groans.

It was too much for Jamie. He opened the truck door, and jumped down, yelling and screaming. He rushed over to the men, and began pummelling them with his fists. 'Stop it! Stop it!' he shouted. 'Stop it, or I'll get Miss Abraham!'

Weak with the effort, he stood back, near to tears, and suddenly felt hands on his shoulders. 'What the bloody hell's going on here?' said a deep voice. Jamie whipped round, and saw his mum's cleaner, Bill.

The attacker rapidly got to his feet, abandoned Walter, who lay motionless on the ground, and began to run. He was very fast, and though Bill chased him halfway up the track, he lost him. In any case, as he said to Lois afterwards, he thought it best to make sure Jamie was OK, and have a look at the old man.

Minutes later, Derek's van drove into the yard, and Lois ran over to Jamie, hugging him as if she'd never let him go. 'Mum, please!' he said. 'Is Mr Abraham all right? That man was trying to kill him!'

But Walter had moaned and, with Bill's help, sat up, rubbing his head. 'Ruddy burglar!' they heard him say. 'Took me by surprise. Is the lad all right?'

Now Enid came rushing out of the house, and helped get Walter to his feet. When he was sitting safely in his chair by the fire, assuring them he needed no doctor except a glass of whisky, Lois, Derek and Bill stood in a huddle by the door. 'Will you be OK with him, Enid?' Lois said. Her tone was not friendly. 'I'll ring the police when I get home.'

'No need,' said Enid, very firmly. 'I shall do it, thank you, Mrs Meade. I can give them all the details, and Father can help. We're grateful to all of you . . .' Here Walter nodded, and muttered his thanks.

'And as for Jamie, and what has happened here tonight,' said Lois coldly, 'I will be in touch tomorrow, Enid. And you'd better have a bloody good explanation for all this.'

Enid stared at her. 'But Jamie said you knew he was here . . .' she said, her confidence collapsing. Surely the boy wouldn't have lied to her?

'Yeah, well, we'll see,' said Lois. 'But there's a lot more questions I want answers to. Like why you didn't answer the phone just now. I'll see you tomorrow.'

'I never answer the phone in the evenings . . .' said Enid dully, unable to explain how much she dreaded hearing her brother's voice, knowing that whatever he had to say would inevitably involve her in something she did not want to do.

'For God's sake, why not!' said Lois, but Enid turned away sadly.

Bill went off into the darkness on his bike, now elevated to hero status in the eyes of Jamie, and the three Meades returned to Long Farnden in total silence.

Thirty

Next morning, Wednesday, Enid was due to be at the Charringtons', just up the road from the mill. Rosie looked around at her untidy, grubby kitchen and looked forward to the clean-up miracle Enid could be relied on to work on it. However, at nine o'clock, half an hour later than Enid usually arrived, Rosie looked at her watch and said to Anna, 'Where on earth is she? It's not like her to be late. Perhaps I should give her a ring.'

Anna, whose dislike of Enid had not abated, replied that even Miss Perfect slipped up sometimes. Like last night.

'What *do* you mean?' Rosie asked. 'And where did you get the "Miss Perfect" from? Not from the children, I hope. They are very fond of Enid, and I'll not have them calling her names. Please don't say that again, Anna.'

Rosie's little homily closed the conversation, and it was not until she had gone outside to feed the rabbit – the children could not be trusted – that she remembered Anna's remark about 'last night'. When she came in again, she reminded her, and saw Anna hesitate. 'Well,' she said. 'It was not really about Miss Abraham. I took the puppy for a little walk – to do a pee-pee, as you say – and saw a boy with his bicycle. He said he was Jamie . . . I think . . . yes, Jamie Meade, and had got off to fix his light. I asked him where he was going . . .' She paused.

'And where was he going?' said Rosie. She did wish Anna would not invest every story with high drama.

'To the mill, he said. For a piano lesson with Miss Abraham. Do you not think that curious? What about the mother, the recluse? And the grumpy old father?'

'And the villainous son,' said Rosie grimly. 'Well, I'm

going to ring Lois Meade and hope that she can send someone else in Enid's place. I could ask after Jamie, too.'

Lois's answered immediately. 'Morning, Mrs Charrington,' she said. 'Nothing wrong, I hope?' She was feeling tired. They had had a long post mortem last night, once they'd got Jamie home and put his bike safely in the shed. Gran had been anxious to get the boy to bed, but Derek had put him through a grilling, wanting to know exactly what had happened at the mill, and whether he had been frightened or hurt. Jamie had been defensive. 'They were very nice to me,' he'd said. When he'd described the noise from Enid's mother's room, he had played down his fear. He'd been worried that Dad would stop his piano lessons if he thought there'd been any kind of danger. And, anyway, even though he'd been terrified for a while, he was sure none of them would have harmed him. It was just that burglar . . . And that hadn't been the Abrahams' fault. He hoped the police would catch him. Poor old Mr Abraham . . .

Lois had been sitting at her desk, about to ring Cowgill, when Rosie rang. Although Jamie had been pretty convincing, Lois knew him too well. He'd been frightened by something, she was sure, and was covering up. She knew why, of course, and felt sorry for him. When Derek had finished with him, she'd gone in and tucked him up as if he was still a little lad. 'Dad's been very worried,' she'd said. 'We all were. Don't do a silly thing like that again, will you? Night, love,' she had added, and kissed him lightly. He'd sighed deeply and turned on his side, but it was a good hour before he fell asleep.

For all Jamie's efforts to make light of the circumstances, Lois had known the minute they got out of the van in the mill yard that something was nastily wrong. It was the so-called burglar. She and Derek had seen nobody on their way down the lane, and Bill had said the intruder had crashed through a gap in the track hedge and disappeared across the field into woods. Would a burglar do that? And wouldn't he have had a getaway car? No, it all felt very much awry. She would ask Jamie no more questions. He must put it out of his mind. The piano lessons were another matter. It would all depend on what Enid had to say when she came in this morning. Meanwhile, Cowgill should know the details so far.

Rosie was saying something, and Lois tried hard to focus on a long rambling speech about the puppy and Anna, and the people at the mill. When Jamie's name was mentioned, she snapped to attention. 'What did you say?' she asked.

'Well, nothing to do with Enid not coming this morning, really, but . . .' She relayed what Anna had said. Lois muttered, 'Oh yes, we know about that,' and asked more urgently if they'd had a call from Enid saying she'd be late, or anything?

'No, nothing,' said Rosie. 'It's not like Enid, is it? I'd go down and make sure she's all right, but I'm not really keen on . . . well . . . you know . . .'

Lois did indeed know, and had now decided that though she was far from keen herself, the time had come for her to ignore Enid's warnings and pay a visit herself. She'd had enough of all the fiddle-faddling about – Gran's words here – and with Derek's accusation ringing in her ears – 'trusting that woman in the face of plenty of warning' – she told Rosie she'd send Sheila Stratford instead. Then she telephoned Cowgill and filled him in, and told Gran she might be out for lunch.

As she opened her car door, she was surprised to see Hazel drawing up outside. 'Can I have a word, Mrs M?' Hazel said, unsmiling.

'I'm in a hurry,' Lois said. She'd had no apology from Hazel, and was not in the mood to be indulgent, even if she was the daughter of her best friend.

'Right, I'll make it snappy. First, I'm sorry I sounded off about Enid Abraham. Out of order, I know. Very sorry. Next, I hope you'll take me back, because I like it . . . and I like you,' she added, with a very uncharacteristic wobble. 'But more important, I want to warn you.'

'Warn me, Hazel? What of?' said Lois, feeling a huge relief that Hazel was back in the fold. If she'd gone, it would have been a failure for New Brooms.

'The Abrahams,' Hazel said baldly. 'I hear all kinds of things, mixing with the undesirables as I do.' Lois knew that good things had come of Hazel's work with Cowgill. It was a pity there wasn't a better word for snout, grass, informer. Hazel had put her life at risk on occasion, knowing full well that involvement in drugs could, and did, provoke dangerous reactions in a murky world. It was a kind of mission for the girl, and Cowgill made full use of it.

'What things?' said Lois.

'There's trouble down there. The kids say they used to go down to see if they could fish in the mill pond . . . and other things, o'course. The old man sent them packing every time. And they said the curtains were always drawn across one of the windows, but they twitched, like someone was watching. They notice things, the kids. They get wary.'

'Oh my God,' Lois said wearily. 'Thanks, Hazel. And, by the way, we'll forget our little barney. I do trust you, Hazel, but I have to stick up for Enid unless there's something solid against her . . . Must go now. Cheers.'

Lois drove off, relieved that at least one problem was solved. But her irritation with Enid was growing. Why hadn't she phoned in if she was sick? And shouldn't she have checked that it was all right for Jamie to be there last night? One phone call would have done it. There was a definite chilly centre to Enid Abraham. Like the way she took charge in the yard, more or less forbidding Lois to call the police. She was very like her brother, people said. How much like? And was it more than a physical resemblance? By the time Lois turned into the track to the mill, she was simmering.

The early sun had disappeared behind heavy clouds and the mill was shrouded in its usual gloom. Lois shivered as she got out of the car. Nobody about. Well, that was nothing new. Chickens cackled from a barn across the yard, and a cow called out in what sounded to Lois like a soul in torment. Blimey, talk about Cold Comfort Farm!

She marched across to the back door. Well, the only door, as far as she could see. Folk at the mill for centuries had had no need of a front door. The mill stream ran alongside the house, and the rotting remains of the big mill wheel still clung uselessly to the wall. The big pond was covered over with blanket weed, an unpleasant light green, hiding its depths. What a place. No wonder Enid didn't want visitors.

Lois listened before she knocked. No sound came from inside. No friendly conversation, or a Hoover cleaning up. Nothing homely. Then a dog barked twice, a sharp, warning yelp. Lois knocked loudly, and waited.

Nothing happened. The air in the yard seemed to have thickened into something old and stale. Lois had a strong impulse to get out, to find somewhere fresh and wholesome and take some deep breaths. But she had a job to do, and she knocked again. This time the dog barked for longer, but still no one came.

Lois put out a tentative hand and gave the door a slight push. It opened a fraction, and creaked loudly, but nobody appeared. Lois looked all around, especially behind her, before pushing it wide enough for her to step gingerly over the threshold. An old sheepdog with rheumy eyes barred her way, snarling.

Lois gritted her teeth. She was not going to be put off by any bloody dog. Grabbing an old rubber glove left abandoned by the door, she clouted it round the head and pushed her way into the Abrahams' kitchen. It was gloomy, but neat. The cats dozed, not bothering to get up. A shelf clock, its plain face worn away by time, ticked over the fireplace. The kitchen table was covered with a chenille cloth bordered by bobbles, just like Lois had seen on her grandmother's table years ago. In the corner, in a high-backed wooden chair, sat the old man, not moving, but staring at her with eyes that were very much alive.

'Oh, God!' Lois said, startled into retreating a few steps. 'Sorry . . . Mr Abraham, is it? . . . I knocked, but . . .'

'What d'you want?' Walter Abraham spoke flatly, as if hypnotized.

'Where's Enid?' Lois's anger was returning. 'I'd like to speak to her . . . urgently.'

The old man said nothing for a few seconds, then to Lois's horror, tears began to fall unchecked and ran down his cheeks, some into his half-open mouth. He shook his head. 'She's gone,' he said.

'Gone shopping? When will she be back?' Lois was daunted now, uncertain what to do about this old man weeping in front of her.

Again he shook his head. 'Not shopping. Gone. Gone away. And I don't know when – or if – she's coming back.'

Now what? Lois frowned, and made a decision. She pulled a chair out from under the table and sat down. 'You look terrible, Mr Abraham,' she said. 'Why don't you tell me what happened, then I can make us a cup of tea and see what help you need.' She sighed. She was a cleaner, not a ruddy social worker.

He made an attempt to get up from his chair, but sank back, his eyes closed. After another moment of silence, he opened them and said, 'We had a big row. Worse than usual. About your lad coming down here. It upset Mother, and I was angry.'

'But no harm was done, was it?' Lois was gentle. She knew if she stormed on about Enid's irresponsibility, he would dry up, or defend his daughter with excuses.

He shook his head. 'You don't know how we live down here, Mrs Meade,' he said. 'Always on a knife-edge, waiting for Mother to explode. Start throwing things. Screaming. We walk on tiptoe down here.'

'And Enid broke the rules, letting Jamie stay?'

'Right,' he nodded. 'I think she cracked. I suppose I knew she would, one day. Couldn't stand it any longer. She's not taken any of her things . . .'

'She probably means to come back later.'

'No, we had this terrible row. She said she'd send a postcard when she got where she was going, and I wasn't to try and get in touch. No one must try, she said.'

The old man had brightened. The tears had stopped, and he sat up straighter. He told Lois he could manage on his own, and, yes, look after Mother. She wasn't to worry. He was sorry about the job, and about the piano lessons. Jamie had seemed a nice lad.

Lois stood up. 'I'm sorry too, Mr Abraham,' she said. 'Enid was a good worker. Let us know if you need any help.' As she left the kitchen, she heard sharp rapping sounds from inside the house. What a bloody awful situation.

As she got into her car and started the engine, she stared at the house. Her anger had subsided, and she supposed she should feel sorry for the old bugger. But she didn't, and for a good reason.

She was convinced he was lying. Lying through his rotten teeth.

Thirty-One

L ois sat in her office next day, trying to make sense of revising the schedules. She picked up the phone. She'd talked to Sheila yesterday about extra work, but needed to extend it, at least temporarily. 'Sorry, Sheila, to bother you again,' she said, 'but I'd really appreciate it if you could take on a few more hours, just until I can get a replacement for Enid. The others are giving more time, as and when it's needed. Bill's been great. Says he doesn't mind how long he works. Better than waiting for Rebecca to come home from endless school meetings, he says.' She regretted the last remark at once.

Sheila rose to it swiftly: 'Should keep him out of mischief, too,' she said acidly. She had absolutely no evidence that Bill had made any approaches to Hazel, and was disappointed. The job needed a bit of spice now and then. Still, her daughter in Waltonby had phoned her with a bit of gossip earlier, and she was anxious to relay it to Lois.

'Um, there was something you might like to know about,' she said.

'Yes?' Lois had ignored the jibe about Bill, making a mental note to be more careful in future.

'My daughter . . . said she's heard somebody saw Enid. In a car. Not her car, but in the passenger seat. An old banger, it was, she said. She was laughing, she said. Laughing at the bloke sitting next to her, she said.'

'When?' said Lois sharply. News of Enid's disappearance had got around fast, aided, no doubt, by arch-gossip Sheila. Perhaps I should have said to keep it quiet for the moment, Lois thought. Too late now, anyway, and gossip had its uses.

She had already brought Cowgill up to date, but this was an extra, maybe an important extra.

'Yesterday some time.' It was all very vague, most of it hearsay.

'I expect we'll hear all sorts of stories,' said Lois without comment, and signed off.

Gran came in with coffee and asked if anything had been heard of Enid. Lois shook her head. 'Did she say anything to you?' she asked. She had been pleased that Gran had struck up a friendship with Enid. They'd been for one or two walks together, strolling round the village, while Enid reported local legend and history and Gran listened with interest.

'Nothing at all. Nothing about going away, or even wishing she could, though I reckon she had every reason to.' Some of Enid's apparently casually dropped remarks about life at the mill had shocked Gran. If she'd been Enid, she had told her firmly, she would have made sure there were changes, or else left them to it. But afterwards, when she'd thought about it, she could see the poor woman was in a trap. It was like a spider's web down there, with the old mother as the spider. Gran had not discussed this with Lois, as she was anxious not to prejudice Enid's job. She knew some of the other cleaners disliked her, and wouldn't make it worse by setting Lois against her.

'What d'you mean?' Lois was on to her at once.

'Oh, you know, that mother bein' a recluse. And the weak old father.'

'And the criminal brother,' said Lois sternly. 'Mum,' she continued, 'if you know anything about Enid goin' off, or anything else you can think of, you got to tell me. It might be . . . well . . . a matter of life and death.'

'Lois, I really don't know anything. Enid was friendly, but a very private person. You know that. When we went on walks together, she'd chat about this and that, but never much except what we know already about the Abrahams. She talked a lot about her childhood, an' happy times she had with her brother. I reckon she's very upset about the way he turned out. Still fond of him, though, like you would be if it was family . . . Got to get on, now,' she added, and left the room.

Lois sat for a while, staring out of the window but seeing nothing. In her mind's eye she had a picture of the mill kitchen. Neat, gloomy but clean. And next to the fire, two pairs of boots put there to dry. *Two* pairs of men's boots?

In the middle of what seemed to Enid Abraham like nowhere at all, she sat on a broken old chair and shivered. It was cold and she was alone. She couldn't get up to move about and warm up, because her hands were tied together and anchored behind the chair. She couldn't see, because a grimy handkerchief had been tied round her eyes. Her sense of smell was not restricted, however, and she sniffed. Mushrooms? Not quite, but the damp, sharp smell was like mushrooms. She remembered how she and Edward used to go collecting them, early on summer mornings. He had taught her which ones were edible . . . ah, that was it. The smell was toadstools. Damp, acrid and poisonous.

No light penetrated through the blindfold, but she knew it was daytime. She had heard a cock crowing from far away, waking her up hours ago. She had no idea how long she had slept, but was in an agony of cramp when she awoke. She had managed to wriggle enough to get her circulation going, and had then decided to sit it out and not struggle. She would listen hard, and wait. He would be back. She could rely on that.

Thirty-Two

W hen someone had seen Enid Abraham in the passenger seat of an old banger, Enid had not been laughing. She had been gasping between terrified tears. She had stopped crying after a while, and tried pleading. It had made no difference. She had promised everything demanded, reminding Edward that she had always done her best to support him, even when it meant putting herself on the wrong side of the law. In her own defence, she had said her crime – to allow Jamie to come into the house and have a piano lesson – had been a very small one. And no harm had been done. And why had he attacked Father in that way? He was an old man, and broken by all the trouble. No longer the real head of the family, and if it was anyone's fault it had been Enid's. None of it had made any difference.

Manhandled and restrained, she had ended up in what she now knew for certain to be a cave, now that she felt the warmth of a little sunlight filtering in through the undergrowth. The sounds and smells, birdsong and dampness, convinced her she was in the cave in Alibone Woods, where they had picnicked in happier days. It was more a deep hollow in the hillside than a cave, made by quarry workers years ago, and now surrounded by thicket and trees. The perfect hiding place. She was still bound and blindfolded, and was beginning to feel faint. He hadn't gagged her, fortunately. She supposed he was confident that she wouldn't shout for help, sure of his hold over her. He had assured her he would be back, and had returned to feed her cold soup out of a tin before disappearing once more, saying that when he returned he would have decided what to do next. She begged him to take off the blindfold, saying she would do whatever he wanted.

Hadn't she always, telling lies and covering up? She'd even buried a dead dog for him, and not asked questions when he kept appearing and disappearing.

The blindfold was soaked with tears, and Enid's cheeks were hot and sore. But all her physical discomfort was nothing to the pain in her heart. Just when she'd thought things at the mill were improving, it had all got much worse. She had so loved working for Mrs M, feeling a real person again, with a place in the world and even the beginnings of a friendship with Gran. Although Lois's mother was much older than she was, she felt at ease with her, and that was rare. Well, now that was well and truly scuppered.

And Father had been so much better lately, even though Mother had become a total recluse – maybe *because* she had! Now he was back to the fearful, grim old man he'd been for years. Why hadn't he tried to help her when she'd been taken off, struggling and crying? It was no good asking, and anyway, in her heart of hearts she knew why. So many secrets, so much emotional blackmail. How would it all end? Not well, she was sure of that now, and began to cry again.

'For God's sake shut that row!' The voice was harsh.

'Edward?' said Enid, stiffening in alarm, recognizing at once that Edward's mood was black.

'Who else are you expecting? Your precious Lois Meade, come to rescue you from your evil brother? Maybe her pal the cop? No, dear Enid, no chance of that. I'm very good at covering tracks now. Nobody will find you. Anyway, you're not staying here much longer. I've decided what we'll do next.'

'What?' Enid's voice was cracked and nearly inaudible.

'You'll know soon enough. When I'm ready. Here, open your mouth.' He fed her bread and cheese, piece by piece, held a bottle of water to her lips for her to drink, and then said more gently, 'I'm off again now. Things to do. Here, put this rug round you. Gets cold at nights.' She felt his hand touch the top of her head, lightly, like he used to. A gesture of affection. Another change of mood. In spite of the prospect of more fear and discomfort, Enid felt a glimmer of hope.

Then, from the rustling and alarm calls from woodland birds, she knew he had gone.

Alibone Woods had other visitors. Lois, accompanied by Bill, was walking systematically through the trees. They were not speaking, but listening and looking. It had been a sudden impulse to search the woods. Conversations with Enid had been running through Lois's head, and mention of a secret place known only to Edward, and regular picnics in Alibone Woods had rung bells. Wouldn't such a hiding place be as good a place as any to start looking for Enid? She knew the police had searched, but had good reason to question their thoroughness.

'But Mrs M,' Bill had said, when she'd phoned him at lunchtime, 'you said the old man told you she'd gone away and didn't want to be followed?'

'Yes, but he was lying,' said Lois shortly. 'Don't bother, Bill. I'll go on my own.'

Before she could put down the phone, he'd said that of course he would come with her. He would meet her by the lay-by bordering the woods, when he'd finished with his afternoon client.

'It's a bit of a long shot, isn't it?' he'd said as she got out of her car.

'Not as long as all that,' she'd said, and explained. 'If Edward has taken her off, he could've hidden her for a bit. After all, Jamie goin' down to the mill was a surprise. If Edward was around, it could have made him do something daft, bein' caught on the hop.'

'Do you reckon he's dangerous?' Bill had asked.

Lois had nodded. 'Blokes on the run, like he is, must get desperate. God knows if he's a threat to Enid. They're supposed to've been close. Still, that don't always mean anything.'

Now, trudging slowly up and down, working from one side of the wood to the other, they said nothing more. After a while, Bill broke the silence. 'They're big, these woods, Mrs M. We shan't do it all in one go,' he whispered. 'I'll have to get back in a hour or so. Me and Rebecca are goin' over to Tresham.'

172

'That's OK,' said Lois. 'We'll do as much as we can, and if we haven't found anything, we'll do the rest tomorrow.' Her spirits were sinking. She had started off with high hopes, pleased that Bill was with her. He was such a solid chap, and a reassuring one, too. She was sure nothing would happen to her with Bill there.

They had found nothing, no traces of undergrowth beaten down or footprints in soggy ground, and although she was tired and fed-up, and very much aware of Bill's growing scepticism, she had a strong feeling that somewhere in this paradise of trees in fresh leaf and buds of bursting bluebells was Enid Abraham, hidden from sight and contact with people who could upset her brother's plans.

Another hour had enabled them to cover about half the acreage of the woods, and they walked back to the car. 'Well, nothing there,' said Bill cheerfully, seeing Lois's long face. 'I'll come back with you tomorrow.'

'You've got a full day's work,' said Lois. 'Don't bother, Bill, I can manage.'

She had it in mind to alert Cowgill. Perhaps he would be interested. If she could stop him filling the woods with boys in blue, and persuade him to search quietly with her, then if they did find Enid, with or without her brother, it would be a lot easier to do something about it.

'Righto,' Bill said. 'But take your mobile, and give me a bell if you need help.'

Cowgill *was* interested in what Lois had to say. 'Trouble is,' he said, 'there's a high-level meeting tomorrow. All day. I've got to be there.'

'What? You mean even *you* have to obey orders?' Lois was irritated, and more so when Cowgill suggested local bobby Keith Simpson should come and help her instead.

'For God's sake!' she said. 'This is a woman disappeared! Probably abducted by a murderin' lunatic . . .'

'Only murderous with dogs,' replied Cowgill mildly.

'So far!' said Lois sharply. 'I wouldn't give much for Enid's chances if she crosses that madman. And,' she added angrily, 'dogs are just as important as humans, I reckon. More

173

so than some I could mention,' she ended up, and put down the phone.

Just let him wait until he wanted her to do something urgently! Well, she'd go on her own. She had an idea. Talk of dogs had reminded her of the old collie she took for walks for the old lady. He'd still got a bit of life left in him, and she'd borrow him tomorrow morning to give her a bit of protection while she combed the rest of the woods. Perhaps have a word with Miss Clitheroe first? In her long stint at the school, she'd have heard all the local lore from the children, and might just know where the secret places were. It could save Lois a lot of time.

Thirty-Three

M iss Clitheroe proved useful. Yes, she'd heard the children talking about a hiding place in Alibone Woods. It had been years ago, but a young teacher she'd had in the school at that time had organized a trek with the older children, their aim being to find the cave.

'And did they?' said Lois, anxious to get going.

Fortunately Miss Clitheroe had a class waiting, and cut short reminiscences. 'Yes, they did. Had a picnic there. It was over by the railway line, where the stream goes underground. I don't think the quarry people found what they were looking for. It was soon abandoned, and lost in the undergrowth. I don't think anyone's been there for years.'

'Thanks a lot.' Lois was grateful and left swiftly, not wishing to be a nuisance. A cave lost in the undergrowth sounds very promising, she said to herself, and she walked quickly round to collect the collie.

'I'll bring him back in a couple of hours,' she said to the old lady. 'Not car sick, is he? I thought I'd take him to Alibone for a good walk off the lead.' Assured that the collie had ridden on more bumpy farm vehicles than Lois had had hot dinners, she set off with the dog on the back seat. He looked at her trustingly. Curiosity roused him from his usual aged apathy, and his ears were pricked, eyes roaming from side to side as they drove along.

It had begun to rain, and Lois pulled on an old hat that Derek had left in the boot. 'Come on, dog,' she said, and opened the door. The collie bounded out, given a new lease of life by the smells and sounds of the wood. This time Lois knew exactly where she was going. All the times she had waited for Cowgill at their meeting place stood her in good stead. She had a feel for the geography of the wood, and made straight for the stream, turning in the direction Miss Clitheroe had described. When she came to the place where the trickle of water disappeared underground, she stopped. She could see the edge of the wood, and the railway line beyond. All around her were thick bushes and small trees, growing faster at this place where sunlight penetrated. She listened. Nothing strange. Bird calls, rustling from animals running from the scent of dog. She could see no place where a cave might be. Then the dog began nosing and scrabbling fiercely at a dense patch of couch grass. She went closer, and caught her breath. He was uncovering a narrow pathway made through the bushes. He disappeared then, and she followed, pushing her way through thorns and scratching her legs on brambles.

Suddenly she was there, at the edge of the cave. For a moment she could see nothing but blackness and was terrified at being so exposed to whatever – whoever – was in there. Then her eyes adjusted, and she saw the dog rooting around among tins and bottles. She saw a chair tipped over on its side, and lengths of rope on the ground. The back of the cave was now visible, and there was clearly nobody there. The bird had flown, if there had ever been one.

She was about to leave, calling the dog to follow her, when she saw something glinting on the ground. It was a pen, a ballpoint with a silvery clip. She picked it up, looked closely, and felt a jolt of recognition. On the side, printed in black letters, she read '*New Brooms – We sweep cleaner!*' Well done, Josie. It was proof that Enid had been here. And was now gone. Lois did not need three guesses to identify her captor.

Poor Enid. Poor little woman. But then, as Lois walked back through the wood, Bill's doubts about the Abraham family came back to her. Was Enid really a poor little woman? Had she been taken, or had she gone freely, laughing, hiding with her brother until it was safe for them to vanish together? And why should they choose this particular time? Had they both thought that as a result of Jamie's incursion into the inner sanctum of the mill, the police would be hotter on the trail of Edward?

And then, that recurring question: what had he done to make his escape so vital? Killing a dog, blackmailing a sick man? Neither of these seemed so desperate that Enid would have to go with him . . . unless she was implicated.

Lois shook her head. She didn't know the answer, but she was still stubbornly on Enid's side, whatever was said by Bill or Derek – or Hazel, or any of the others. Innocent until proved guilty, she thought, and smiled wryly at something so easy-sounding. She came back to the track that led to her car, and whistled the dog. He'd been distracted by a fleeing rabbit, and she turned to look, whistling again, a shrill two-fingered whistle she'd learned from the boys.

'Not bad for a woman,' said a voice behind her. She froze.

Cowgill stood there, smiling. Her heart slowed down to its normal beat and she said angrily, 'So they let you out, did they!'

'That's a very fetching hat, Lois,' was all he said, and began to walk into the wood, heading for their meeting place. 'Come on,' he said, as she stood still, undecided what to do. 'You've got things to tell me, I expect.'

The dog growled at Cowgill, and Lois patted him approvingly. She had a lot of thinking to do before revealing all she had found to Inspector Cowgill. And anyway, where was he when she was faced with a dangerous-looking cave in the dark wood?

'Stuff you,' she said, and headed for her car.

Derek was home early. 'I finished the job,' he said, 'and it wasn't worth starting anything else. Where you bin?' he added, watching as she took off muddy shoes.

'Alibone,' she said shortly, and continued, 'and yes, I met Cowgill there, and we had it off in the mud, 'cause that's what turns him on.'

She watched Derek's face fall and felt very ashamed of herself. 'Sorry, sorry, love,' she said, and put her arms around his neck. 'It's just that bugger really gets to me. I've a good mind to forget the whole thing.'

'But you won't,' said Derek, stroking her heavy, damp hair. 'Come on, now. Tell us what happened.'

Lois gave him all the details, and he whistled softly when she got to the tipped-over chair and the New Brooms pen. 'Blimey, so she was there,' he said.

Lois nodded. 'Sure of it,' she said, and went on to describe her meeting with Cowgill and his stupid arrogance.

'He could have had a bad day at his meeting,' said Derek tentatively.

'Whose side are you on?' said Lois.

'Enid's, funnily enough,' he said, and hugged her more tightly. 'If you think she's a victim, that's enough for me. And now we got to find her,' he added, as Gran came into the room and said she was glad to see love's young dream was alive and kicking.

She smiled as she said it though, well aware that it was their kitchen, their house, and she was just a guest. But a paying guest, she thought happily, as she set the table for tea, and took out a cake she'd spent all afternoon baking.

'I suppose you were talking about Enid?' she said. Lois had gone off to change and Derek sat at the table with a cup of tea.

He nodded. 'Seems she was hidden in the woods, but he's taken her off again.'

'He, meaning Edward?' said Gran.

'Yep. Lois is convinced. But where we start, God knows,' he added. 'The police still don't seem too bothered about it . . . yet . . .'

'What d'you mean by that?' Gran looked at Derek suspiciously. Had he told her all of it? They knew she was fond of Enid Abraham, and perhaps wouldn't want to worry her more than necessary. But she probably knew the woman better than any of them. She believed strongly that Enid had done nothing bad. She wouldn't be capable of it. But there was this other thing . . . Enid's affection for her brother, whatever *he* had done. She had heard it in Enid's voice, when she spoke of their childhood together. Sibling affection could be strong, in spite of everything. And if they really were twins, well . . .

'I just mean,' answered Derek, 'that it is possible, from what is known of that ruddy brother, that if he's in a tight corner he could do something violent. He's killed a dog.'

178

'Oh yes, somebody who's capable of that could do anything,' said Gran. 'I had a neighbour in Tresham who kept a dog so's when her husband came in drunk, he could kick it instead of lashing out at her. When the dog died, he stopped her getting another – said it wasn't so much fun . . .'

Lois had come in, followed by the kids who'd been watching television until summoned for tea. 'Now,' she said, 'let's forget all about Enid Abraham and have our tea. What's new from Tresham School?'

'Nuthin',' chorused Josie and Douglas.

But Jamie said, 'What about Miss Abraham? Why haven't they found her? What's happened to her, Mum? Can't we do something?'

Thirty-Four

Enid was lying curled up on the back seat of a car. She did not know *which* car, as the blindfold was still on. Edward had taken her, not too roughly this time, out of the cave, leading her by the hand. He'd not answered when she had asked if it was her car, but the smell was wrong. It was unpleasantly musty, old.

'Don't pull me too fast, dear,' she had said kindly, as they stumbled through the wood. 'I can't see where I'm going, you know.' In the long, solitary hours in the damp darkness, she had thought everything through very carefully. She knew that Edward had worked out a plan, calculated to avoid discovery of something he had done that was so bad that it had unhinged him. Temporarily, she hoped. The best thing would be to humour him, and wait for her chance. Edward had always been unreliable and unstable, and Mother had explained many times to Enid that he couldn't help it, it was the way he was made. And so excuses had been made, cover-ups engineered. People he had cheated or annoyed had been paid off or pacified. No wonder they were so hard up at the mill! The money she had earned at New Brooms had been the first she had had to spend on herself for years.

Now they drew to a halt. The journey had been only about fifteen minutes, Enid reckoned. Edward turned off the engine, telling her to stay down until he came to fetch her. She did as she was told.

A short while later, the car door opened and her father's voice said, 'Good God! What has he done now?' She felt her blindfold being untied, and sunlight flooded in, blinding her. Then she felt gentle hands helping her out of the car, and when she finally opened her eyes, there was her father, and tears were once more running unchecked down his sunken cheeks.

'Father! You look terrible! Where's he gone?'

Walter gestured towards the mill house. 'Come on in. I'll get you a cup of tea,' he said, and they walked across to the door hand in hand, Enid stumbling with a sudden loss of balance.

'What time is it?' she said.

'One o'clock,' said her father. They were in the kitchen now, and the old dog rushed across to greet her. The cats, too, came over and rubbed against her legs.

'Where's Edward?' Enid said.

'Around,' said her father, and put on the kettle.

'I must ring Mrs M,' Enid said. 'Explain what's happened . . . well,' she added, seeing her father's face, 'I'll make a good excuse. Then we can get back to normal.'

Walter slowly shook his head. ''Fraid not, dear,' he said.

'Why not?'

'Edward'll tell you,' he said, and poured boiling water into a teapot, swilling it round and tipping it out into the sink. The tea-making ritual was the same as ever, but nothing else was, Enid realized. In the corner of the kitchen stood three suitcases, bulging and ready for transit.

'Where are we going?' she said, and her voice quavered. No answer from her father.

'And what about Mother?' Enid felt panic rising. Nothing would get her mother to leave her room now, let alone leave the mill. Three suitcases? Why not four?

She looked wildly around the kitchen. 'Where is he! Please tell me what's going on, Father!' He did not look at her, but continued to fill the teapot.

Desperate now, Enid walked quickly over to the passage and into the hall. Before her father could stop her, she was knocking at her mother's door. 'Mother!' she shouted. 'Let me in, *please!*'

'Enid! Come back here!' shouted her father.

But Enid continued to knock, hurting her knuckles, until she heard a voice from inside the room.

'It's not locked.'

She stopped knocking, her heart pounding. Very gently she turned the doorknob and stepped gingerly into the dark interior. A figure sat at the small table where Mother wrote her notes to the outside world. Enid peered through the gloom. 'Mother?' She could see the old cardigan over bent shoulders and a tousled head turned away from her.

'Mother?' she repeated.

Suddenly the figure whipped around. And laughed.

Enid screamed. From under the unkempt hair a white face with burning dark eyes looked out at her. 'Edward!' screamed Enid. And then: 'Where's Mother! What have you . . .'

She fainted then, and between them Walter and Edward picked her up and laid her gently on her mother's unmade and unsavoury bed.

Thirty-Five

Lois drove slowly towards Bell's Farm. She had arranged to clean today, not Enid's usual day but the best she could do under the circumstances. Rosie had said the afternoon was not very convenient, but in a saccharine voice had sympathized with the difficulties Lois must be having. Lois bit her tongue, and set off early, planning to stop by the bridge over the mill stream and think. It was quiet and cool there, and she could watch the moving water and try to work out what Edward Abraham would be likely to do if he needed to vanish for good.

Bright sun percolated through the newly leafed trees, and the stream, now tamed and sparkling, flowed gently under the bridge. It was a lovely place, Lois reflected. The mill, too, could have been idyllic. The Abrahams must have had high hopes when they arrived here from Edinburgh. Lois had never been to Edinburgh, but imagined it as a cold, northern, granite city, with its castle looming over the columns of bagpipers she had seen on television, marching and playing their haunting music for shivering tourists.

Why had the Abrahams chosen Cathanger? Hadn't Enid said something about her mother coming from round here? She stared down into the water, running clear now over mossy stones, and guessed it was because Cathanger was comparatively remote. Nowhere in the middle of England was really remote, but this was a place you could certainly keep yourself to yourself. If nosy neighbours had been the problem, then Cathanger was the answer. It had obviously worked, too, for years. Stories about the Abrahams had circulated, but nothing really worrying. A spot of embezzlement, a reclusive woman and an unfriendly old man.

No, it had all gone along smoothly until Enid had decided to join New Brooms. Lois could see that clearly. The poor woman had finally made a stand, and in opening up the closed world of the Abrahams, had landed herself in this mess. Lois turned away from the bridge. Then the night of the flood came back to her, and she looked again at the stream, with its dam of thicket and undergrowth. She had been terrified that night. That rolling *thing* in the swollen, muddy water. That white shape so like a face flashing out into the dark and quickly disappearing. She shuddered.

Time to get going. She drove on to Bell's Farm, scarcely glancing at the mill, certain that Enid was not there.

'Ah, there you are, Mrs Meade.' Rosie was bright and forgiving, relieved to see Lois. After all, she would be getting extra service from the boss. 'No news of Enid?' she added.

Lois said she'd heard nothing, but asked if Rosie had seen any sign of activity at the mill, anything odd going on.

Rosie shook her head. 'It's difficult to see down there,' she said, 'with all those trees and the hedges allowed to grow so high.'

'How about Anna?' Lois knew the girl took the new puppy for walks. 'Is she around?' She might have seen something, without knowing it was important.

'Gone to college, I'm afraid,' Rosie said, 'but I'll ask her when she comes back. Really, I don't know why she bothers to go to English classes. Her English is nearly perfect now.'

'Love,' said Lois flatly. She had heard through the grapevine that Anna the au pair had an Italian boyfriend from college.

'What? Did you say "love"!' Rosie was all ears. This would jolly up things a bit. She had always heard that au pairs were a danger in the house, seducing the husband and causing ructions, but so far Anna had seemed bloodless, uninterested in men or boys. Now this was more like it!

Lois told her what she knew, and they agreed it was a promising development. 'She's been altogether too shut in on herself. Spends hours in her room, brooding. You know

184

the sort of thing, Mrs Meade.' Rosie went off to make a cup of tea, humming happily to herself.

Lois carried on cleaning. Upstairs, she adjusted the curtains in Rosie's bedroom and looked out. She could see over the field and high hedges towards the mill. The roofs of house and barns were visible, but the yard and the mill pond were hidden. A dark, private place.

Then it struck her. A dark, private place, and the perfect spot to hide. A double bluff, then? She hadn't even bothered to look down the track when driving past, sure that Enid was not there. But supposing she was, still held captive?

Lois flew downstairs, and, yelling as she passed Rosie that she'd be back shortly, she ran as she hadn't run for years, out of the farm gate and down the lane towards the mill. As she approached the track, she slowed down. Nearly there, now. No good storming in, all guns blazing. She would make it a normal, reasonable call to enquire after Enid's health, checking that she really did not intend to return. Yes, that would be best.

She walked briskly, and just as she was about to turn down the track, a car came up it towards her, going fast. It was a dull blue, patched clumsily here and there with paint that did not quite match.

She realized in time that it was not going to stop. Jumping on to the verge, she looked as closely as possible through the dirty windows. She was almost sure it was Mr Abraham in the passenger seat, and probably Edward driving. On the back seat she caught a brief glimpse of a woman huddled in the corner, looking out at her. It was Enid. Her expression was blank, her face dirty, and tears made tracks down her pale cheeks.

Thirty-Six

The rest of the afternoon went slowly. Lois determined not to say anything to Rosie Charrington, and invented a fairly plausible excuse for running off. She thought she saw Douglas on a bike, she said, and since he should have been at school, she had rushed out to catch him. But it hadn't been him, and she was sorry for the interruption.

Rosie accepted this without question. She was chiefly concerned with the news that Anna had a boyfriend. At coffee time, she pestered Lois with questions that she could not answer, and in the end, Lois said why didn't she wait until Anna returned, when she could have all the juicy details straight from the horse's mouth? This had caused a small chill to descend, but Rosie quickly forgot, and the afternoon ground on.

At last it was time to leave, and Lois drove slowly and carefully down the mill track, pulling up outside one of the barns and looking around to make sure the car had not returned. A terrible din came from the chicken shed, and a cow contributed to the chorus from the barn opposite. Good God, thought Lois, they've gone off and left the animals shut up! Well, she had a remedy for that. Bill, farmer's son, would know exactly what to do. But first, the house. After all, the whole carful might return any minute. Prepared for a confrontation with the reclusive old mother, who had certainly not been in the car, Lois marched across to the door. To her surprise, she found it half-open.

They'd left in a hurry. That was immediately apparent. Dirty pots and pans stood in the sink, a pile of overalls for the wash scattered around the floor. The dog growled, standing at bay and prepared to attack this intruder. The cats fled through the open door.

'Here, boy,' said Lois, holding out a friendly hand, and hoping to God it would not be bitten off. But the sheepdog crawled slowly towards her on its belly, suspicious at first, and then, this time deciding she was friend not foe, wagged its tail tentatively in greeting. First hurdle cleared, then. Lois knew the way to the mother's room was through the hall, and walked boldly through. Take the enemy by surprise, that would be her strategy.

The first door she opened led into the dining-room Jamie had described. And there was the piano, the cause of all this trouble. She backed out. Next, the one opposite. She knocked, sure that this must be the mother's, and then noticed that it stood ajar. There was no reply to her 'Hello? Mrs Abraham?', and so she pushed open the door and went in. The room was empty, and the smell was overpowering.

A quick glance told her, once more, that the exit had been hurried. Clothes strewn everywhere, and a tray of food left half-eaten. On a small desk she saw a pile of books tipped over, and, turning to get out as quickly as possible, caught her foot against a rucked-up rug. She looked down and saw a book, half-hidden. She picked it up and found that it was a leather-bound diary. Opening it at random, she saw handwriting so small that she was unable to read it in the gloom. She slipped it into her pocket and left the room swiftly, holding her nose. Bloody hell! – what was Enid thinking of, allowing it to get into this state?

Lois walked quickly round the rest of the house, and found nobody. She had seen a large key hanging by the back door, and, sure now that nobody was coming back, took it, locked up and went back to her car. There she phoned Bill.

'A job for you, lad,' she said. 'When you've finished eating, come straight over to Bell's Farm. And bring your wellies.'

Bill said that his lump of cheese and hunk of stale bread could wait, and he'd be there in ten minutes. Lois grinned. He was a comfort, was Bill. At least I chose well with him, she reassured herself, even if Enid Abraham had turned out to be more liability than asset. Where the fault lay for that had yet to be discovered, and until it was, she determined to find Enid and bring her back into the fold.

Now she dialled Cowgill's number, and as she did so, realized the enormity of what she had found. *Where was old Mrs Abraham?*

'OK, I'll stay here 'til you come,' she said, and was thankful that Cowgill seemed at last to have grasped that something bad enough had happened to command urgent action.

'Oh, and I've asked Bill Stockbridge to come over and see to the animals. They're goin' to be eating each other if they don't soon get fed. What did you say?' she added, and his reply made her smile to herself. 'You'd do very well without me, I expect,' she said. 'Plenty of willin' snouts about, though not many goin' for free . . . yeah, OK, I'll wait.'

Much later, after Bill had dealt with the animals and Cowgill had come over to inspect everything and make his plans, Lois remembered the diary. She checked that it was still in her pocket and said only, 'Right, well, I'll be getting home. Got work to do.'

'I'll be in touch,' said Cowgill. He turned to Bill. 'I'd be glad if you'd keep this under your hat for the moment,' he said, but without much hope. From long experience, he knew that people could never keep secrets for long. Still, he might not need long to sort out this one. A battered, patched blue car with three oddly assorted people in it shouldn't be too difficult to find.

Chugging along, Enid had much the same thoughts. If Mrs M was worried, and Enid was sure she would be, she'd most likely tell the police. They were supposed to be looking for Edward, after all. This old banger would be easy to spot, and easy to catch. She stopped crying, and silence fell over the three of them. Father was hunched down in his seat, and though he had his eyes closed Enid was sure he was not asleep. Edward drove carefully, negotiating twisting lanes that Enid did not recognize. She had no idea where they were, but they had been going less than half an hour when Edward turned the car into a rutted track, worse than the one down to the mill. 'Where are we going?' she said in what she hoped was a casual voice. Edward had started humming quietly for the last five minutes, and Enid recognized one of their childhood songs, '*Frère Jacques, Frère Jacques*'. To Enid's ears it had a sinister sound. This lighthearted Edward, singing as if they were on a picnic jaunt, was terrifying in his unpredictability. She couldn't even guess where they were going, or what he would do next, but she knew from experience that he was not to be underrated.

'You'll see,' he said lightly. 'It'll be a treat for you, Enid,' he added, and smiled to himself. After five minutes bumping along, being thrown from side to side, they stopped outside an old barn. It was falling to pieces, and clearly never used by whoever owned it. 'See, Enid?' Edward said. 'I've had to find all the best hiding places around, and this one is perfect for the purpose.'

'What purpose, dear?' said Enid.

'Come with me,' he said, and got out of the car. She had a swift image of herself trussed up in the corner of a dark barn with Father, both of them abandoned to a terrible fate.

But Edward asked her to help open the battered doors of the barn, and inside she saw, with a sinking heart, another car, a much better, newer car. It was an anonymous black, with the opaque windows she associated with film stars and criminals. Not what the police would be looking for at all. Edward had lost none of his cunning, she reflected sadly. No wonder he'd wanted her out of the way in the cave. He'd had a lot of organizing to do.

'Come on, quickly,' he said now. 'Help me transfer the cases, and get Father into the back seat. I want you in the front to map read . . . just for the first few miles. Then I know the way, after that.'

He was excited, full of enthusiasm. They completed the transfer in minutes, put the old car in the barn and shut the doors, and then they were off again, back down the track and out on to the road. 'Here,' said Edward, giving Enid the road map, 'tell me which way to the motorway, then I'll be fine. You can have a nap.' He turned and looked at her briefly. 'Sorry, Enid,' he said, 'about the cave business . . .

But it was necessary . . . part of the plan. Sorry if I hurt you . . .'

She managed a smile in return. 'That's all right,' she said. 'No harm done. I expect you'll be telling me more about it later. Now, take a right turn at this junction, and then it's straight on for about five miles.'

Once on the motorway, Enid put down the map and closed her eyes. She knew they were heading north, and now had a good idea where they were going. Father was snoring now, and she was glad. At least he had found an escape from this terrifying flight. He must be worrying about Mother. After Enid had come round from her faint in the house, Edward had explained that they had taken Mother to a nursing home the other side of Tresham. 'We had to do it while you were out working,' he'd said. 'Knew you wouldn't agree. Father wasn't too keen, but I convinced him.' He had grinned conspiratorially. 'Anyway, she's settled down well, they said.' Then he'd added, 'It was a good joke, the dressing-up, wasn't it? Fooled you for a minute, didn't I?' His laughter had been like a blow, and she'd recoiled.

Enid could sometimes read Edward's mind. Twins were renowned for this. She had tried for years to deny their twinhood, not wanting to be associated with Edward's excesses more than necessary, but there had always been a kind of silent communication between them. It had been a comfort at times, when they were little. The two of them in league against the world. But after a while, when Edward began to be difficult, she'd tried to shut it down. Most of the time she had succeeded, but now she felt it strongly. He was lying. Somewhere in his account of what had happened to Mother, there was a lie.

'We'll go and see her . . . see for ourselves, when we go back,' Enid said. 'She'll want to have visitors, Edward.'

He laughed, more of a bark than a laugh. 'Huh! I don't see why,' he said. 'She's not wanted visitors for years now, so why should she change?'

Father's voice came from the back, weak and croaky. 'We're not going back, anyway,' he said.

'Shut up!' All Edward's amiability had vanished. His hands

190

tightened on the steering wheel. 'How can I concentrate on the driving if you two keep babbling on! Shut up, both of you!'

They drove on in silence for another hour, and then he started singing again: '*Frère Jacques, Frère Jacques, Dormez-vous? Dormez-vous . . .?*' Over and over, the same refrain.

Enid dozed off, but woke again when the car came to a halt. They had turned off the motorway, and were in a lane bordered by high hedges. This was not what she expected, and she said, 'What are we doing here?'

'Father needs a pee,' said Edward, getting out and opening the rear door. He helped the old man out, and they disappeared. Enid had wild thoughts of making a run for it, but knew that Edward would soon find her, and she could not risk his anger. She needed the toilet herself, but decided she could hold on for a while. It was dark now, and she dreaded stumbling about in the woods, bopping down and peeing into her shoes, like in the old days of picnics. Supposing Edward went off and left her when she was crouching down? No, she would wait, stay here in the car and do her best to protect Father.

She saw the silhouettes of the two men coming back to the car. Edward, tall and thin, very much in charge, and poor Father, a broken, beaten, old figure. What dreadful things had Father done at Edward's behest over the years? And what now? Enid tried to imagine her mother, a stranger amongst people over whom she had no control, but the image was illusive. She couldn't picture it, and gave up.

They were on the road again, back on the motorway and still heading north, and Enid recognized a sign. 'Welcome to Scotland' shone out at her in the car's lights. She was right, then. They were going back, returning to Edinburgh. But what then? She tried to tune in to Edward's thoughts, but found only an incoherent jumble. She began to cry silently, but quickly stopped herself. The thing now, she told herself firmly, was not to antagonize Edward, but to act calmly and normally. That would be best. She settled in her seat and, with a great effort, tentatively joined in his chorus: '*Frère Jacques, Frère Jacques . . .*'

Thirty-Seven

'**O**h, sod it,' said Lois to her empty office. She had urgent New Brooms work to do before tea, lists to make, visits to organize, and she had sat down with good intentions. But the red leather-covered diary on the corner of her desk caught her eye, demanding attention. She'd had a quick look when she came home, but the writing was tiny, and she had put it aside for when she could find a better light and had more time to examine it properly.

Now, under her desk lamp, Lois knew she could read it quite easily. She cursed her own weakness, put aside her lists, and gave in to temptation. It was more of a journal than a diary, she discovered. It was not divided into days, but with plain, lined pages, and Mrs Abraham had written her thoughts and accounts of happenings as they occurred. Fortunately, she had dated most of these, and Lois could see that the journal had been started three years ago. Was this when she had become a total recluse? She read an entry:

> Nice dinner. Enid a good cook now. Not as good as me, but not at all bad. Walter suggested a walk round the fields, where we wouldn't meet anyone. I declined with thanks!

Lois flipped forward through the pages. The mood had darkened.

> Edward in trouble again. Not his fault, poor boy. Walter unsympathetic. It upsets me dreadfully. Early bed, and slept badly.

There were several more entries along these lines, and then the next date was many months later:

> Haven't seen Edward for weeks. He doesn't care about his poor old mother. Walter makes excuses, but he's probably shown poor Teddy the door. Had a go at Walter and ended up throwing a plate at him! Enid talks about getting a job. What nonsense! Her place is here, looking after me. The light hurts my eyes, and I keep the curtains drawn. Not much appetite.

Turning to the last entry, Lois saw that it was dated a few weeks ago:

> Dreadful rain again. Very depressed. Walter no help. Driven to slapping his face yesterday, but he turned away from me. Haven't seen my Teddy for so long. Very unhappy Mummy.

The words were smudged here and there, where, Lois guessed, tears had fallen.

Nothing more. The rest of the journal was blank. Lois checked the date of the last entry. She thought back, remembering the days of endless rain and imagining how gloomy it must have been in that awful room at the mill. She looked in her own desk diary, and found the date. Oh my God. Lois stood up and looked out of the window to see if Derek was back. His van stood outside, and she rushed out of the room, calling for him. 'Here, Derek! Come here! I want to show you something!'

He came at once, and Lois shut the door behind him. 'Don't want Gran to hear this,' she said. She handed him the journal, open at the last entry.

'Whose is this?' he asked suspiciously.

'Mrs Abraham's,' Lois answered. 'I've borrowed it. Read that last bit, and see the date.'

Derek read it carefully, then looked up at Lois. 'Old bag,' he said. 'But I don't see . . . ?'

'The date,' repeated Lois. 'It's the day of the big flood. That night I went down to the mill and got stuck in the water.'

'And?' said Derek patiently.

'And I looked over the bridge and saw a big *thing* in the stream and . . . Oh God, Derek . . . I saw a *face!*'

'Here, steady, Lois,' Derek said, seeing her colour draining away. 'It doesn't mean anything. Remember? They said it could've been a cardboard box, or an old feed sack caught up on that dam. And they looked afterwards, and didn't find nuthin'.'

Lois took a deep breath. Derek was right. She was jumping to conclusions. The woman probably gave up writing because she was too depressed. She took back the journal and closed it up. 'I'll just keep it for a day or two,' she said. 'I expect Cowgill will have found them by now, and we'll get an explanation.'

'And it's time for tea,' said Derek, taking her hand. 'Gran's cooked us something from a WI recipe, so watch out. Could be curtains for the lot of us.'

After tea, when Derek had gone out to the garage to reorganize his van, Lois looked at her watch and decided to phone Cowgill. Surely they must have spotted the car by now. It couldn't have been an easier target to find: an old blue car with a crazed-looking driver, an old man and a weeping woman in it? She'd heard from Bill that he and Sebastian Charrington were going to take care of the Abrahams' stock, until it became clear what had happened. That was one thing Cowgill didn't have to worry about.

'Hello? Can I speak to Inspector Cowgill, please?' Lois was accustomed to him answering on his own line, but this must be a passing office girl.

'Hold on, please.' There was a minute's pause, and then Cowgill came on. 'Sorry about that, Lois,' he said. 'I was just out in the corridor getting a cup of tea. Things round here seem to have ground to a halt.'

'Specially important things like cups of tea?' said Lois sourly. 'But on a trivial matter,' she added, 'where are the Abrahams? I was expectin' you'd let me know.'

194

There were a few seconds' silence, and then Cowgill said, 'Well, actually, Lois, we are not absolutely sure at this moment in time.'

'You mean you lost 'em!' Lois was disbelieving. *Surely* that must have been the easiest manhunt on record!

'Well, it was more a case of never finding them,' Cowgill said apologetically. 'No trace of the car as you described it . . . and we put out a countrywide alert. We're still looking, of course. We do want to talk to Edward urgently.'

'But . . .' Lois was speechless.

'As soon as I get news, I'll let you know, of course. But anyway, Lois, I shouldn't worry. For all his many and unattractive faults, Edward Abraham has no record of physical violence.'

'Except murdering a dog,' said Lois quickly. 'And attacking his father in his own farm yard. *And* putting his own sister under such a reign of terror she's disappeared against her will! How much more violence do you want? Are you really goin' to wait until Enid is found dismembered in a cupboard somewhere? And, for God's sake, *where is the old mother?*'

'Calm down,' said Cowgill irritatingly. 'We have no proof they didn't take the mother with them. Perhaps you just didn't spot her. We are still keeping an eye out for the car, and have several other leads we are pursuing.'

'Huh! Heard that one before!' said Lois. 'And don't tell me to calm down . . . Enid is one of my team, and a friend of my mother's. And,' she added with emphasis, 'while you are pursuing your "other leads", I'll be following my own.'

She listened to his flat voice for a minute or so, and then cut in, 'Oh, I'm fed up with this. You do it your way, and I'll go mine. There's not much point in my telling you things if you don't act on them, is there?' He was still talking as she cut him off.

Thirty-Eight

It was dark now, and Enid dozed in the front seat of the car. Her father had been deeply asleep for a couple of hours, and she was glad. The longer he was absent from this nightmare the better. She watched Edward's profile from time to time, and was not reassured to see him calm and relaxed. She could feel the tension in him, and had decided in the long hours of travelling northwards that he must be handled with great care. It was his unpredictability she feared, as always. Perhaps there was something in his swings of mood that could have been put right, but she considered he was, and always had been, spoilt, selfish and naturally wayward. He'd got away with all kinds of minor misdemeanours as a child, and gradually, as he grew up, the seriousness of these had increased. But, unfortunately, his confidence in his own invulnerability had also increased.

It was really Mother's fault, Enid reflected sadly. Father had tried to discipline him, but each time Mother had stepped in with excuses, pleas for leniency, promises that she would correct him in her own way. He was an attractive child, a handsome teenager and a charming adult – when it suited him. All his life he was bolstered through numerous sticky patches by the knowledge that his mother would defend and protect him. She had lied for him, given him false alibis, and persuaded Enid to do the same. *Her* childhood, teenage years and adulthood, had been very different. Edward had always been given first place. 'He *is* the boy,' she'd heard her mother say repeatedly, and though Walter had retorted that they were not living in the dark ages and women were now supposed to be equal, even he had finally given up and colluded in the primacy of Edward's position. 'He *was* born first, you know,' he would say weakly.

She had loved Edward so much. Guided by her mother, she had looked up to him and followed his lead in all that they did together. Despite everything he had done and made her do, they still had the closeness of twins. He had demanded so much. In spite of his good looks, he'd never had a real girlfriend. Mother again! She had given such a cold shoulder to any girls brought home for inspection. And so Edward had gone underground. Enid knew he had women who supplied his needs. She shivered and hunched down in her seat. 'Edward?'

'What?'

'How much further?'

'Nearly there,' he said. 'You must know where we're going by now?'

'Mmm,' said Enid.

'Well?'

'I suppose it's Edinburgh,' she said reluctantly. She could hardly deny the existence of a band of light across the night sky, where the city awaited them.

'Brilliant deduction!' Edward was cheerful, humming that tune again.

'Where are we going to stay?' They would certainly not be going to any old friends of her parents. By the time they left, Edward had alienated all their friends. No chance that a welcoming house would be opened up for them.

'You'll see,' said Edward. 'I've got it all arranged. Been busy, you know. I may look like a tramp, but my organizing talents have not deserted me. And speaking of looking like a tramp, Enid, when we get where we're going, I'd like you to do a spot of washing and ironing. Smarten me up!'

'Like Mother used to?' said Enid quickly, without thinking.

His hand left the steering wheel, fist clenched, and Enid recoiled. But he collected himself in time, and said tersely, 'Shut up about Mother! She's OK where she is. Father'll only get upset.'

Enid said nothing, but found herself trembling. She hadn't been able to imagine Mother in that nursing home, and wondered why. Could he be lying? Again?

197

'Where was that place you took her?' Enid was risking a lot, but had begun to think she hadn't a lot to lose. Her job was finished, her home abandoned. She had sailed too close to the wind with Edward too many times. He'd *almost* got her into trouble more often than she could count, like that time at Waltonby vicarage when he'd come looking for her. More lies, and to that nice old vicar, too. She would never be free of him, and she feared him. But he needed her, just as he had needed her in the past, and she could make use of that.

'Didn't you hear what I said!' Edward's angry voice caused Walter to stir in his sleep, and he mumbled something. Enid caught the word 'mother', but nothing more.

'Yes, I did. But I want to know,' she said calmly. 'After all, I shall want to send her a postcard of her old home, shan't I?'

Edward said nothing, but she could hear his quick breathing. Finally he sighed, and his shoulders dropped. She knew she had won.

'It's over the other side of Tresham,' he said. 'St Mary's Residential and Nursing Home, in that development on the eastern side. New, well-run, and very comfortable. They took her in without notice, luckily, and the minute she got there she seemed to relax. Even talked to the woman who gave us tea. Quite an eye-opener, Enid, to see our mother behaving almost normally!'

'She always loved you, Edward,' Enid said simply.

She again felt the tension, but ignored it. 'You could be more understanding, you know,' she continued. 'It's really an illness with her. She can't help it.'

'Didn't seem ill when they brought her a plate of cream cakes!' said Edward. 'Gobbled them down, like she'd been starved.'

In a way, this reassured Enid. Edward's typically hard-hearted reaction, and his telling the nasty story about Mother and the cakes, sounded convincing enough. Still, he was good at being convincing. Enid sighed. Well, if it was true, perhaps it would be the best thing for her. They might be able to bring her out of her self-imposed isolation, where Enid had failed. Maybe she should stop worrying about Mother, and start thinking about how to deceive Edward into thinking she was happy to go along with him. Her one goal now was to escape, and this would mean abandoning him. Her heart missed a beat, but she reassured herself that he would survive somehow, as he always did. She would return to Cathanger by some means or other, and prepare the way for her father to go back home. She had no idea yet how she would do it, but her mind was quite made up. She just hoped Edward could not tune into her thoughts . . . and she also hoped he was, for once, telling the truth about Mother.

'Enid? Are you asleep? For God's sake, I need you to map read now. We're on the edge of the city, and you bet all the one-way streets have been changed! Wake up, woman!'

Enid had not been asleep. She had her eyes shut, and she was thinking. From now until she reached Cathanger again, she would not stop thinking, nor relax her guard against Edward's suspicious watch. This time he would not win. This time she would be strong.

Feeling much cheerier, she unfolded the city map, and began to direct Edward towards the centre. 'Where are we going to stay?' she said.

'You'll see,' he answered, and drove on.

When they were right in the heart of the old town, he drew the car to a halt against a high pavement. Enid recognized Lawnmarket, where she used to meet a friend for coffee.

'Help me to unload the stuff,' said Edward. 'We can't park here, of course, but I'll get you and Father settled in with the luggage, and then go and find a place to leave the car. Wake up, Father! We're there . . . back to your old hunting grounds!'

Walter showed no signs of pleasure, but grimly did as he was told. They tramped through the quiet alleyway to the back of a tall building, and then up a stone spiral staircase to the second floor. Walter was puffing and struggling, but Edward forced him on from behind. 'Nearly there!' he said, and then opened a door with keys he took from his pocket.

'Lucky I still have friends somewhere,' he said, ushering them into a tiny kitchen. 'Old Donald from school has this flat as a bolthole in Edinburgh. He's done very well, has Donald.

Chairman of the Board and all that. Big estate in Galloway. I've been useful to him now and then. They come here to escape pressure of business, apparently. No phone, nobody knows when they're here, except for his loyal secretary. Good idea, eh, Father?'

Walter stared at him, breathing hard.

'And now,' continued Edward, oblivious to everything except the success of his plan so far, 'now he and his wife are off in some godforsaken tropical holiday spot for three months. Sent me the keys, bless 'em. Still,' he added with a grin, 'they owe me a favour or two.' He turned to Enid. 'Get the kettle on, and we'll have a bedtime drink when I come back. I'll get a few supplies from a late-night opening place I saw on the way in. Shouldn't be more than half an hour. All right, Father?'

Walter nodded mutely, his eyes half-shut.

'Right,' said Enid brightly. 'Off you go, Edward. Bring enough food for a couple of meals. I'll sort things out, and make up beds, and then we'll get Father settled. He can sleep as long as he likes tomorrow.' She patted her father's hand, and closed the door behind Edward with relief. She heard him put the key in the lock and turn it. So they were to be prisoners, in case she should alert someone to their whereabouts. Well, she would think of a way round that one, too.

Her father looked poorly, with a blue line around his lips. Those stairs had been too much. She was sure of that. It was even more urgent to work out a way of getting him back home, and she began to unpack and make up beds as rapidly as possible. The sooner she convinced Edward that they were staying with him, the easier it would be to escape.

Thirty-Nine

G ran had woken up in the middle of the night, certain that she had heard a strange noise from downstairs. She had tiptoed down, holding the old golf club that she always kept under her bed, and now saw with a shiver of fear that a light was on in the kitchen.

'Mum? What on earth is that in your hand?' Lois sat at the kitchen table, mug of hot milk in hand, staring at her mother.

'And what on earth are *you* doing down here at this time of night?' said Gran crossly. She felt foolish, standing there in her nightie holding a golf club.

'Well, one thing's certain,' said Lois, starting to laugh, 'I'm not goin' out for a quick round of golf!'

Gran sat down at the table and put the club down at her feet. 'You know perfectly well I keep it under the bed in case of intruders,' she said. 'It was your father's idea, and a very good one, too. Now, you haven't answered my question. Why aren't you in bed asleep?'

'I woke up and couldn't get off again, so I came down to do a few jobs and not wake Derek.'

'You're worried about something,' said Gran baldly. 'Same thing as me, I expect. I can't stop thinking about Enid Abraham.'

'And her mother,' added Lois. 'They all seem to have disappeared off the face of the earth.'

They were quiet for a minute, and then Gran said, 'It's that Edward, isn't it? He's taken them away somewhere, and we'll never see them again.' She rubbed her eyes, and her lip quivered.

'Oh, yes we will,' said Lois. 'We'll find them, Mum, even

if the lousy police have given up. Between us, we ought to be able to think of something that'll put us on track.'

'What about that car you saw them in?' Gran looked at Lois hopefully. 'Surely the police can catch up with that?'

Lois shook her head. 'They've been keeping watch,' she said, 'but there's no trace.'

'He's switched cars, then,' said Gran, who loved detective series on the box, and knew all the dodges.

'Very likely,' said Lois. 'But that shouldn't stop them being seen. They've got to eat, and pee, and end up somewhere. People don't just disappear for good.'

'Some do,' said Gran gloomily.

'Maybe one on his own, but not four, and one of 'em a frail old man,' Lois answered.

Again they fell silent, Gran frowning with the effort of trying to recall something useful.

'Where did they come from before they moved to Cathanger?' said Lois.

'Somewhere up north,' said Gran. 'Can't remember where. I expect the police have made enquiries.'

'I wouldn't bet on it,' Lois said sourly. They were silent for a moment, and then Lois slapped her hand down on the table. 'Blimey! Why didn't I think of it before? Enid's job application . . . had all the details.' Lois stood up briskly and left the kitchen. She was back in seconds, holding the application letter. 'Here we are!' she said triumphantly. 'Edinburgh! That's where they lived. And Enid worked in a chemist. Her father was caretaker in a school, and her mother came from round here.'

'So we know quite a lot,' said Gran, cheering up. Then she subsided. 'There must be dozens of chemists in Edinburgh,' she said. 'And schools. And we don't know her mother's maiden name.'

'Well, thanks for the vote of confidence!' said Lois, picking up the golf club and handing it to her mother. 'Tomorrow, first thing, you're going to see your pals in the WI. One of them'll know who Mrs Abraham was before she married, you bet. Nothing escapes that lot. And I shall get busy on the web. Can't be too difficult to find a list of Edinburgh chemists and schools and make a few calls. Now, back to bed, Mum. We shall have Derek down here in a minute.'

On cue, the door opened and a sleepy, irritated Derek came in. 'What the bloody hell are you two doing?'

'Practising our golf swings, o'course,' said Lois, turning him round and patting his pyjama'd bottom. 'Off we all go, now. Busy day tomorrow. Night-night, Mum. Put the lights out for us, will you?'

Next morning, Lois decided her first priority was to do something she'd decided on last night, but not told her mother. The real reason she had come down in the night had been a recurring nightmare she could not shake off. She was standing in pouring rain on a dark, stormy night on the bridge by Cathanger. The water was rising and she felt it slowly submerging her. Then she was afloat, over the edge of the bridge, and being tossed in the dark water. Carried downstream, gasping and trying to keep her head above water, she had felt the blow as she hit the dam, and this woke her, shaking and bathed in sweat.

There was only one thing to do, and she intended to do it this morning. The sun was shining in a clear blue sky, and nothing down by the bridge would be sinister or likely to inflame her imagination. She would walk by the edge of the stream, past the dam and beyond, as far as she could go. If she found nothing untoward, it would be her best chance of putting the nightmare to rest.

By the time Lois drove through the tunnel of trees and parked in a field opening, the sun had gone and heavy clouds threatened rain. She pulled on a waterproof jacket and headed back down the lane towards the bridge. A vehicle passed her, and somebody waved. Rosie Charrington, on her way to the shops in Tresham. Lois reflected on how quickly the Charringtons had been absorbed into the area, quickly accepted by the natives. He was a vet, and a vital part of farming life. No matter that the inside of Bell's farm looked like the interior décor department of the smartest store in Tresham, or that the kids were looked after by an au pair most of the time. Vets were OK, and their wives and kids and etceteras likewise.

Not so the Abrahams. They hadn't tried, mind you, and even discouraged friendly overtures, if any. Poor Enid.

Lois climbed over the end of the bridge, and stepped gingerly along the muddy bank. She pushed her way through thicket, now in leaf and difficult to negotiate. She came to the dam, and looked back along the quietly flowing water to the bridge. It was rippling and clear, and concealed nothing but an old oil drum, rusting and open at both ends. Nothing there, then. She examined the dam, and saw the division of the stream into two rivulets. They had been rushing torrents on that dreadful night, but now ambled gently round the dam and joined up again the other side. Lois peered down into the thickly woven branches and bits of old timber and saw nothing out of the way. Then a white flicker at the water's edge caught her eye. She leaned over precariously, and managed to grab a small piece of cloth, closely entangled in the twigs. She pulled, but it didn't shift.

Then she leaned over too far, and put out one foot to save herself toppling in. Water came in over her shoe and up to her ankle.

'Damn!' Lois steadied herself and retreated up the bank. The white cloth still flickered tantalizingly in the water, but now Lois could see it had a scalloped edge and traces of embroidered flowers in one corner. A lady's handkerchief, then? A quick flash of alarm sent signals to Lois's ready imagination. She took a deep breath, told herself it could have belonged to anyone, any passer-by who leaned over the bridge to look into the flowing stream.

She pushed her way out of the bushes which grew thickly at the edge of the wood, and followed the path of the stream out into the field. It was pasture, and she could see cows – she hoped they were cows and not bullocks – in the distance by the hedge. They were lying down, a sure sign of rain, Gran said.

Lois plodded on, putting up her hood now that the sun had disappeared and heavy drops were falling steadily. Something quick and reddish rushed into the wood and disappeared. A hungry fox. Lois shivered, and not entirely because of the drop in temperature. She stopped and looked around. The stream was in open country now, and she reckoned nothing would have happened out here, without cover or shelter. Perhaps now she'd sleep more easily.

A small spinney, planted by the farmer as a sop to saving the environment, came into sight. The stream ran through it, and either side mossy banks proved slippery in the rain. Lois decided she'd go to the other side of the spinney, and then call it a day. She'd come a good mile now, and considered that would be a limit to whatever might have been possible that night.

She saw it then, and in terror missed her footing, ending up on her back in dripping undergrowth. Close to the stream, where the soil was soft and manageable, was a patch of fresh, bright green growth. Grass and water plants had grown much more thickly here, nourished by something nameless.

Rising up from all this lushness, something whitish, thin and bony stuck out. Lois struggled to her feet, her heart thumping. She peered closer, saw what it was and gagged. A hand, somehow risen to the surface, and showing quite clearly a wedding ring, washed clean by the falling rain. Lois was gulping deep draughts of air, desperately trying to stop herself vomiting. Finally she allowed herself to turn and have another look. So that was it. That was where Enid's mother had ended up. It *had* been a face that night, and someone had finally followed the tumbling body, snatched it from the stream and given it this indecent burial.

'Mrs M? What the devil . . . ?' She whipped round and saw Bill. She had never been so glad to see anyone, and mutely pointed in the direction of the hand.

'My God!' Bill stared, and without thinking put protective arms round a very damp Lois. He had been on his way to the cows, helping out Seb Charrington with a call from the local farmer. He'd seen a figure in the spinney and had come to investigate. Now he'd found more than he had bargained for, and realized he had no idea what to do next.

But Lois had recovered. She disentangled herself gently from Bill's arms, and said, 'Thanks, Bill. Now, if you can stay with me for a minute or two, I'll decide what we do now.'

Forty

Hunter Cowgill was humble and apologetic. 'You were right, Lois, and I was wrong,' he said simply. 'Must be getting slack in my old age.' He sat uncomfortably on a kitchen chair and looked at Lois. Far from triumphant at the success of her hunch, she was desperately worried. Now she knew that Enid was in the hands of a killer.

Lois said, 'From what Gran and me gathered from Enid, it was the mother who called the tune, and Edward along with her. His mum adored him, and I reckon he grew to hate her. Blamed her for everything that went wrong for him.'

After she'd reported to Cowgill what she had found, the police had gone swiftly into action, and then he'd turned up at the door asking to talk to her and Derek. 'All official now, Lois,' he'd said. 'We'll be interviewing around all the villages, and as Enid worked for you, you're naturally on the list. We've pulled out all the stops, and they'll not be hidden for long.' She didn't ask him what they'd found when they started digging. She knew.

'I've got good news . . . of a sort,' Cowgill said, sitting on the edge of a kitchen chair.

'You know where she . . .' Gran stopped when she saw Cowgill shaking his head.

'No,' he said, 'but we're pretty sure we know who sent those letters.'

Derek stiffened. 'Tell me who the bugger was, then,' he said angrily.

'We have obtained specimens of handwriting of Edward and Enid – not difficult, when you have the resources—'

'Yeah, yeah,' said Lois. 'And?'

'They are virtually identical. And match your letters. But

207

an expert has picked up a quirk in the way the capital "A" is formed in one of them, and it looks like Edward was your correspondent.'

'Why the hell should he want to stir up trouble here?' said Derek.

'I reckon I know,' said Lois, and looked at Cowgill. 'Desperate to bust up my work with you. Much too close for comfort.'

'Right,' said Cowgill. 'Anyway, it's another to add to his list of offences. And it's always a relief to know who sends anonymous letters.'

'Thanks,' said Derek, and held out his hand awkwardly. Cowgill, with considerable dignity, shook it. Nobody said anything for a moment or two.

Then Cowgill cleared his throat. 'So now we're on the move, following up several leads, and it shouldn't be long,' he continued, getting to his feet.

He meant to be reassuring, but Gran looked doubtful. Lois had spent hours on the telephone, ringing round chemists and schools in Edinburgh, but with no success. Staff had changed several times in the shops, and schools were closed. She had found nothing, and began to wonder if Enid's story of their early life in Edinburgh had been true.

Gran, too, had had no luck with the WI. She'd spoken to several of the older women, but no one seemed to know. They had forgotten that Mrs Abraham had been a local girl. It seemed that once the message had got about that the family were reclusive and did not welcome callers, the Abrahams were ignored.

'Lois did some ferretin',' said Derek, 'but nuthin's come up.'

Cowgill gave Lois a wintry smile. 'Thanks for trying,' he said. He recoiled though as she snapped back at him, 'I wasn't trying for you! Enid's on my team, and is in real danger! That bugger Edward is a killer. I'm sure of it.' She saw Gran fighting back tears, and stopped. 'Don't, Mum,' she said. 'We'll get her back.' She turned to Cowgill. 'Mum was a friend for Enid. Her only friend, probably.'

'Better get goin', mate,' said Derek, standing up. 'Sooner

208

we catch up with 'em the better.' He showed Cowgill to the door, but just as he was leaving, Lois yelled out for him to wait.

'Thought of something?' said Cowgill hopefully.

'No,' said Lois. 'I just wondered . . . well, I expect it's too soon to say . . . but d'you know how she was killed?'

Cowgill shook his head. 'Not yet, Lois. We don't even know who "she" is yet. But it looks like it might well be Mrs Abraham. Still, I don't have to tell you all to keep anything I say to yourselves. And Lois,' he added, and risked putting a gentle hand on her arm, 'we'll be doing everything we can. And that's quite a lot these days. I'll keep in touch.' He turned away then, and they followed him to the door. He waved a hand in farewell, and left them standing silently in the hall.

Forty-One

'M rs Meade? It's Rosie Charrington here. I just wondered if you've heard anything more about Enid
Abraham? There's been a lot of activity round here today
– police and dogs, and the police helicopter too. The children
have been so excited! Seb went down to look . . . they were
all round the bridge . . . but it was all closed off, and he was
sent back in no uncertain—'

'No, I've heard nothing,' Lois said abruptly. 'It is very
worrying, I know. But I'm sure we'll be hearing from Enid
soon. Was there anything else?'

Rosie sounded huffy. 'No, nothing else. Just thought you
might have some information about what's going on down
there. Saw you there this morning. Well, keep in touch, then,'
she added, and rang off.

Lois felt a stab of anxiety. If Rosie had seen her, who
else had noticed her car parked as she searched through
the meadow? The incredible disappearing Edward Abraham
seemed to turn up all over the place. Could he have taken his
father and Enid, hidden them somewhere, and come back to
make sure his disgusting handiwork was secure? If he had
seen her, she might be the next on his list. She certainly
knew too much for his comfort. She shook herself. No, of
course that was ridiculous. Wherever he was, surely he would
not come back to Cathanger? The old saying about criminals
and the scene of the crime came unbidden into her head. But
anyway, she argued with herself, if he had been around this
morning, he would have seen the cops arriving with dogs and
helicopter and left as quickly as possible. Even so . . .

She heard the door open, and only one child's voice.
Where were the others? Oh no, not that again, not the dread

210

of something happening to her family: Jamie abducted, or Josie attacked and raped! She rushed out of her office and swiftly made sure they were all there. 'You OK?' she said. 'Jamie? Douglas? Josie?'

They stared at her. 'What's up, Mum?' said Douglas. She hastily pulled herself together, and said nothing was the matter, and they'd better get changed and start on homework.

Relieved, they disappeared, and Gran emerged from the kitchen. 'I know,' she said. 'I bin thinking along the same lines. We'll just have to be careful, that's all.' She did not say that she'd always thought no good could come of this association of Lois's with the police. She'd nearly scuppered her marriage, and now they were deep in it again. Still, to be fair, Gran reflected, the fact that Enid Abraham worked for New Brooms would have dropped them in it anyway.

Walter Abraham, lying awake in a narrow bed in a tiny flat in Edinburgh, was thinking back over the past months, and came to the conclusion that New Brooms was responsible for all that had happened. He wasn't thinking rationally, but it seemed to him that from the time Enid had applied for that job, trouble had begun. Big trouble, this time. He thought of that terrible night of the flood, and all that happened. And all because of Enid and her job.

Walter turned over in bed with difficulty. He could feel his heart pulsing away much too quickly. Those stairs had been disastrous. What was going to happen to him? He supposed he should see a doctor, but had no hope that one would be allowed in. Tears ran down his furrowed cheeks and into the pillow.

His thoughts roamed on, round and round the events of that night. If only he could forget, but he never would. He almost welcomed the idea of death, of oblivion. It would be an escape from the nightmare that haunted him night and day.

Early on, Enid had brought her father a cup of tea and was appalled by his appearance. He seemed to have shrivelled overnight. His colour was bad, and as he'd tried to lift himself up to take the tea, he had begun to shake with the effort. 'Father! Are you all right?' Enid had helped him to sit up and put a pillow behind him. She'd held the cup to his lips, but after a few sips he had shaken his head, and lay back with his eyes closed.

Enid had decided to let him sleep, and now, since hours had gone by and her father was still asleep with an ashen face, she went into the tiny sitting-room, where Edward, with a dirty jersey pulled on over his pyjamas, was reading yesterday's newspaper.

'Edward! Come and look at Father, please. He's not at all well. We'll have to get a doctor to look at him. Please, Edward.' She tried to keep calm, although thoroughly alarmed at her father's condition.

Edward peered at her round the edge of the paper. 'Needs a day in bed, that's all,' he said. 'Journey too much for him, poor old sod,' he added, and went back to his reading.

'No, Edward! It's worse than that! Come and have a look at him. And hadn't you better get dressed?'

Edward put down his paper and turned to Enid with exaggerated patience. 'Now listen,' he said. 'Listen carefully, Enid. We are here in Edinburgh for one reason only. We are in hiding. Not necessarily for ever. But for now, nobody except me comes into this flat, and nobody except me goes out of it. You will stay and look after Father, and cook and clean for us. Should be good at the cleaning,' he added grimly. Then he went on: 'If you want some painkillers for him, I'll get them. I shall buy food, and anything else we need, and you and Father will stay here.'

Enid exploded. 'Painkillers!' she said loudly, and Edward frowned and put his finger to his lips.

'Quiet, Enid! Never know who might be listening . . .'

Enid spoke more quietly, but continued firmly, 'Father needs special care – hospital, probably – and if we don't get it for him, he'll more than likely die! It's his heart – even I can tell that.'

'Nonsense,' said Edward. 'You're exaggerating as usual. A couple of day's rest, and he'll be right as rain. *And,*' he added in a suddenly menacing voice, '*if* you don't mind, I'd be glad if you don't talk about dying . . . nobody's dying, Enid. Forget it.'

Enid had had long hours to think. She had wanted to believe the nursing home story and had allowed herself to think Edward spoke the truth. But she knew in her heart he was lying, knew for sure, in the way she'd always been able to tell. She had faced the worst, and answered, 'Nobody *else*, you mean, don't you, Edward?' Her former resolve to go along with everything, and play the innocent, obedient twin, was fast disappearing. She thought only of her father now.

Edward stood up, sending the newspaper flying. His face was dark and suffused, and he raised his arm. Before he could strike her, a quavery voice came from the bedroom. 'Edward? Come here, son . . . I need your help . . .'

Enid stared at her twin, willing him to give way. After a second or two, to her huge relief, he turned away and went slowly into his father's bedroom.

Across the courtyard from the ancient block of apartments sheltering the Abrahams, in another similar medieval build-ing, a middle-aged couple from the Midlands, life members of the National Trust, were unpacking in the charming little flat done up with excellent taste by the Trust. They'd stayed overnight in the Yorkshire dales, and now were settling in.

'Oh, look,' said the wife, 'there's people in that empty flat!'

'You can't say that, dear,' said the husband. 'If there's people in it, it's not empty.'

Not for the first time, the wife wished she could hit him, not hard, but just enough to relieve her feelings. 'Oh, you know what I mean,' she said. 'It was empty all the time we were here before. Now I can see a man moving around . . . and . . . yes, there's a woman, too.'

'Come away from the window, dear,' said her husband. 'We don't want them to think we're spying on them.'

The wife obediently returned to her unpacking. 'Where shall we eat tonight?' she said. 'Shall we go out to a restaurant? Save me cooking, our first night?'

Her husband considered the matter carefully, as he considered everything. Then he shook his head. 'Let's just have a snack here, and an early night,' he said.

'OK,' she said sadly, and shoved a pile of knickers into a drawer which he had filled with an inordinate number of socks.

Forty-Two

Immediately after an early lunch, Edward said he would go out and get more food and the papers. 'We need to keep an eye on the news,' he said conspiratorially. He was used to Enid as henchwoman, but the new steely look in her eye gave him pause for thought. He agreed – or pretended to – to look up a nearby surgery and ask for advice on Father's condition. 'I can do that without giving away our whereabouts,' he explained to her in his new conciliatory tone.

He knows which side his bread is buttered, thought Enid bitterly, but felt encouraged that she was making progress.

After he had gone out, she went in to give Father a drink, but he had fallen asleep again. She thought his breathing was easier, and relaxed a little. In the tiny bathroom, she cleaned the basin where Edward had left a grimy rim, and noticed a small medicine cabinet over the bath. Might be something in there to help Father, she thought, and opened the door. Cough syrup and a couple of bottles of eye drops. Then she saw something more interesting. A dog-eared packet with a prescription label. She recognized at once the name of sleeping pills she had once been given by a Tresham doctor. A sudden idea made her tear the packet open with hasty fingers. She prayed there would be at least two left. There were three, and she put them into her skirt pocket.

Edward hugged the inside edge of the pavement, walking quickly with his head down. Just up from the alley leading to their flat, a small newsagent and sweetshop made a good living selling a wide range of newspapers in several languages. Tourists had come back to Edinburgh after a bad season when nobody travelled unless they had to, fearful of terrorist attacks.

'Good afternoon,' said the Asian proprietor, smiling pleasantly at Edward. 'May I help you?' He stared at the unkempt figure, and wondered privately where he had come from. He was an unusual customer in this affluent part of the old town. Edward did not reply, but held out a couple of papers and the exact money, still with his head down and face concealed. 'Thank you, sir,' said the newsagent, and glanced at the front page of one of the papers Edward clutched. A large photograph of a haunted-looking face had pride of place. 'Find This Man!' said the headline.

'Looks like a big story, sir,' he said politely, but Edward did not answer and vanished quickly from the shop. He must get back to the flat as quickly as possible. Diving into a mini-supermarket, he picked up some essentials and blessed the checkout girl, who was talking so hard to her neighbour that she scarcely looked at him. He hurried back up the spiral staircase and shut the door behind him with relief. There was much to do before he could venture out again.

'You're back soon,' Enid called from the kitchen. 'Did you remember the painkillers?'

'Tomorrow will do,' said Edward curtly. He looked around the small entrance lobby, searching for a place to hide the telltale newspapers. Ah, that would do. A pile of old magazines, hidden by a vacuum cleaner. He shoved the papers under the pile, and went through to the sitting-room. Enid must be kept in the dark for as long as possible. Thank God there was no television in the flat, nor radio. All part of Donald getting away from it all. Edward had checked, of course, ready to disable any means of communication from the outside world. God, it's just as well I've a good head on my shoulders, he congratulated himself, and then remembered that that had been his mother's favourite phrase. He blotted out the memory, took the shopping through to Enid, and disappeared into the bathroom saying, 'Sudden call of nature! But I got all we need, and I'll get the rest later.'

Next time Enid checked on Father, he greeted her with a

much stronger voice, and her spirits began to rise. Her plan depended on him being at least mobile. She made him a cup of tea, and was surprised to see that Edward was still in the bathroom. When he finally emerged, Enid stared. 'What on earth?' she said. He had shaved off his straggly beard with an old razor of Donald's and, more shockingly, all his hair had gone too. He was completely bald.

'Now,' he said, with a jaunty smile, 'I look like every other yobbo, don't I?' His dark eyes burned into her, and she shivered.

'Yes, you do, Edward,' she said. 'Nobody would recognize you.' Surely that was the right thing to say. But he was advancing on her, and she shrank back. He only patted her shoulder.

'Good girl,' he said. 'Father better? Splendid. Must get going now. I'll be back shortly. Got to get a few new clothes . . . there's an Oxfam shop down the road. Don't want to look *too* smart and new!' He looked around the room, and then pounced on a small table by the electric fire. 'I knew I'd seen them! Must be Donald's,' he said, and put on a pair of rimless glasses, which, as he'd hoped, completed the transformation.

Enid realized with a sinking heart that he was exhilarated by this new game. A challenge, he would have called it, but she knew it was the adrenaline of pitting himself against an unseen enemy that gave him the feeling of excitement he'd always craved.

'Don't forget to find a surgery,' she said, suspecting rightly that concern for Father had gone right out of his head. 'He's much better, but still needs to see a doctor. Don't forget, will you, Edward?'

He shook his head impatiently. Then, unaccustomed to his scalp's sudden exposure to fresh air, ran his hand over his baldness. 'Well, you know,' he said, 'it really feels quite good. Sort of clean and businesslike! Perhaps I'll keep it like this, when . . . well . . .'

'When what, Edward?' said Enid quietly.

'When all of this is over. When I've got it sorted,' he said. He blinked several times and said, 'You know, Enid, I hadn't realized that I do need glasses!' With a grin he went out again, locking the door behind him. She heard his quick footsteps on the narrow spiral stairs, and then silence.

Enid quietly busied herself tidying the flat and piling up their few belongings. Drawers and cupboards were full of the owner's clothes and shoes, but she managed to clear some space. Edward must get no hint that she meant to leave. Oh, Edward . . . She took a deep breath, and continued work. Everywhere was dusty, and she wondered how long since Donald and his wife had been here. Probably one of those couples who wintered abroad, she thought enviously. Still, it was not winter any more. They might be back soon. But Edward was thorough. He would not have brought them here if Donald had been expected back shortly.

She found a duster and went systematically round the flat. I wonder how the Charringtons are managing without me, she thought sadly. Perfectly well, probably. Mrs M will have organized it. Probably forgotten all about me. Out of sight, out of mind. A tear dropped on to the duster, and she sniffed. In the lobby by the front door, she found the cleaner and pulled it out, ready to give everywhere a good going over. Then she saw the pile of magazines. They were mostly colour supplements from old Sunday papers. Still, Father might like to look at them. He could leaf through them, see if anything interested him. She lifted the pile and saw the newspapers underneath.

Edward stared out at her from the photograph. It was an old one, taken when he had won a clay pigeon shooting match in Fletching. His hair was neat, but long, and he had a beard. 'FIND THIS MAN'. She read on, and finally put the pile of magazines back to cover the newspapers. She went unsteadily into the sitting-room, collapsing on a chair and putting her head between her knees to fight the overwhelming faintness.

'Enid? Enid, can I have a drink of water, dear?' It was her father, calling in a much stronger voice. She stood up, and with a huge effort walked slowly into the kitchen to run some cold water into a clean glass. She gulped a mouthful herself, and then took it in to her father.

'Ah, there you are,' he said. 'I'm feeling much better, dear. Perhaps I'll get up soon and maybe manage a stroll outside?' He seemed to have forgotten they were prisoners, and Enid wondered if it had all been too much for him.

'We'll see,' said Enid, and managed a small smile. We're not going anywhere, Father, she wanted to say. At least, not until I've made it safe for you. 'We'll see,' she repeated. 'Now, would you like me to sit with you for a bit? We can have a nice talk.'

'Oh, look!' said the woman from the Midlands, peering round the edge of the curtain down into the courtyard. 'There's another man from that staircase. Must be several of them in that tiny flat. He walks like the other one. Perhaps he's his brother . . . ?'

'For goodness sake!' said her husband. 'We haven't come all this way to indulge in gossip about what you see through the lace curtains. Come away from the window at once!'

'They're not lace,' said his wife stubbornly. 'The Trust would never have lace curtains. And it's not gossip. You're the one who's always saying I'm not observant enough. I'm just taking an intelligent interest in my surroundings.'

'Huh,' her husband replied. 'Sounds like gossip to me.'

She gave up, and came away from the window. 'I think I'll go shopping,' she said.

'Hang on a minute,' he said. 'I'll come with you.' Oh, bugger, she thought, but she waited while he put on his coat and hat, and they went out together.

Forty-Three

L ois ticked off dusters from her list. A robot could do this, she thought, as she went on to the shelves round the corner. Operating mechanically, she continued to push her heavy trolley round the wholesalers, her mind on Enid, captive and miserable. She knew Cowgill had the whole thing well organized now, and she expected a call any minute to say the Abrahams had been found. But she dreaded one thing. It was certain they would be found – but dead or alive? Two dead, and one alive? Anyone who had murdered his mother and buried her in a muddy field would stop at nothing. She was sure that a criminal's first murder, like the first theft, would be the most difficult. After that, the most basic hurdle had been taken. Thou shalt not break the law. Most of us, she thought to herself as she consulted her list, don't even try. We may feel like it sometimes. Some people even have enough provocation . . .

Provocation. That word stuck in her head as she struggled on. What had driven Edward to do it? She knew he had frequent rows with his father. He'd even physically attacked him that night in the yard. It had been him, for sure. But his mother? She adored him. Lois knew that from the diary. She supposed she should give that to Cowgill now, but for the moment . . .

When she returned home, she took it out of her drawer and turned again to the last entry. 'Haven't seen my Teddy for so long . . .' What had happened to stop her just there? It was the day of the flood. And the day Enid said her mother shut herself up completely, and she'd not seen her since. Because she'd not been there at all. Because she'd been rolling down the swollen torrent until she'd fetched up on the bank, and then one of them, Edward or Walter, had dug a shallow grave and buried her. She remembered Enid saying her father had been out very early next day and done a thorough search.

Bridie Reading was also thinking about Enid. She hadn't particularly liked the woman, and nor had Hazel. Particularly Hazel. She knew too much about the Abraham family, and was wary. Her mum said she had a nose for trouble, and meant it as a compliment. Now they sat watching breakfast television, but neither was concentrating.

'Mum,' Hazel said. 'You're sure you don't remember anything about that Mrs Abraham living round here as a girl? You know, Lois asked us.'

'Never heard anything. 'Course, I wasn't in Farnden when she was a girl,' Bridie said slowly. 'When they came back, they were just left to get on with it. Villages are like that.'

'Yeah, but villages are full of gossips,' said Hazel. 'Surely somebody . . . ?'

'Hey, wait a minute!' said Bridie. She sat up, reached for the remote, and turned off the television. 'Why didn't we think of it before? Ivy Beasley!'

'What, that old biddy over at Ringford? Her that nearly married her lodger, and then he done a runner?'

'That's her,' said Bridie. 'Why don't you call in on that old woman at the lodge, just in a friendly way, to check she's OK. Then you'd have an excuse to go on and see Miss Beasley. She's the old one's friend. Nothin' has ever escaped her eagle eye. Chat her up.'

'Chat her up!' said Hazel, grinning. 'She'll have my guts for garters, if what I've heard is true. Still, I'll give it a try. Nice one, Mum.'

'I *know* who you are,' said Ivy Beasley. 'No need to go into all that.' She had opened the door a crack, and peered through at this unwanted visitor.

Hazel stood on the scrubbed white step, and smiled. It was an effort, but she had to stop the woman shutting the door. 'I need help,' she said. 'They say you know everything about what goes on in these parts. Old Ellen said. Can you spare me a minute?'

There was pause while Ivy Beasley considered it. Then, to Hazel's relief, she opened the door wider and said, 'I suppose you'd better come in, then. You'll have to be in the kitchen. Front room's just been cleaned. And it had better be quick.'

Hazel ignored the suggestion that she might sully the best chairs, and went through.

'It's about the Abrahams at Cathanger,' she began.

'Of course it is,' said Miss Beasley sharply. 'D'you think I'm stupid? What d'you want to know?'

'The mother's maiden name. Seems she came from round here.' Hazel realized there was no point in niceties. Straight to the point with Ivy Beasley.

'Ah, yes, well, it looks like your boss has backed the wrong horse in employing one of them Abrahams,' she said. 'Still, that's her affair. But if you ask me, she'd steer well clear of them in the future.'

'Yes, well, as you say, that's Mrs Meade's affair, Miss Beasley. We just think it might be helpful – I don't need to explain why – to discover as much as possible about them. Enid Abraham's a good worker, and Mrs M's very concerned.' Hazel knew she sounded defensive, but could not help it. There were limits.

'No need to get all hoity-toity, Hazel Reading, not if you want me to tell you what I know.'

Hazel sighed, trying to be patient. If this Miss Beasley knew something, it could be worth waiting for.

After settling herself, Ivy began in a different, confiding voice, 'Well, I didn't think nothing of it when Mrs Meade's mother was asking around at the WI. But later on, when I got home and was feeding that cat, it came back to me.'

'Yes?' Hazel diplomatically stroked a big, ordinary-looking tabby that had landed unasked on her lap.

'The Abraham woman. She were a Blenkinsop. Big family o'girls. Father worked on the railways with my dad. She was younger than me, o'course. But I remember her as a whiney, spoilt sort of creature. Good at getting her own way. That kind o'thing. Blenkinsop. She went away when she got married, and then when they came back, didn't want to know any of us. Ideas above her station, if you ask me. Well, that was it. Blenkinsop.'

She was silent then, and Hazel said, 'That's very interesting, Miss Beasley. Thank you. I wonder, could I . . . ?' But Ivy Beasley was on her feet, showing her out of the kitchen. Hazel knew she'd got all the information Miss Beasley was prepared to release, and, standing once more on the white step, turned to thank her. But the door had shut, and she returned to her car.

Lois listened carefully to what Hazel reported. 'Well done,' she said.

'Not much help, really,' said Hazel gloomily, shifting the telephone receiver from one hand to the other. 'Everything helps,' said Lois. 'Now we know what kind of woman she was. That could be very useful, and we might catch up with some other Blenkinsops . . .'

But when Lois finished talking to Hazel, and searched through the local directory, there were no Blenkinsops listed. Well, all those girls must have married and got themselves different names, and the old folk would have died by now. Miss Beasley's comment, faithfully relayed by Hazel, came back to her.

A whiney, spoilt sort of creature. Good at getting her own way. Was that why she became a recluse, discovering that it was a very effective weapon? And where did that leave Enid? Whose side was she on? Lois sighed again. If only she could hear from Enid, just to know she was still alive, then she'd be happy to leave the rest to Cowgill.

She told Derek this when he came in from the garden. 'Don't deceive yerself, me duck,' he said. 'You'll ferret away 'til you come up with somethin' like the truth. And we're all prayin' to God it'll be soon, if only so's the kids can get through to you! Josie's bin asking for new jeans for a week now, and it's time you listened!'

As they ate, Lois told Gran about Hazel's call, and she

smiled. 'Right ole acid-tongue, that one,' she said. 'Everybody knows her, and most of the WI are scared stiff of her. Still, she came up with the goods.'

'Hazel wasn't sure it's much help,' said Lois. 'But it's a start.'

'I'll ask around,' Derek said. 'I'm helpin' next door with his paving tomorrow, then we're goin' to Waltonby for a refresher. Someone in the pub might remember the Blenkinsops. The old farmers get in there, playin' dominoes. Get them goin' on the old days, and you're there for the afternoon.'

'Mum?' Josie smiled pleadingly at her mother. 'Mum, can we go shopping soon? I need some new—'

'I know, love,' said Lois, 'some new jeans. Yep, o'course we can go. I bin a bit busy lately, but we'll go to that new shop in the centre. Get you some T-shirts as well. I reckon you're goin' to be busty like your gran!'

'That's quite enough of that, Lois Meade,' said her mother huffily. 'Your dad used to say I'd got a better figure than Betty Grable.'

'Betty *WHO?*' chorused the kids.

Forty-Four

Edward Abraham was looking for a chemist. In his new guise, he strode along, head held high, smiling to himself and seeing miraculously more clearly through Donald's spectacles. He was quite unrecognizable, he was sure of that. He even *felt* like a totally different person! Whoever would have thought that it would be as easy as that? He should have done it years ago.

'Afternoon!' he said, passing an old newspaper seller, who was offering papers with Edward's photograph emblazoned on the front page. The seller nodded at him without a second glance. Wonderful! He walked into a small supermarket and picked up supplies for Enid. Now for a chemist to find some pills for Father. He was sure Enid had been exaggerating, trying to worry him about the state of their father's health. He was clearly better, and after a day's recuperation would, Edward was convinced, be as good as new. The change of scene would do him good. Still, better humour Enid for the moment.

He walked on down Nicholson Street, and saw a green cross sign coming up. That would do. As he walked into the light, airy chemists, it seemed familiar. Had he been here before? Certainly not this visit. Then it came to him: this was where Enid had worked. Everything had changed, of course; a completely new interior, but the general layout was the same, and a panel of coloured glass over the door had survived. Ah, yes, and there was the huge bottle filled with bright blue liquid that had stood in the window for as long as he could remember. He was the only customer, and a woman assistant had perched herself on a stool in the corner, leafing through a newspaper.

He stopped to look around, and muttered to himself, 'Well, bless me . . .'

'Excuse me?' said the assistant, coming forward. 'Can I help you?'

Edward smiled at her. He dared to do that now! Perhaps he would mooch around a bit, indulging in memories. 'In a minute, thanks very much,' he said. 'Just looking around. I used to come in here in the old days. It's changed a bit!'

'Yes, well . . .' The woman lost interest. She had thought she knew him from somewhere, school, maybe. But he was too old to have been at school with her. He was drifting about the shop now, picking up things and putting them down again. One of those. Still, what was it to her if a couple of packets went missing? She wandered back to her stool and picked up the newspaper again. She turned the page, and a face stared out at her. She frowned, and looked up to where Edward had picked up a small hand mirror and was looking admiringly at himself.

He caught her eye.

He turned and saw the newspaper and her startled expression. In a second, he was out of the shop and running.

'Mr Gordon!' The woman rushed out to the office at the back of the shop. 'Look, here . . . this photo! He's just been in the shop . . . honest, it was him!'

The manager took the paper from her and stared. 'Are you sure?' he said, but he knew the woman was reliable, not one of the flibberty young ones. He picked up his telephone and dialled. 'Hello? Police?'

Edward, out of breath and slowing down, found himself approaching Forrest Road, and calmed down sufficiently to give a quick pat to Greyfriars Bobby on his doggy plinth. No harm done, he reassured himself. The chemist woman was probably thinking of something else entirely. He ambled along George IV Bridge and turned left into Lawnmarket. Nearly home. Home? His mood darkened again. They were more or less homeless now. They could never go back to Cathanger, but this did not worry Edward. He hated the place, just as his mother had hated it. But then, she was full of hate.

Hatred of his father, of Enid, of anyone who tried to help her . . . Still, the three of them would make a life in Scotland somewhere. Enid was good at homemaking.

As he went through the little arched passage leading to the courtyard and the flat, he stood aside to allow a couple to pass. 'Thanks,' said the woman. 'Lovely day.' He kept his head down and grunted. Musn't make the same mistake again. He was still a wanted man, however good his disguise. He walked through the passage and into the door of their building.

'That was the bloke from the flat opposite,' said the Midlands woman to her husband. 'Now I've seen him up close, he is very like the other one, except not so hairy.'

'Really!' exploded her husband. 'Don't you ever listen to anything I say?'

Enid took the ham, lettuce, tomatoes, and fruit. 'And the painkillers for Father?'

Edward waved the question aside. 'Doesn't need them now, surely,' he said. 'Seems a lot better.'

He was pleased with himself, thought Enid suspiciously. But not quite so jaunty as before. What had happened out there on the streets? She was beginning to feel claustrophobic, shut up in these small rooms. She could see out of the window that the sun was still shining, and tourists wandered slowly in and out of the courtyard, visiting a museum in an ancient building across the way.

She prepared the salad, and Edward helped his father to the table. There was no doubt the old man was a lot stronger, and Enid was encouraged. This suited her plan. She could not have carried it out if Father had been ill and bedridden. The time Edward was out shopping had not been wasted. She'd found a current railway timetable shoved in amongst cookery books in the kitchen, and rejoiced.

After their meal, Father sat in an armchair and dozed off. Enid and Edward sat at the table, drinking coffee. Edward had taken a book of old photographs of Edinburgh out of the shelves, and was leafing idly through it.

Might as well forget the sunshine, Enid told herself. When she went out, it would be in the dark, preferably with just enough light for her to see where she was going. It would be difficult with Father, but they would manage. Meanwhile, she must keep her mind empty, in case Edward tuned in to her thoughts. Conversation, then, about ordinary things.

'Where else did you go, when you were out?' she asked.

He pushed his chair back suddenly. 'Nowhere much,' he said casually. 'I'll help you wash up,' he added, and picked up their coffee mugs.

As she washed the plates, stacking them on the draining board for Edward to dry, Enid risked starting a conversation on a more dangerous topic. 'Um, I was wondering,' she said, 'whether Mother sent a message for me at all?'

She could almost feel the temperature drop, and Edward's reply was icy. 'No message for you, Enid,' he said. 'Concerned only with herself.'

Enid was silent, hoping he would continue. She was desperate to know how he had been driven to such violence against his chief champion, the one who had blindly adored him all his life.

'I'd like to think,' he said eventually, after minutes ticked by, 'that senility was settling in. Making her worse in every way. Exaggerating her bad points. It does, you know, Enid,' he added, looking at her closely, as if needing her agreement.

She obediently nodded. 'I know,' she said, and scrubbed round a dish that was already very clean.

'I couldn't stand it,' he went on. 'All the recriminations if I didn't see her every day to bring her flowers and swear undying love. And then, when I stayed away, she stored it all up and was hysterical the times I did call in.'

'What times? Where were you, Edward? I never saw you coming and going . . .'

He grinned, a sudden flash of the old, invincible Edward. 'Of course you didn't,' he said. 'I made sure you were out of the way, doing your extraordinary cleaning jobs. My hiding places were many and various, I can tell you!'

'So how did you persuade her to go into the nursing home?' Enid said.

His eyes changed, the guarded look returning. 'Father did

most of it,' he said. 'He was very firm, just like the old father we remember. That voice that had to be obeyed. I helped her dress in her best, and then she got quite girlish and demanded lipstick and a comb. Went off without a backward glance, Enid. The confirmed recluse! Makes you wonder, doesn't it.' He hung the drying-up cloth on its hook, and turned to smile at her, quite fond again.

She shivered. 'It does indeed, Edward,' she said.

Forty-Five

Jamie was not feeling so good. At least, that is what he had told his mother first thing this morning. Lois had looked at him doubtfully. 'You look all right,' she'd said. But when he answered her, his voice was hoarse, and he coughed painfully.

'Well, you'd better stay there today,' she had said.' I'll get Gran to make one of her specials. She swears hot lemon, brown sugar and a splash of something stronger will cure anything.'

'Kill or cure,' muttered Jamie, who'd had specials before, and hated the taste.

The real reason for his not feeling so good was a session fixed for tomorrow with the history teacher. They were doing the Second World War, and had some facts to learn.

Jamie had been bored with the subject, and done no work. He'd promised to have it learnt by tomorrow, but couldn't see any hope of it. It wasn't that he hadn't tried. He'd sat in his room with the book open in front of him, and gone over and over. But it didn't stick. This morning, he'd decided on evasive action. Maybe if he asked Gran to help him, he could do it. No good asking Mum. She never had a spare minute. Yep, Gran would do it. And if it didn't work, he could still be ill tomorrow. It'd be more convincing. Relaxed by this consoling thought, he had shut his eyes and when Lois came in with the special, he'd given a very convincing imitation of being sound asleep. She put the drink by his bed, and smiled down at him. My baby, she had thought. Looks so innocent, bless him.

Derek had gone off early to help with the paving stones, and she knew he'd be late back. They'd have a real thirst on them. She went into her office to check messages, and saw 'Blenkinsop' written on her pad. Damn, she'd meant to remind him. She dialled his mobile, and got a breathless Derek. 'OK, I won't forget,' he said. 'What? Oh, yep, it's goin' fine. Cheers.'

Sheila Stratford had surprised her husband at breakfast. 'Nothing much in the larder for dinner,' she said. 'Shall we go to the pub?'

'What?' said Sam. 'On a Sunday? What about that leg o' lamb?'

'You got that last Sunday,' she said doggedly. 'Anyway, it's our anniversary, in case you'd forgotten. It'd be a little treat.'

Sam was cornered. 'Oh, well then,' he said grudgingly. 'I suppose it'd be all right, just this once. Can't spend more than the hour . . . we're very busy on the farm. I shall be there most of today, Sunday or no Sunday.'

When he'd gone, Sheila was chagrined to answer the door to the florist from Tresham, who handed over a bouquet of roses with a professional smile. 'Happy anniversary, Mrs Stratford,' he said.

'Best love, Sam,' she read. So he'd not forgotten. Damn. Still, there was an ulterior motive to her pub idea, and she put the roses in water gratefully. She'd made a special fruit cake for his tea, so that should put things right.

'Hello, Derek! Fancy seeing you here!' Sheila and Sam walked into the bar, and Derek rose to his feet.

'Could say the same,' he said. 'What're you havin'?' He introduced his neighbour, who said he must be off for his dinner. Derek intended to follow, but couldn't duck his round when Sam and Sheila came in.

'No, it's a special day today,' said Sam, rising to the occasion. 'Another half?' Derek nodded his thanks, and congratulated them.

A voice from the corner chimed in, 'How's about one for the oldest inhabitant then?' It was old Alf, one of several who made the oldest claim. He was on his own and feeling left out.

231

'I known you two since you were knee-high,' he said. 'That counts for summat, don' it?'

The four of them sat around the table swapping tales of old times like the Stratfords' wedding day, when it had rained right up to the time when Sheila got out of her dad's car at the church, and then the sun had come out like a spotlight, and not gone in again for the rest of the day.

'We seen some times,' said Alf, shaking his head wisely. Sheila judged it the moment to mention the subject she'd planned to bring up all along. She'd known Alf would be in his regular corner.

'Speakin' of weddings,' she said, 'I were trying to remember who that Mrs Abraham – her down at Cathanger – was before she married. D'you remember, Alf?'

'Who wants to know?' said the old man, automatically suspicious.

'I do,' said Sheila. Silly ole fool. It wouldn't do to tell him Mrs Meade had asked, else he'd clam up like an oyster. Or oyster up like a clam. Sheila chuckled to herself. Alf said, 'What's the joke? Think I'm senile or somethin'? O'course I remember the Blenkinsops. Big family o'girls. He were a railway worker. Wife was a right harpy. Still, all them girls got wed.'

'Good lookers, were they?' said Derek. Thank goodness Sheila had brought up the Abrahams. He'd forgotten, and Lois would have crucified him.

'Some of 'em,' said Alf. 'One especially. The youngest, she was. Spoilt rotten. Lovely lookin' gel. Dark hair and very pale skin. Black eyes. Used to say she were a changeling. Didn't look like neither of her parents.'

'Who did she marry?' Sheila knew she was on the right track.

'Some bloke from away.' Alf looked scornfully into the distance. 'She got above herself then. Still, she was always uppity, what with her mum and dad tellin' her all the time how marvellous she was.'

'So what happened to her?'

'Went away. I 'ad a soft spot for 'er meself once, so I kept me ears open, though I weren't good enough for 'er. They said she went to Edinburgh. Then I heard the whole family come back, but I don't know n'more about them. Now,' he continued, 'how's about fillin' up for the toast?'

Derek took three brimming glasses back to the table, then excused himself and phoned Lois. She listened carefully, and when Sheila rang a bit later and related proudly what Alf had said, she listened all over again and pretended it was new and vital information.

'Blenkinsop, did you say?' Cowgill held the phone closer to his ear. Lois must be speaking quietly for some reason. He heard her thank Gran for something, and knew what she was about to say must be about Enid, and not for Gran's ears. A pause, and then she was back talking to him.

'Yep, a Blenkinsop. Big local family. There wasn't nothing much new in what Derek and Sheila heard from Alf. But Edinburgh has cropped up again. I expect you got the word out there?'

Cowgill smiled to himself. She was indomitable. He could do with a bit of that. 'Oh yes,' he said quickly, 'we have everywhere on the alert, Edinburgh especially.'

'Do you know yet?' Lois was hesitant. 'Whether it was her . . . Mrs Abraham?'

There was a pause, and then Cowgill said, 'We've not confirmed the suspicion yet, but between you and me, Lois – and I mean that – we are now almost positive. I think you can be sure we're treating it as matricide.'

'Blimey!' said Lois. 'Fancy that!'

Cowgill put down the phone, uncomfortably aware that he was being mocked.

Around the middle of the afternoon, Gran peeped into Jamie's room and saw an empty bed. He'd managed quite a good lunch, and she had suggested a nap. 'Jamie!'

'What?' He was over in the corner, busy with a computer game.

'What would your father say?' Jamie made a face. Gran opened the window and said, 'Your Mum's gone out cleaning at the estate agent's, while they're shut. I don't think it's right on a Sunday. Still filling in for Enid. Sooner we get a replacement the better. Poor Enid.' Her voice broke, and she squared her shoulders and added, 'You'd better get dressed and come downstairs. I'm just making tea – or would you like another special?'

'No, no thanks, Gran,' said Jamie quickly. He had tiptoed out on to the landing where Mum had a plant in a pot, and given it the benefit of the first special. He expected the plant to be dead by the time Mum came home.

It was warm in the kitchen, with Melvyn the cat snoring peacefully in the big chair by the Rayburn. With his school book in Gran's capable hands, Jamie found it much easier to absorb the facts. Gran said the war wasn't history to her, and had told him interesting, gossipy details to help him remember.

'Well, then,' she said, finally pushing the book over to him. 'I reckon you'll be fine. And restored to health, too,' she added, with a sideways look at him. He nodded, and they were silent for a few minutes.

'Gran . . .'

'What?'

'You know Miss Abraham?'

'Of course I do! What about her?'

'I thought of something she told me. It was about school, an' her own times, an' that. I just remembered, with us doin' stuff about the old days.'

Gran looked at him closely. 'What did she say?' she said urgently.

'Said when she went to school in Edinburgh, her dad was caretaker, an' it was a bit embarrassing. She got bullied, but her brother stuck up for her. Him an' his best friend Donald. Got into fights about it. She likes her brother a lot, you know.'

'Well, maybe so,' said Gran. 'Probably did once, but not so much now. Donald, did you say?'

'Yep. D'you think her brother did that terrible thing, Gran?'

'Looks like it,' said Gran, trying desperately to think of a way of changing the subject. 'Anyway, Jamie,' she said, 'we'll probably see Enid again soon, and get going on the piano lessons.'

'I've remembered something else,' he said, and she could see his eyes were glistening with tears. 'That school, where she was bullied, where her dad was. It was called St Cuthbert's Junior. She said it several times, and told me who St Cuthbert was.'

'Who was he?' said Gran automatically, her mind churning.

'Some ole saint . . . don't remember,' said Jamie, shrugging. 'Think I'll go upstairs now and have a rest.'

'You don't fool me, young man,' said Gran. But she let him go, and went to the telephone. 'Lois? Listen, I got something to tell you. What? Well, stop in a lay-by, or something. This is important. Ready? Right, listen then. It's important, and you'll want to get hold of your cop. Jamie said . . .'

Lois listened, then took a deep breath. 'Right, thanks Mum,' she said. 'I'll need to make a quick call now. Not much chance of an answer, but worth a try. How's Jamie?'

'Right as rain,' said Gran. 'As always.'

In St Cuthbert's school in Edinburgh, the school secretary frowned. She'd just returned from holiday in Spain, and had come into the empty school to make a start on the pile of work waiting for her. The temp, as usual, had been useless. She could break the back of it today, and be ready for the onslaught tomorrow. Now the telephone was ringing, and she considered not answering it. But it might be her husband, or one of the family.

'Helloo? Well, school's closed. Oh, I see. A serious personal matter. Go on, then.' Lois told her a prepared story, and crossed her fingers.

'It's a long time ago, Mrs Meade,' the secretary said. 'We do have school records, of course, and I could look in there for them.' She sounded very reluctant, and Lois stressed the urgency. 'Oh, all right. Abraham? If you could hang on for a wee while . . . or can I ring you back?'

Lois said she was on a mobile, so would sit and wait for a return call. 'Sorry to bother you,' she said. 'It is really urgent. Thanks a lot.' Finally, the call came.

'Got it!' said the secretary, more cheerful now she had a

result. 'Edward Abraham. What did you say? I'm not getting you very clearly. A boy in the same class called Donald?'

There was a pause, and then Lois grinned. 'Great! You're a star,' she said. 'What was his surname? MacDougall? . . . Donald MacDougall. Thanks ever so much. Yes . . . very helpful . . . Bye.' Lois signed off before the secretary could pursue the conversation, and immediately rang Cowgill.

'Yes, Lois, of course I'm listening carefully,' he said. His eyes opened wide as she told him all she'd discovered. 'That's my girl!' he said, and immediately knew he'd said the wrong thing.

'I'm nobody's girl, least of all yours!' said Lois. 'Just get on with it. There's probably quite a few Donald MacDougalls in Edinburgh. If I get any more info, I'll be in touch. And let me know what's happening, *if* you can spare the time.'

Hunter Cowgill sighed deeply, and did as he was told. He got on with it, very rapidly.

Forty-Six

After a long, dreary and claustrophobic day in the flat, Enid drifted towards the sitting-room window. She must avoid at all costs giving any hint that she was up to something. She tried hard not even to think of her plan, terrified that Edward would pick up on her thoughts.

'It's raining,' she said.

He lowered the old magazine he was reading. 'Come away from that window at once, Enid!' he said in a harsh voice. 'How many times do I have to tell you? We're in hiding!'

'Sorry,' said Enid, and backed away, but not before she'd seen a woman's face at the window across the courtyard. The woman was looking straight at her, and then, before she could duck out of sight, Enid saw her give a little friendly wave. That's torn it! Still, what Edward didn't see wouldn't annoy him. 'Sorry,' she repeated, 'but there's nobody about. It's raining quite hard.'

She sat down and picked up a magazine from the pile Edward had brought in from the hall. The newspaper had disappeared.

'Would you like a cup of tea, Father?' Enid was deeply relieved that her father seemed to be more or less restored to health – or such health as he'd had before his ascent up the spiral staircase.

'How about you, Edward?'

'Rather have something stronger,' grunted Edward, 'but I suppose I should keep a clear head. Yes, all right then, I'll have a cup.'

Enid went into the kitchen and put on the kettle. Under cover of the noise of water coming to the boil, she took out of her pocket a little screw of paper. Whilst Edward had been out on an errand, she had crushed two sleeping pills into a fine powder. She made the tea and tipped the powder into the cup destined for Edward, stirring it well.

'Here you are, Father,' she said, 'and this one's yours, Edward. I know you like it strong.' Oh dear, that sounded silly. Why should she suddenly say that, out of nowhere?

He was looking at it suspiciously, and she held her breath. 'Could've been a bit stronger,' he said, and she nearly laughed with relief. But she made a big effort to appear casual, not to watch as he drank it down to the bottom of the cup.

'Did you put sugar in it?' he said, putting his finger into the empty cup and licking it. Enid shook her head. 'Of course not,' she said. 'Must be the milk. Was it fresh?'

He shrugged, not bothering to answer her, and went back to his magazine.

When his eyelids began to close, Enid got up and went swiftly into her father's room. Thank goodness he hadn't dozed off too. She stuffed his warm jacket into a holdall, then went into her own room and collected her coat.

'Father . . .' She was whispering, and he did not hear her. She risked more volume, and this time he turned and saw her, carrying the bag, beckoning to him with her finger to her lips. His mouth dropped open, and he turned to look at Edward. But Edward was deeply asleep, his head back comfortably in the chair. Enid put down the bag, and picked up a small rug draped over the sofa. She wrapped it gently round Edward's legs, and then took her father's arm, retrieved the bag, and made for the hall.

'Door's locked,' whispered Father. His voice trembled, and Enid could feel him shaking. She felt in her handbag and pulled out the key.

'Pickpocket!' she whispered, and smiled, hoping to relax him. He stared at her and nodded. She had never seen him look so terrified, not even when Edward had threatened him at home.

It seemed to Enid to take a lifetime to negotiate the spiral staircase. She dared not hurry her father, unless he tripped. The stairs were stone, narrow and unforgiving. At last they were at the bottom, and she quietly opened the door to the courtyard. She helped Walter into his jacket, and said, 'Off we go,' as if they were setting out for a picnic in Cathanger fields.

'Where're we going?' Father said at last, glancing back at the flat window, as if he expected to see his son's angry face.

'Tresham,' said Enid. 'But first, Waverley Station. It's not far, but there's steps, so we'll take it gently. Plenty of time, Father,' she added, though she had looked at her watch and seen that they would only just make the train from Edinburgh to Kings Cross. She hoped there had been no changes to the timetable. Trains were fewer on a Sunday. They should be in Tresham soon after midnight, and Enid hoped against hope she'd be able to telephone for a taxi. Her father leaned on her as they made their way through the darkening streets. She prayed that he would be up to the long journey. The rain had stopped, luckily, but the skies were heavily overcast, and streetlamps had come on early.

Having safely descended the steps, they were making good progress down Market Street when Walter suddenly stopped. 'What about Edward?' he said. 'What'll happen to him?'

Enid gulped, but urged him on, saying that Edward would be fine. He'd always managed to get out of trouble before. He would find a way this time. Now it was important to get back to Cathanger, where they could help him more than if they were shut up in that flat. 'Did he say that? Did he tell you why we had to come to Edinburgh?' Father said anxiously.

'Sort of,' said Enid. 'Just wouldn't let us go back again straight away. And you need to see a doctor. So that's why we've escaped. Come on, Father, I can see the station. Nearly there.'

It was a rush, first buying tickets and then finding the right platform. Enid had nearly given up when her handbag flew open and scattered its contents all over the station forecourt. But Walter, suddenly galvanized into action, had helped her collect it up, and at last they were in the train, subsiding gratefully into their seats as the guard blew his whistle and they moved slowly out of Edinburgh on their way south.

Forty-Seven

The taxi cruised down Long Farnden main street and drew to a halt outside the Meade's house. It was after midnight, and the village was asleep. No lights showed, except for security lights in the big house by the shop.

'There's Melvyn!' said Enid. 'Oh, do be careful, driver! I couldn't bear him to be run over.'

'What are you talking about, Enid?' said Walter, peering out. 'There's nobody about.'

'She means the cat,' said the taxi driver. 'It's all right, missus,' he said. 'I seen it already.'

'Pull up here, please,' Enid said, leaning forward to put her hand on the door. She felt comforted, reassured, just from the look of Lois's solid house, full of people she knew. Now they would be all right. Her father had slept during most of the train journey, but now he was awake and querulous.

'Where're we going?' he repeated, over and over, as the taxi left the station.

'To get help,' Enid said. 'No good going to Cathanger first. It'll be bolted and barred, for sure. We'll go to Mrs M's and find Gran, and then we'll be fine.'

Walter was not convinced. 'I'm hungry,' he said now. 'And cold. I wish we'd stayed in Edinburgh.'

Enid gritted her teeth. She opened her handbag, paid the driver, and got her father out on to the pavement. 'Now,' she said firmly, 'be very quiet. We won't wake the children, if we're lucky. Come on, Father, best foot forward.'

Lois struggled out of sleep. She'd been dreaming that she was down at Cathanger, and bulldozers had arrived to knock the place down. Bang, crash! They wouldn't listen as she

240

pleaded with them to stop. Bang, bang! Now more or less awake, she could still hear the noise. Then she realized it was the door knocker. 'Derek! Derek! Wake up! Somebody's at the door!'

'Let them bugger off then,' said Derek, turning over and burrowing under the duvet.

'No, we'd better go and see. Might be an emergency in the village. Fire or something.'

Derek groaned. 'Oh, all right,' he said and stumbled out of bed. Minutes later, he was back. 'Lois,' he whispered, 'you'd better come straight away. Visitors.' He helped her on with her wrap, and they went downstairs. When she asked who they were, he just put his finger to his lips, motioning her to be quiet.

The light was on in the sitting-room, and the curtains still drawn. On the sofa, sitting as primly as when she came for interview, sat Enid. Next to her, her father slumped in the corner. Enid was holding his hand.

'So sorry to disturb you, Mrs M,' she said, and burst into tears.

Much later, when the story had been told, and Gran had appeared, embraced Enid and clucked about like an old hen, preparing food and makeshift beds, they all sat quietly, calming down before sleep.

Lois looked at Enid's exhausted face, and decided the necessary call to Cowgill could easily wait until morning. There would be much to do, and she could see that Gran intended to help her friend as much as possible. It was not going to be easy. Enid would be betraying her own brother . . . more than that, her twin. And then, afterwards, there would months and months of repercussions, all the horrors of evidence and trial. She hoped Enid and Walter could stand up to the strain. Old Walter was looking frail and ill. His only son, finally facing the music. What would it do to him?

'Come on, then,' said Derek, taking the lead. 'Everybody back to bed. Tomorrow's another day.'

They began to stir in their seats, when Walter said, 'Just a minute. I got something to say.'

'Can't it wait, Mr Abraham?' said Lois.

He shook his head. 'No,' he said. 'Sooner the better. Sit down Enid.'

They all stared at him, and Lois had a sinking feeling. Old Walter looked grim, grasping the arm of the sofa so hard that his knuckles were white.

'It was me,' he said. 'Couldn't stand any more. I killed her. It was the storm, and she was wild. Hit out at me with a poker, an' I grabbed her. Pushed her on to the bed and put a pillow over her head, and suffocated her. She struggled . . . stronger than I thought . . . but I held on until she stopped. Then Edward came in and saw what I'd done. He was beside himself. Dunno why,' he said reflectively. 'Wasn't that fond of her himself. Still, I thought he'd go for me, he looked so mad. Tried to take it out on me later, that night your lad came down to the mill.' Lois barely nodded.

The old man took out a grubby handkerchief and blew his nose hard. Then he sighed, and continued in a quiet, remote voice, 'After he'd got over the shock of seeing what I'd done, Edward pulled himself together and took over. We carried her on the path by the stream to hide her until next day, and I slipped. She went in. Gone in a minute. It was that deep, the night we had the flood. You'd gone to bed early,' he added, turning to Enid, whose expression of anxious concern did not change. 'So we had to be back quick, in case you woke up. It was a noisy night, with the wind banging about an' everything.' He turned to Lois. 'Then you come down, looking for help with your car, and asking awkward questions.' He looked accusingly at her, and she stared back at him, remembering only too well that dreadful night.

Walter shook his head, as if trying to clear his head of tumbling thoughts. 'Edward said we'd find her first thing, and we did,' he continued. 'We put her to rest, down by the stream in the meadow, under a nice bit o'grass . . . Then we planned what to do next. Edward thought up the nursing home story, and he moved into Mother's room. Pretended to be her.'

The silence was complete. Gran coughed and broke the spell.

'My God,' said Lois, and Derek took her hand.

'God help us all,' said Gran, and moved across to put her arm round Enid's shoulders.

The old man looked at his daughter, and she turned to him. She gently removed Gran's arm, and stood up.

'Time for bed, Father,' she said, and he meekly followed her out of the room.

Forty-Eight

Lois was up at six. She crept downstairs, hoping not to wake the others, though she doubted if any of them had had much sleep. Gran had made hot toddies all round, so perhaps Enid, who had looked completely beaten, had managed a few hours. The old man had seemed in a daze, once he'd made his great revelation. Lois had re-run those staggering few minutes over and over. He had seemed honest and straightforward enough, but was all of it true? Or was he just continuing the habit of those past years, protecting his son from retribution?

As she opened the kitchen door, a strange sight awaited her. Jamie, hair sticking up like a brush and sleepy-eyed, was filling the kettle from the tap. He had a tray ready laid with one mug and a plate of biscuits in an untidy heap.

'What on earth . . . ?' Lois stared at him. 'Do you know what time it is?'

'No, haven't looked,' said Jamie mutinously. 'But I know Miss Abraham is back. I heard her voice in the middle of the night. I'm takin' her a cup of tea.'

Lois walked over to where he stood, put her arms around him and hugged. 'Very nice of you, Jamie,' she said. 'And yes, you're right, she is back, with her father. They came in late last night. Now they're upstairs, fast asleep, I hope.'

'Oh,' he said, and put down the kettle.

'Too early to wake them,' said Lois, seeing his disappointment, 'but I could really do with a cup. Let's both have one, an' a biscuit. Then you can nip back to bed for a bit. School today.

Jamie made a face, but told her the session with Gran had worked. 'I can still remember the dates,' he said confidently.

'Cold all gone, then?' said Lois with a grin. Jamie tried an experimental cough. It wasn't much good, so he nodded and said he'd be OK for school, just about.

Before the others appeared, Lois went quietly into her office and rang Cowgill's emergency number. He received the news with serious concentration, and told her to keep Enid and Walter with her until they came over later. 'We won't come too early – they must be exhausted. It'll be about half nine. As you say, it'll be crucial to check Walter's story. Oh, yes,' he added, 'and we are already on Edward's track, thanks to you. Located his friend MacDougall's secretary, and she gave us the address. From what you said about the sleeping pills, Edward should still be dead to the world.'

'I hope not,' said Lois flatly. 'We could do without another.'

'Unfortunate phrase, that's all, Lois. No room for sentiment in our job. And by "our", I mean you too. I'll be in touch.'

Lois sat very still in her office for several minutes, reluctant to begin a day which could only be a nightmare.

Derek stuck his head round the door and said she was to come and have breakfast at once. 'Lot to do today, me duck,' he said, 'and you'll be no good to nobody without somethin' hot inside you. Gran's down, and got things going.' He smiled at her and disappeared. It was still very quiet in the house.

Lois sat down to a quick plate of cereals, hoping Gran would leave it that. She heard light footsteps in the hall and Enid appeared. 'Good morning,' she said tentatively. She tried a small smile. 'So sorry about last night,' she said. 'I expect you are all tired this morning. Your toddy was delicious,' she added to Gran. 'Seems to have given Father much needed rest.'

'What about you?' said Gran, noticing dark shadows under Enid's eyes.

'So-so,' Enid replied. 'But I'll never be able to repay your kindness, you and Mrs M.' Her voice quavered a little, and Lois said, 'Never mind about that. Come and get some breakfast. Shall we let your father sleep on?'

'Well . . .' Enid was hesitant. 'I had hoped we could be out of your way first thing, but he was sleeping so

245

peacefully . . . and goodness knows what's going to happen today . . .'

She bit her lip and looked away, out at the sunny morning.

'You're not going anywhere, not today,' Lois said firmly. 'You're no trouble to us. Mr Abraham needs to gather strength.'

Enid nodded. 'And I expect you've had to tell . . . ?' Her voice trailed off in the familiar way, and Lois felt a pang of guilt.

'Yes,' she said gently. 'Afraid I had to. The police'll be round in a while to ask some questions. But don't worry,' she added, 'they know the score. Inspector Cowgill will make sure your father is handled with care.'

Gran put a plate of scrambled eggs in front of Enid and said, 'Thought you wouldn't be able to manage the Gran special fry-up this morning. This'll go down easy. And don't look like that, Lois. There's more here for you.'

Enid took a few mouthfuls and then put down her fork. 'Mrs M,' she said.

Lois looked up from her struggle with eggs whipped up with cream and butter. 'Yeah?' she said. 'Something wrong?'

Enid shook her head. 'No, it's just that I need to explain about what Father said last night. It came as a great surprise to me. He'd said nothing about it previously, not even hinted. Of course, I always went up to my room at Cathanger very early. Could have been asleep that night. And Edward told me just recently that he'd found ways of coming and going to Cathanger without me knowing . . .' She shivered, remembering Edward's nightmarish trick, dressing up in Mother's clothes.

'On our journey north, Father and Edward told me a cock-and-bull story about Mother being in a nursing home. I knew there was something wrong about it . . . I get this feeling, you know, with Edward. Almost like being in his head . . . But I could never imagine Father doing anything really bad . . .' Every sentence was an effort, and Enid's voice was fading away.

246

'So d'you reckon he's telling the truth?' said Lois bluntly.

Enid was silent. Then she said slowly, 'He might be. It fits. I hadn't seen Mother since the night of the flood. It was next day Father stopped me going into her room. If what he says is true, then that explains it.'

She was having difficulty continuing, and Lois waited, saying nothing. Finally Enid began again, 'But Father changed after that. Nicer, more quiet. It's an awful thing to think,' she added, words coming at a rush now, 'but maybe, without her, he felt some relief. Oh dear, oh dear . . .' She buried her face in her hands.

Gran walked over to her, and held her steady. 'Don't think about it any more,' she said. 'Take the day as it comes.' She turned to Lois and said sternly, 'The truth'll come out soon enough. Leave the poor woman alone now.'

It was difficult getting the kids off to school, but they left finally, Jamie still asking questions. At nine thirty precisely, the police arrived. Inspector Cowgill was formal but kind. He said he would talk to Enid and her father separately, and Derek went off to help Walter to get himself ready for the ordeal.

'This could take all morning,' whispered Lois, as he went.

'Don't worry,' said Derek. 'I've fixed it. I'll be around while you need me.' He kissed her cheek lightly, and carried on upstairs.

Forty-Nine

D awn had come up over a chilly Edinburgh. In the old town, one or two early risers had walked down echoing streets, pulling up their collars against the wind. In a silent flat, two floors up, Edward Abraham had opened his eyes with difficulty. Good God, what time was it? He had found himself still sitting in the chair, and remembered nothing about the past hours. And what was this rug doing over his knees? He had fought the impulse to close his eyes again, but given up. Enid's treacherous pills were too strong for him, and he had drifted back into sleep.

When he next surfaced, he could hear sounds from outside that told him the morning had got going. His watch confirmed it, and he struggled to his feet. God, why was he so drowsy? He must have been sleeping for hours. And where was everybody?

'Enid!' Why hadn't she woken him? 'Enid!' Where on earth was she? He walked unsteadily through to the kitchen, and then into her bedroom. Empty. His father's room was empty, too, and he panicked.

'*Enid*!'

How could they have gone? He felt in his pocket, and knew the key had been taken out. Oh, no . . . no, Enid wouldn't desert him, surely . . . and Father, too, after all he'd done for him?

In Lawnmarket below, a police car drew up outside the National Trust for Scotland shop, and the engine was switched off. Two sober-faced policemen conferred, reminded each other that they were looking for a murderer, then got out and went through the passage into the courtyard behind.

Edward, thinking it might not be too late to catch up with

248

Enid and Father, pulled on his coat and went towards the door. Halfway there, he heard knocking. It was loud, insistent. Then a voice: 'Open up, Mr Abraham. Police. Open this door, please.'

Edward stood motionless. Steady now. Think clearly. I've always outwitted them before. Open the door, yes. They'll break it down, otherwise. Open the door, stand back and let them in, and then . . . yes, then make a run for it. Take them by surprise. I'm fitter than they are, idle lot.

'Coming!' he shouted, and then walked through to open the door. It went exactly as he had planned. Edward triumphs again! But he was still heavy-limbed from the pills. He missed his footing on the narrow spiral steps, and with a terrified yell, went spinning down and round, on and on, crashing against the stone walls, until he ended up a tangle of twisted limbs at the foot of the stairs.

At exactly that moment, hundreds of miles away, his twin Enid stopped mid-sentence and stared at Cowgill. All colour drained from her face, and she screamed.

'Ed . . . ward! No! *No!* Ed . . . ward!'

Cowgill, toughest of policemen, said afterwards that it was the most chilling sound he'd ever heard.

Fifty

'What's all that commotion?' The Midlands woman came through from the kitchen, where she had been washing up after a late breakfast.

'Can't hear anything,' said her husband. He was studying a town map, planning their itinerary for today.

The woman went to the window, and gasped. 'Oh, good heavens!' she said. 'Come here quickly! There's been an accident!'

They stood at the window, united for once in their curiosity, and looked down.

'Oh no,' the woman said, and put a hand up to her mouth. 'It's that man . . . I can see it's him . . . Now they're covering him up . . . oh, no, right over his head. He must be dead!'

The man took his wife's arm and led her away from the window. 'Sit down, dear,' he said. 'We should just let them get on with it, I think.'

'I want to go home,' she said, beginning to cry.

'But we've paid for the full week,' he said.

She looked up at him, tears streaming down her face. 'They've left the washing out . . . on the balcony . . . and it's raining again,' she said.

'I know,' he said. Silence fell.

Lois sat in her office. She had heard Enid scream and began to get up. Then she heard Cowgill's calming voice, and sank back into her seat. The telephone rang.

'Hello? Mrs M? Bill here. Just checking where you want me to fill in next week. No news of Enid yet?'

Lois couldn't speak for a moment. 'Well, yes,' she said. 'There is news. Not good, I'm afraid. But go on over to the Charringtons, and I'll speak to you later. I'll speak to you all later. Thanks, Bill.'

Something sticking out of her desk drawer caught her eye. It was Mrs Abraham's journal. She opened it near the beginning, and began to read.

> Walter gave me this diary, and told me to write it every day. He said it would help. And he said to tell the truth, because only the truth would do.

Lois frowned. As on other occasions, she felt ashamed, as if overhearing a private conversation. Probably why I've not handed it over to Cowgill, she thought. Perhaps she should give it back to Walter, let him decide whether to make it public. But no, it had to go to Cowgill. Should have gone before. She read on, leafing through a few pages.

> So here goes. The truth is that I don't love Walter any more. Edward is everything to me. I don't need anyone else. Walter knows it, too, though he won't admit it, won't let me go. I don't want him near me any more. There, Walter! You said to tell the truth, so that's it. All for now.

Lois realized she was trembling. Poor old man. She opened it again at random. The handwriting was wild, all over the place.

> I wish Walter and Enid would go away and leave me with my Teddy! While she's here he loves her more than me. He says he doesn't, but I know different. Always the same, even when they were babies! That look between them! Why did I have to have twins? Walter's fault . . . Twins in his family, not in mine. I wish . . .

The entry ended with smudged ink. Tears. What a pitiful woman, thought Lois, and shut the diary wearily. She left her office and met Cowgill coming to find her.

'I think Enid needs help,' he said.

She looked at him bleakly, handing over the diary. 'She always has,' she replied.

Weeks later, weeks of tension and unhappiness for all of them, and another staff meeting had come round. Monday, midday, and the team was assembled in Lois's office.

'Right,' said Lois briskly, 'let's get on with it. I'm interviewing some new possibles, you'll be glad to hear. Now let's look at the schedules for next week. Bill . . .'

There was a light knock at the door. 'Come in,' said Lois, irritated at the interruption.

'Hello, everybody.' It was Enid, and she came forward tentatively, apparently unaware of their shocked faces. 'Move up, Sheila,' she said, sitting down in her usual place. 'Sorry I'm late.'

Lois hesitated. 'Are you sure you're . . . ?'

'Quite sure,' said Enid quietly. 'Now, Wednesday at the Charringtons, as usual?'